"I can't do this, Nicholas. . . . Would it truly be making love? Do you love me now or would we just be . . ."

"Sharing the expected relations between a husband and wife?"

"Please, Nicholas. Try to understand." Andrea kept her gaze fixed firmly on his closed face. "Our reunion has been less than ideal."

Nicholas seemed so different, so changed . . . so fascinating. There was no denying her attraction to him still, but he also aroused a spark of fear. She didn't know this Nicholas. He was nothing like the smiling, teasing man she'd married. She watched him move around her, but she was unable to stop herself from flinching when he began to unfasten her gown. Andrea struggled to focus on the words, trying to ignore the rising hunger of her body. For so long she'd gone without a husband's touch, and her physical senses were clamoring for satisfaction. . . .

Her emotions, on the other hand, were swiftly withdrawing. On their wedding night, she had surrendered herself to him, heart and soul, only to be left hurt and bewildered. Could she allow herself to become that vulnerable again? Would he take her hard-won confidence and wound it as he had once done to her feelings?

PORTRAIT OF DREAMS

VICTORIA MALVEY

POCKET BOOKS
New York London Toronto Sydney Tokyo Singapore

This book is a work of fiction. Names, characters, places and incidents are products of the author's imagination or are used fictitiously. Any resemblance to actual events or locales or persons, living or dead, is entirely coincidental.

An *Original* Publication of POCKET BOOKS

 POCKET BOOKS, a division of Simon & Schuster Inc.
1230 Avenue of the Americas, New York, NY 10020

ISBN: 0-671-02070-6

First Pocket Books printing September 1998

10 9 8 7 6 5 4 3 2 1

POCKET and colophon are registered trademarks of Simon & Schuster Inc.

Cover art by Harry Burman

Printed in the U.S.A.

To my incredible husband, Steve,
who always believed in me,
encouraged me to follow my dreams,
and loves me without limitations.

To my wonderful boys, Sean and Dylan,
who were always patient and loving,
giving up their computer games while Mommy
worked.

And lastly, to my terrific parents, Jim and Pat Frey,
who taught me to dream.

This is for all of you. I love you guys!

Acknowledgments

To my enthusiastic agent, Pam Hopkins, who took a gamble on an unpublished historical writer when the market was tight, never faltering in her belief that someday I would make it. Guess what, Pam? That day has come! Thanks for believing in me.

And, most important, to my fantastic editor, Amy Pierpont, who saw raw potential and sculpted it, blending our talents to create a terrific story. I can't thank you enough for all you've done for me, Amy. You are a great editor and we make an incredible team. I am honored and blessed to have had the opportunity to work with you. Thanks for making my dream a reality.

Prologue

Chelmsford, England—June 1803

Their cries of repletion echoed in the darkened room, mingling with the chime of the clock, as Andrea bound her husband to her in the timeless way of passion. Unimagined delight cascaded through her as Nicholas leaned down to rest upon her body. A sigh broke from Andrea before she wrapped her arms around her husband's glistening flesh, her hands stroking against the relaxed muscles on his back, love for the man she'd wed that morning filling her.

"Nicholas," she whispered, pressing a soft kiss against his shoulder. "My husband."

He brushed her tangled hair back from her face, a chuckle rumbling in his throat. "And to think I balked when my father told me that I was to marry you."

"I fear I reacted far worse," Andrea admitted.

"Now why doesn't that surprise me?"

Her lips twitched. "To hear your question, one would think that I'd been less than the ideal lady."

1

"You've always been a lady, Andrea. A high-spirited one, admittedly, but a lady nonetheless," Nicholas said, rolling to his side.

"High-spirited indeed," she scoffed, lifting herself up onto an elbow in order to look at Nicholas fully. "Why is it when a woman expresses an opinion, she is considered high-spirited at best, while a gentleman is thought bold?"

His chest shook as he laughed. "I believe it the wiser course to simply leave that remark unanswered."

"Coward." Her voice was tinged with a smile.

"Certainly not. It's a prudent man who knows when to hold his tongue," he responded in kind.

Her expression grew serious. "You can't possibly comprehend what it's like to have someone always judging what you say or how you act and informing you of what is best for you."

"Pardon me, Andrea, but I believe you've met my father, haven't you?"

"But you're his heir."

"Which only makes the expectations that much higher." Nicholas turned his head to stare up at the velvet canopy on the bed. "It is wearisome to be forever seeking approval and never receiving it."

"I understand," Andrea said softly, laying a hand upon his chest. "I could do little right by my parents. Their wishes and mine were seldom the same."

"But you were constantly forging ahead with your own, weren't you?"

"Unfortunately for my parents, that's true."

A corner of his firm mouth lifted, making him even more devilishly handsome. With his thick, dark hair, mussed from her fingers threading through it, his sparkling golden eyes, gleaming in the muted light from the fire, and his aristocratic features, Nicholas took her breath away. First figuratively, as she gazed at him, then literally, as he eased her toward him for a passionate kiss, their lips tangling in a dance of seduction.

Her green eyes widened. "What inspired that lovely kiss?"

"You."

"What about me?"

He smoothed a strand of her long, auburn hair over her shoulder. "Nothing in particular. Just because."

The answer melted her heart. "Oh, Nicholas."

He shifted her on top of him, pressing her close. "I'm so glad I found you."

"Found me? Your parents announced our engagement. There was no 'finding' involved."

"Perhaps," he conceded with a grin. "Still, once I saw you, I was clever enough to readily agree with my father's announcement."

Her hair brushed against his chest as Andrea's laughter spilled from her. "The first night we met, I was planning on acting so horrid that you would bow off."

"And risk the anger of both our fathers?" he asked with a mocking tone. "Never would I dare."

"Certainly not," she agreed tongue in cheek. "After all they'd gone through to make sure that their neighboring estates would become one!"

"Still, I was furious with my father for calmly informing me that I was to marry . . . without so much as a by-your-leave."

"As was I." Andrea lightly trailed her fingertips over his forearm. "How was I to know that I'd fall desperately in love with you the moment we met?"

Nicholas's shout of laughter made her smile. "You did no such thing."

"I most assuredly did!"

"Hardly, but it is true that all I had to do to captivate you from the very beginning was one tiny act."

"And that would be?"

"Laugh."

Andrea remembered how she'd tried to put him off by giving him her haughtiest of glares before snubbing him, rudely turning away. With her back toward him, she'd been expecting an angry outburst, but had received his laughter instead. Instantly she'd been intrigued. She'd wondered if she'd finally met a man who would appreciate her fortitude, rather than try to squash it.

Because of that one sound, she'd turned around to give him another look.

Andrea smiled demurely. "You are quite right, Nicholas. You won me with your laugh."

"Now, if we'd met as children, then you, naturally, would have been madly in love with me the entire time and merely awaiting my attentions."

"Undoubtedly," she returned with a chuckle. "When my father inherited the title and property five years ago, I was but a girl of ten and two while you were an ancient gent of ten and nine. So, it is indeed fortunate for your reputation that you were off at Eton for years. After all, it would hardly do to have such a mature gentleman entranced with such a young lady . . . lovely though she may be."

"For true, my dear. I would have lain at your feet and declared my heart yours at first glance," Nicholas agreed, his humor earning him a light swat on his shoulder. "But honestly, I do believe that it was all my clever maneuverings to outwit my father's attempts at matchmaking that finally led to his startling pronouncement of our engagement."

"I found your avoidance of me amusing." She rubbed one foot along his calf. "Imagine, if you will, your parents, my parents, and me sitting down at a table that has been arranged with an extra setting . . . every time. It was so amusing for me to listen to your parents upbraid the servants as if it were a mistake they continually made. Did they think me so lacking in wits that I would not realize that the setting had been meant for their son? They actually thought I would believe it a mistake after I'd been *told* you would be attending."

Nicholas curved a hand across her hip. "My father is of the mind that if he says something with enough conviction, everyone will believe him."

"The opposite is true, for I was beginning to wonder from what dreadful disease his son suffered."

"You were *what?*"

His incredulous question made her laugh. "All I ever heard from our parents was how wonderful you were, incredibly handsome, utterly charming, unfailingly kind. Yet, because you'd never seen fit to grace our intimate soirees, I was beginning to think that you might have something horribly wrong with you. In the beginning, I'd had no idea that they were interested in a match between us, so I wondered why they were so insistent we meet."

"Did you never consider that perhaps they were trying to sway you into favorably viewing a future suit, since you'd done nothing but fight your parents over their past choices?"

"I did after the first few dinner parties, but their intensity surprised me. For some reason, they seemed doubly intent upon their course."

"Because of our neighboring properties," Nicholas provided. "We wed, and our lands become one glorious estate. A goal worth striving for, don't you agree?"

"It's despicable to treat people as assets."

5

"I can certainly attest to your worth," Nicholas murmured, shifting his hips beneath hers. "However, I'm a bit more interested in your ivory limbs than your golden coffers at the moment."

She twisted lightly beneath his stroking hands. "I'm perfectly serious, Nicholas."

"As am I."

"Our parents should not have the right to position us however—"

"Don't fret, love. I'm rather fond of your current position." He arched upward, stroking her softest of flesh with his budding hardness.

His breath caressed the nape of her neck, distracting her further. "I truly believe we need to discuss this, Nicholas."

"I've more . . . pressing issues entertaining my thoughts at the moment, Andrea."

Nicholas slid his hands down her thighs, pulling her long leg over him, leaving her utterly vulnerable to his intimate caress.

"Don't you find this more interesting than worrying about our parents?"

His husky murmur barely penetrated her consciousness, all logic burning away beneath his magical touch.

A discreet knock on the door sent Andrea into a sitting position, eliciting a groan from Nicholas. "Someone's at the door," she whispered, stating the obvious.

"I don't care," he murmured, reaching up to cup her full breasts.

His bewitching thumbs did little to aid her concentration as he moved them back and forth across her nipples. She clasped his hands, holding them still. "I hardly feel comfortable doing this with someone standing on the other side of the door!"

"Fine," Nicholas assented, his hands still pressed

firmly against her breasts. He turned his head toward the door. *"Go away!"*

His loud bellow made her jump. "Nicholas!" she hissed. Really, he could have been more discreet!

"I was merely doing your bidding, my sweetness." He levered himself up to nuzzle at her shoulder. "Now, shall we resume our pleasures? I believe we were right . . ."

Another knock, this one louder than the last, brought a sharp curse from Nicholas as Andrea scrambled from his lap, clutching the bedcovers to her chest.

"Who is it?" she called out, ignoring Nicholas's frown.

"Andrea, they'll simply abandon their rude interruption if we ignore the—"

"Many pardons, Master Nick, but it's a most urgent matter."

Andrea recognized the voice as belonging to Nicholas' manservant, Hampton.

"I'm going to thrash him soundly," Nicholas vowed as he climbed from their bed.

His continued grumblings brought a smile to Andrea's face. He sounded like a disgruntled codger who'd just lost his last farthing.

Wrapped in his dressing gown, Nicholas opened the door, grousing, "Pray for your soul, Hampton, old fellow, for I'm about to dispatch you on your way."

"Ah, get on with you, Master Nick," chuckled Hampton, shaking his head. "Dispatch me? That's a fine tale."

The expression on Nicholas's face was one of resigned exasperation. "The urgent matter?" he reminded his manservant. "Quickly, man. My hands are beginning to itch with the need to wrap around your throat."

"Now how's a body supposed to deliver an important message with you jesting like that?" The top of Hampton's head barely reached Nicholas's broad shoulder, and with Nicholas practically standing on top of him, the manservant had to crane his neck back to speak with his master.

"I'll attempt to restrain myself." Nicholas's tone was dry enough to straighten Hampton's white curls.

"Then I'll get on with it."

"Please do. There's no rush, of course. It is only the eve of my nuptials."

"And a man needs his privacy, don't he?"

"When denied, the value only increases."

"What's that?"

Nicholas rolled his eyes at Andrea, before turning back to Hampton. His patience with his manservant warmed Andrea. She had to smile when Nicholas said, "Allow me to clarify matters, Hampton. I will be closing this door in one minute, regardless of your urgent message."

"But what of this note?" Hampton waved a slip of parchment.

"Perhaps it would be a good time to deliver it?" Nicholas prompted, holding out his hand.

"Oh, yes. It would be at that." Nodding once, Hampton cleared his throat. "This missive was just delivered from one of the King's own men. He said it was urgent and he's awaiting your reply."

Andrea watched as her husband accepted the note without further comment. Nicholas's expression grew serious as he read the message, but Andrea could see the underlying spark of excitement in his eyes. He walked swiftly to his writing desk, scribbled out a quick response, sealed it, and handed it to Hampton. "Please give this to the messenger."

"What's this all about, Master Nick?" Hampton asked, accepting the missive.

Nicholas straightened. "You go too far," he said quietly.

Hampton sniffed, drawing back his shoulders. "Can't blame a body for wondering about all these peculiar happenings," he muttered, turning away from Nicholas. "Got to admit it's fairly unusual for a gentleman to be receiving urgent messages from the King on his own wedding night. Why, a body could ask himself if—"

Nicholas shut the door, closing out Hampton's mumblings.

"What is it, Nicholas? What has happened?" Andrea asked, trying to push down the sense of alarm that filled her.

When Nicholas glanced at her, his expression was blank. Andrea grew cold at the distance she felt forming between them. "What is it?" she asked again, dreading his answer.

"I've got to prepare," Nicholas murmured in a distracted tone as he headed toward his armoire. "I'll have Hampton send on my clothing in the morning. It wouldn't do to have him in here packing my bag while you're in my bed," he said, flashing her a quick smile.

At her silence, he glanced back at her. "I'm only thinking of you, Andrea. I don't wish to cause you distress."

What did he expect from her? Thanks for his consideration of her privacy when he was obviously preparing to leave her without one word of explanation? She eased from the bed, keeping the bedcovers wrapped about her in an elegant fall of silk. "Thinking of me? No, I don't believe you are. I asked you a question, Nicholas," she said with quiet dignity. "And I believe I am due the courtesy of a response."

Her formal tone must have reached him, because

Nicholas stopped dressing and gave her his full attention. "You're quite right, Andrea. My apologies for my abruptness. I also apologize for the ill timing of this assignment, but it can't be avoided."

"What assignment?" There was nothing she could do to keep the ice out of her voice.

His entire body stiffened in response to her tone. "I'm afraid that I'm not at liberty to discuss the particulars," he returned, softening his voice. "Suffice it to say that I volunteered for this mission a few weeks before my father announced our engagement. I've been expecting to be contacted, but had no indication that the timing would be so ill-advised."

"And you didn't see fit to inform me of this?"

His brows drew together in consternation. "What do you think I am attempting to do at present?"

Did he honestly believe that this constituted fair warning? If he'd told her of this possibility even a few days ago, she wouldn't be as devastated as she was at this moment. Tears threatened to fall, but Andrea hardened herself, unwilling to allow a single one to streak down her cheeks. "Your attempt, my lord, has fallen far short of the mark."

She could almost feel the anger beginning to radiate off him . . . and she reveled in it.

"I am trying to be exceedingly patient with you, Andrea, but you are weighing upon my attempt."

He was leaving her on their wedding night without an explanation and she was supposed to worry that she was trying his patience? Good heavens! Did Nicholas have no understanding of her feelings? Was he truly unaware of his insufferable attitude? Andrea shook her head slowly. "Why couldn't you have told me earlier?"

A sigh of sheer exasperation escaped him. "Andrea, I've already told you why this matter was not discussed before this evening." Nicholas moved over to her, laying a gentle hand upon her cheek. "I vow to explain everything to you upon my return in a few weeks."

His voice was soft and gentle and she found it completely insulting. Gone was the teasing from a tender lover, replaced by the slow tones of a husband trying to placate his wife. The polite nothings were meant to calm her jittery nerves. Nothing of depth. Nothing of meaning. When she'd married Nicholas, she had honestly believed she'd found someone who would trust her, give her an equal voice, yet with the very first event of their married life, Nicholas relegated her to a position of subservience.

"I'm not sure what you'd like me to say, Andrea. I've told you all I'm at liberty to explain."

She took a single step backward, breaking contact with his hand and allowing it to fall away from her cheek. "You don't need to say anything further. I understand completely."

His relief couldn't have been more obvious. "Wonderful. I can head off now without leaving you overwrought."

It was all she could do to keep from flinching.

He retrieved his jacket and slipped on his boots. "Once more, I appreciate your understanding and, upon my return, promise to be as attentive a husband as possible going forward." Nicholas's smile was a thing of beauty . . . and it made her want to cry.

"Yes." The single word held immense power, undoubtedly reassuring Nicholas while sentencing her to a life she'd vowed never to live. A life where she'd traded the dominance of her parents for that of her husband.

Andrea pulled her painful thoughts to a halt, drawing inward, wrapping her inner strength about her like a shield. It was the only way she could think to protect her aching heart. She'd sworn never to enter into a marriage of duty, yet here she sat, not married an entire evening, and already she'd been dismissed by her husband.

It was too late to alter her fate. They were husband and wife. A husband who wore a smile and a wife whose heart lay frozen, broken and small, within her breast.

Nicholas returned to her side, leaning down to kiss her. At the last moment, Andrea turned her head, offering him her cheek like a dutiful wife. She felt him pause before he pressed a light kiss upon her cool flesh.

"I can only offer you my abject apologies once more and promise that I will make amends upon my return."

She turned her gaze upon him. How did one make amends for shredding a person's dreams? "Godspeed," Andrea said finally, aware that Nicholas was waiting for a response.

He ran a single finger along the line of her jaw before walking across the room. At the door, he paused, glancing back at her, his handsome face set in serious lines so unlike the laughing man she'd grown to love.

Softly, Nicholas closed the door behind him.

Just like the considerate husband he was.

Paris, France—August 1805

Two years.

He'd been rotting in this dark hellhole for two long, horrible years . . . without a word, without an indication that anyone knew or even cared if he was still alive.

King George's assassination plot against Napoleon had gone terribly wrong when one of their compatriots, Méhée de la Touche, had betrayed Nicholas and the others to the French government. Everyone involved in the plot had been arrested and tossed into the Bastille, a prison that embodied all the attributes of Hell. One of the guards had told him of the fate that awaited the other royalist members in his group. King Louis's own grandson, Louis-Antoine, the Duc d'Enghien, had eluded the French forces, only to have Napoleon's personal bloodhounds Talleyrand and Fouché track him down in Germany and drag him back to France to be executed. Instead of unseating Napoleon by reclaiming his throne, the rightful heir had been shot down like a common criminal.

Their mission had been all for nothing. King Louis's heir was dead, and Napoleon was preparing to declare himself emperor of France.

Nicholas closed his eyes to the darkness, leaning his head back against the cold stone wall. What alarmed him most was that these thoughts no longer had the power to disturb him. It was as if he were slowly becoming deadened to everything around him. Little by little he'd been shutting out the horrors that constantly barraged him. No longer did the fetid water and maggot-ridden food disgust him. Instead, he simply shut himself off from his senses and ate.

Survival.

Nothing else mattered. Soon, he reassured himself. Soon, someone would negotiate his release from this pit. He'd been told that they were attempting to ransom him back to his family, but he couldn't understand the delay. No, he wouldn't, couldn't, allow himself to begin thinking that he'd never be released. To lose hope would be to lose himself.

His mind wandered over the scene of his homecoming, the images of Andrea throwing her arms around him, sobbing in relief. His father would clasp him by the shoulders and proudly speak of the honor that his son had bestowed upon the Trent name by his brave actions. It would be the approval he'd long since sought but never received. It would not matter to anyone that the outcome of the mission had been horrific. No, the result would not detract from his honorable actions. The deceit of one of their agents did not affect his bravery.

Soon, he thought again, allowing the word to echo over and over in his mind, a mantra of promise. He could hold on for a bit longer and then this nightmare would be over. He could go home to his beloved Leighaven, his wife, his family, and resume his life, putting these torturous years behind him.

Soon.

One

Chelmsford, England—April 1810

Her rump was beginning to ache.

Andrea shifted once more in her chair, trying to get comfortable, but after two hours of sitting and politely conversing, she was, in truth, getting rather sore. Her area of discomfort was rather apropos for the current topic of conversation. Her smile was strained as she replied to Lord Whiting's inquiry. "While I do believe it is important to fertilize your crops, I'm not sure I agree that the manure from Arabian horses is more potent than that of other breeds."

Lord Whiting shook his head sharply. "I beg to differ, my lady. I have found considerable improvement by simply—"

"Don't be a ninny, Whiting," Lord Valcourt tossed out, his handsome face displaying his scorn.

"Lord knows, horses are Whiting's passion," added another young dandy who had been introduced to her just that evening.

15

"Nothing else seems to incite his interest, by God," snickered Lord Hawthorne, nudging Lord Valcourt's arm.

"Now see here . . ." sputtered Lord Whiting.

"Your pardon, gentlemen, but I was wondering if I might borrow my daughter-in-law for a spot."

Lady Miriam's polite interruption was welcome indeed. Though difficult, Andrea managed to keep from wincing as she eased her stiff body into a standing position. She ignored the outstretched hands of assistance being proffered by the four young bloods surrounding her. "Excuse me, gentlemen," Andrea murmured, moving gracefully to Miriam's side.

"Perhaps you will honor me with your presence as my dining companion in the near future. I have great interest in concluding our discussion."

Lord Whiting's inquiry made Andrea's smile wilt, but she still managed to reply, "I look forward to it."

"And I'd appreciate your insight into a problem I've been having with this lovely filly I recently purchased at Tatersalls." Lord Valcourt's earnest request couldn't be denied.

"At your convenience." Bowing her head slightly, Andrea guided Lady Miriam away from the gaggle of men before anyone else had the opportunity to detain her.

The crisp evening air was a welcome respite from the stuffiness of the drawing room where her mother-in-law was hosting their party. The candlelight glistened through the window glass onto the garden terrace as Andrea looked back into the room. "Are you quite certain that we must hold these monthly weekend parties?"

"Positive," Lady Miriam asserted. "All of these people have sought your assistance with their thoroughbreds. It is exceedingly important to thank them for their patronage, for without their support of your expertise, Leighaven would have gone to creditors years ago."

Andrea gazed into the room, watching as her mother, smiling and happy, conversed with their guests. "At least my mother is in her glory," Andrea remarked, relaxing for the first time that evening.

"She does love our parties," acknowledged Lady Miriam. She brushed back a few loose tendrils of gray-streaked brown hair. "Almost as much as you dislike them."

Andrea laughed in agreement. "You know me far too well, Miriam."

"You have hardly kept your distaste of these affairs a secret," a deep voice returned.

A guilty look on her face, Andrea spun to face her brother-in-law, Thomas. "Perhaps not, but you're hardly one to talk. After all, you've sought refuge in the garden once or twice yourself."

Thomas's laughter was a soft chuckle as he moved toward her. "True enough," he conceded, leaning down to press a warm kiss upon her brow. "You look lovely this evening, Andrea."

She lifted a length of gauzy skirt. "My mother assured me that this was the height of fashion."

His brown eyes, so like Miriam's, sparkled down at her. "Something which Lady Anne keeps well in mind."

"Are you implying, my lord, that I do not?"

The teasing question brought a quick grin to Thomas's handsome face. "Of course not," he responded lightly. "I am positive that you are well aware of what is fashionable . . . for those wretched horses of yours, that is."

Lady Miriam tapped her fan on her son's arm.

"Mind your tongue, Thomas. Remember that those 'wretched' animals have rebuilt our family fortune."

His mother's gentle chiding brought a dull flush to Thomas's cheeks. "Fortune that needed to be replaced since I lost the original one," he said, bitterness coloring his words.

Something inside Andrea softened at Thomas's pain. She lay her hand against his forearm. "We all have unique gifts, Thomas, and no one ever faulted you for doing your best."

"Indeed not," agreed Lady Miriam. "I was merely trying to point out that—"

"Good heavens, what a gloomy lot you three are!"

Her mother's exclamation caught Andrea's attention. "Good evening, Mother," she murmured politely.

Lady Anne smoothed a hand across her forehead. With auburn hair lightly dashed with gray, and bright green eyes, there was no mistaking that she and Andrea were mother and daughter. "I've near worn myself to exhaustion trying to provide proper comfort for our guests, while the three of you hide out here on the terrace."

Andrea shifted uncomfortably. She was an adult and yet her mother still possessed the power to make her feel like a guilty child. "You're quite right, Mother." Andrea glanced at both Miriam and Thomas, who seemed to be suffering from the same reaction. "Shall we all return?"

Lady Miriam nodded. "So sorry, Anne. I merely needed a breath of air."

"Understandable, but one must always remember one's duties." Lady Anne patted her powdered cheek before flashing a smile at Andrea. "Lord Hartnell has arrived, Andrea, and he is seeking your company."

Andrea forced herself to keep her pleasant expression firmly in place at this news, knowing that her immediate future would be filled with more discussions on manure and the like. The string quartet played in the corner of the room, filling the air with muted notes, as the foursome entered the room.

"Look, Miriam, Lady Dabney has arrived." Lady Anne discreetly peered about the room. "We simply must greet her together."

"Certainly, Anne," Miriam replied.

Andrea watched the two women move across the room.

"Your mother's ability to spot a title in this crush inspires nothing less than awe."

She slanted an amused look at Thomas, who stood behind her. "One must never be remiss in her duties," Andrea said, mimicking her mother's tones.

Thomas shivered. "Lord, you frighten me when you speak like that." He placed a hand on her shoulder. "Promise me you'll never become a social paragon like our dear Lady Anne."

Andrea's laugh drew the attention of the people around them. Flushing, she lowered her voice, leaning back into Thomas. "As if that would ever happen." She glanced up at him. "I fear I run a greater risk of turning into a bluestocking."

"And what of being unfaithful, Andrea? Do you run the risk of that as well, or has it already come to pass?"

Every muscle in her body froze. *That voice.* Slowly, she turned her head, her very breath snaring within her breast at the sight before her.

Nicholas.

After seven long years. He'd returned to her, to them. Emotions cascaded through her: joy, shock, wariness. In a daze, she took a step forward, ready to hold him, to reassure herself that he was real.

His words stopped her.

"It would appear that you and my brother have become, shall we say, close friends in my absence."

The statement halted her steps and made the weight of Thomas's hand burn into her shoulder. She could imagine how it appeared with her leaning back into Thomas and his hand resting familiarly upon her. Still, Nicholas hadn't even given her a chance to explain before he tossed out an accusation, stopping her welcome.

Lifting her chin, Andrea took another step away from Thomas, breaking contact with him, to stand at equal distance between the two brothers. "Welcome home, Nicholas." She was aware of the curious, avid gazes of their guests fixed upon the scene playing itself out. Slowly, she leaned forward, pressing a cool kiss upon her husband's cheek. "I am so very happy to have you home again."

He lifted his shoulders in a shrug, the elegant cut of his jacket stretching across them perfectly. "I am so very happy to be here."

His sardonic tone made her flinch, but she ignored it, instead turning toward the man standing next to her husband. He was the agent they'd hired to arrange for Nicholas's release. "Mr. Grant," she said warmly, reaching out to clasp the shorter man's hands between her own. "At last, you were successful."

Mr. Grant bobbed his gray head. "It took quite a bit of money and negotiating, but we finally agreed upon a price, those French thieves and I. I meant to send a note, telling you of our arrival, but we came on directly and I never had the opportunity or time to do so."

"What is important is that you found your way back to Leighaven." Andrea felt Nicholas's gaze upon her. "I thank you for my husband's freedom and I will see you compensated handsomely."

The smile she'd given to Mr. Grant remained on her face as she faced Nicholas once more.

"Seven years, Andrea." Nicholas's harsh whisper grated upon her ears. "Seven years."

Those two simple words held a wealth of pain, bringing tears to Andrea's eyes.

Nicholas shook his head. "Why?"

Before she could answer, Lady Miriam's cry broke the tension.

"Nicholas!"

The small woman launched herself across the room, straight into her son's arms. Andrea's heart ached to see him so eagerly enfold Miriam while he gave her, his wife, nothing but cold indifference. With his eyes closed, she was free to gaze at him, hungry for the sight of his once beloved form. How many years had she cried herself to sleep, fearing the thought of his fate? Regardless of their parting, she had loved him, completely.

His once black hair had gray strokes at the temples, his body was leaner and harder than she remembered, and the expression in his startling golden eyes harsher than she'd ever imagined possible. He seemed a different man from the one she'd married.

A man who was her husband and a stranger all in one.

A man who sparked to life a sensual awareness that she'd thought long dead.

A man who was so cold.

Andrea took a step back as people began to surge forward, clapping Nicholas on the back, giving him happy greetings. Another step backward brought her up against a hard form. Spinning about, Andrea looked up at the solemn face of Thomas.

"Don't worry, Andrea. I'll explain everything to him. He'll come around as soon as he understands."

And would that take away the pain radiating within her heart, the heart Nicholas had once managed to break so soon after he'd claimed it for his own? Did Thomas not see that she'd longed for nothing more than to be taken into Nicholas's arms, held close to him?

The tears she'd tried so desperately to contain spilled forth, staining her cheeks. Andrea wiped them away as she skirted around Thomas, heading for the darkness of the cool garden.

"Andrea."

Nicholas's voice made her pause, but she didn't turn around, unwilling to show him how much he'd distressed her. "I need to speak with you," he added.

"If I might interject, Lord Leigh—" interrupted Lord Whiting.

"Who are you?" Nicholas ground out, glancing around the crowded room. "What the hell are all of you doing in my home?"

"I can explain, Nicholas," Miriam began, only to be cut off by her son.

"Andrea, where are you going?" he asked again as she continued for the side door.

The tears fell faster as she increased her steps.

"Andrea!"

She ignored him, slipping outside. On the terrace, she heard Nicholas's frustrated voice ring out. "Will someone please explain to me what the devil is going on here?"

Two

The only sound in the room was the hissing of the fire as Nicholas stood still in front of the window, looking out over his lands. He doubted he'd ever seen a more beautiful sight.

Except for the glory of his wife.

Nicholas shook his head, trying to loose that thought, but it stayed firm, teasing him. A vicious curse burst from him. Nothing had happened as he'd dreamed of for years upon years. No welcoming embrace from his wife; no expressions of pride from his father. Instead of the hero's welcome, he'd received nothing but more crushing blows.

On their journey back to England, the agent had informed him that his father had passed away a year after his imprisonment. It had rocked him to the core. He'd never have the chance to see acceptance in his father's gaze, nor prove that he would do justice to the title of his heritage.

Still, he had his home, his wife, and the rest of his family. It had sustained him during the long journey from war-torn France to England. Those images had helped him gain back his strength and pushed him forward as nothing else could have done.

And what was his reward for his efforts?

To walk into a room and see his wife leaning against his brother with obvious intimacy, Thomas's hand curved around Andrea's shoulder, the two of them so absorbed in each other they hadn't even noticed him enter the room.

In an instant, his dreams of reuniting with a loving wife were gone, replaced by the bitterness of disillusion.

It infuriated him further to realize that despite his disenchantment, he still found himself wanting her. He longed to crush her cool mouth beneath his own, drinking deeply, while he pressed each luscious curve into his own hardness, until he cleansed himself of his passion. He'd dreamed of the way her auburn hair had wrapped around his body, silken strands enticing his flesh, and how her startling green eyes had narrowed, heat burning in their depths, as she'd beckoned him into her fiery embrace. The images of their wedding night were forever seared upon his memory.

When he'd first glimpsed her standing in the drawing room, beautiful, alluring, he'd wanted to pull her into his arms and lose himself in her.

It had been then, however, that he'd noticed her familiar position with Thomas. His sense of loss had caused him to lash out at her in anger, tossing the accusation at her with no regard to their audience. Worse still, she had spoken not a word of denial. No, instead she'd walked toward him, given him that polite kiss, and bid him welcome.

Nicholas's hand shook as he reached out to touch the elegant drapes hanging from his canopied bed. The simplest of luxuries, yet it was the grandest of textures. Ever since his release from prison, he couldn't stop touching things, testing them, making sure that they were real and not another mirage summoned by his mind when the walls of his prison cell had begun to close in upon him.

It still seemed impossible to him that he was finally home at his beloved Leighaven. He could touch it, smell it, see it, but part of him was afraid that he would soon awake in his filthy cell. He needed to forget the past and reclaim the life he once lived, to overcome the nightmares that had haunted him for years.

And yet, earlier in the evening, when he'd been surrounded by strangers, he'd felt trapped, overwhelmed by the sheer presence of so many people after being alone for so long. He'd had to fight back a sense of panic to keep from walking away, finding a solitary haven.

And those emotions terrified him.

A knock at the door brought Nicholas from his disturbing thoughts.

"Nick? Do you have a moment?"

Thomas.

He forced a bland expression onto his face. "Come in."

It only took a glance to see Thomas's anger. "What's happened to you, Nick? How could you have done that?" He shut the door with a firm push. "You walk in after seven years and the first words out of your mouth are accusations against Andrea and me. Good God, man, has prison truly destroyed your sense of decency?" Thomas rubbed the back of his neck. "I can't begin to claim that I understand the horrors you suffered, but, devil take it, Nick, surely it didn't change you completely."

The moisture trapped in Thomas's eyes took Nicholas aback.

Thomas came to a halt in front of him. "Blast it, Nick. Don't you realize how much I've missed you?" He reached out and enfolded Nicholas into a strong embrace.

With the touch, memories flooded Nicholas: Thomas riding after him on a pony; Thomas hiding in the library with him to sneak some port; and when they'd nabbed one of their father's cigars, Thomas sharing both it and the bout of sickness to follow. Nicholas closed his eyes.

Here was home.

Nicholas pulled back, clasping his brother by the shoulders. "I missed you too, Thomas."

"Good God, man, how could you even think for a moment that I'd cuckold you?"

"It's been seven years."

Thomas shrugged himself free of Nicholas's grasp. "What the bloody rot does that have to do with anything? It could be a lifetime and I still wouldn't do it."

"Andrea's a very beautiful woman." He should know. Even hours after their reunion, he still felt the desire simmering in his gut.

"She's your wife!"

Thomas's shout made Nicholas smile. He lifted his hands. "Ease up, Thomas."

"How can you request such a thing of me when I have been accused of lying down with your wife? I am more than fond of Andrea, I'll admit, but I love her as a dear sister. Anything more, well, it's . . . it's just obscene, is what it is!"

The vehemence in his brother's statement was enough to convince Nicholas of his sincerity. "Then I owe you my apology."

Thomas ran a hand through his hair. "And one to Andrea."

"True enough."

A sigh broke from Thomas. "There were things that occurred during your absence."

A corner of Nicholas's mouth quirked upward. "I would think so."

Thomas smiled in return, but his was edged with nervousness. "Some of them shame me."

The darkness of the past feathered in Nicholas's mind. "We are all plagued by that which we'd rather forget," Nicholas said softly.

Thomas took a deep breath. "I'm the reason behind your lengthy imprisonment."

Nicholas jolted at the statement. *"What?"*

"A few months after you departed, we began to make inquiries as to your whereabouts."

"I want to know why you feel responsible for my capture."

Thomas waved his hands. "I'm heading toward that part, Nick. Andrea had shown all of us the note you'd received from the King on your wedding night and she'd informed us that you would only be gone a few weeks."

Nicholas thought back. His memories of that night seemed to belong to another man.

"When you didn't return, we began to search for your whereabouts," Thomas continued. "It took Father nearly a year to finally discover that you had been captured and thrown into the Bastille."

"Why did it take a year? Why didn't Father seek information from the palace?"

"His Highness denied your mission existed, despite the proof we had in his note," Thomas explained. "In fact, the palace declared the note a forgery."

There was nothing Nicholas could do to stop the

shiver from racing down his spine. He'd been dismissed and forgotten, completely expendable.

"It was around then that Father suffered his stomach ailment and died within a few days." Sorrow darkened Thomas's brown eyes. "I'm thankful he passed so quickly. He was in a tremendous amount of pain."

An odd ache centered in his chest at the news, but Nicholas forced himself to concentrate on Thomas's explanation.

"Soon after his death, we found that he'd been paying large sums of money to various members of parliament in order to secure your whereabouts."

"So, why didn't you arrange for my release then?"

Thomas thrust both of his hands through his hair. "This is most difficult, Nick."

Nicholas allowed silence to spin between them.

"I don't know if I can . . ."

"Tell me."

The request brought Thomas's head snapping up. He nodded, inhaling deeply once more. "You're absolutely correct. You deserve to know. Our financial situation at that point was less than secure, so I decided to make a few risky investments in order to recoup our losses as quickly as possible."

It was all too easy to follow. "And you lost everything in the process," Nicholas concluded.

Thomas closed his eyes, nodding, guilt etching harsh lines upon his face. "We were virtually destitute. I'd sold off most of our secondary properties, except for our town house in London, and borrowed against Leighaven. We stood to lose it all."

"What happened?"

"Your wife is what happened."

"Andrea?"

Thomas nodded firmly. "Andrea. One night she came upon me when I was deep in my cups and got the nasty story out of me. You see, I'd hidden it from the family as best I could . . . which only made it harder on our finances. You know, keeping up appearances and such."

"So what did she do?"

"She told me to hie myself off to bed and when I finally awoke the next morning, I found out she'd not only reviewed our books, but she'd set upon a plan to save Leighaven."

Nicholas sat down. "Amazing," he murmured. "Dare I inquire as to this plan?"

Thomas sat down across from him. "First, she gathered the family and explained our financial situation to everyone. It was mortifying, but at the same time a huge relief. Finally, the burden was off me."

And settled onto Andrea. Nicholas kept that thought to himself, unwilling to add to Thomas's obvious guilt.

"She calmly stated that we needed to pull in close ranks; no more parties, no extra expenditures, no clubs. Now that one hurt. Our family had been members of White's for years and I had to forgo our membership. After that blow, she pointed out that we still had two remaining assets: our London town house and Leighaven."

"Pray do not continue if she was forced to sell our London property."

Nicholas's protest brought a crooked grin to Thomas's face. "No, she wasn't, but she did let it for five years."

He was too stunned to respond.

"Indeed she did. She routed about for tenants and had them maintain the property. In doing so, we would remain the owners of a well-tended property rather than the debtors on a ramshackle town house . . . without so much as a farthing expended to do so."

"Brilliant," Nicholas conceded, now that he'd gotten over his initial shock of having the Leigh ancestral London house up for lease.

"Then she informed all of us that the only way to regain our fortune was to utilize our one remaining asset."

"Leighaven."

Thomas nodded. "She sold off all of our thoroughbreds in order to quiet the loudest of the moneylenders, then she began to restock the stables."

"How did she manage that?"

"None of the horses she stabled were ours."

"She began to board them," Nicholas said slowly.

"At first, she simply boarded them, but as she spent more time there, she began to train them."

Nicholas was glad he was seated. "Train them? Where did she learn how?"

"Books."

His incredulous stare caused Thomas to laugh.

"It's the God's truth, Nick. Every night she'd settle in with this pile of books and devour all she could with regard to horses. Why, now she even heals them, recommends good matches for breeding—"

"Good Lord."

"—and has built up such a reputation that everyone wants her to care for their thoroughbreds."

"Which is why all of the young bucks filling Leighaven tonight had naught but the best to say of Andrea," Nicholas concluded, his ears still fairly ringing from all the compliments he'd received about his wife.

"Anyway, she toiled like a drudge, still does in fact, to rebuild our fortunes. Two years ago, she hired Mr.

Grant as our agent to negotiate your release. It had taken her years to regain the monies necessary."

"And what occupied you during this time, Thomas?" It took considerable effort for Nicholas to keep the anger out of his question. It seemed his wife had bartered herself in a humiliating fashion in order to save his family, while Thomas, the only remaining Leigh male, had apparently done nothing but damage.

"I was in London most of the time, making the investments that Andrea recommended. Her recommendations caused our fortunes to double over and over again."

"While I sat in prison and rotted," Nicholas concluded.

"Absolutely not," Thomas protested vehemently. "We continued to funnel money into securing your release, but it never seemed to be enough."

Nicholas felt the tightness in his throat ease. He hadn't been forgotten. He thought of his wife, here in the country, slaving over other people's horses in order to make money, and felt queasy. As a gentlewoman, she should not have had to worry about anything other than maintaining her social status. Instead, she had been laboring like a commoner.

His head began to ache.

"Andrea is wonderful." Thomas's insistent voice only made the ache turn into a dull throb, pounding against his temples.

"Apparently," Nicholas murmured, walking to the window, gazing blankly over his lands. One thing was abundantly clear to him.

The wife he'd callously insulted was the very reason he'd had anything to come home to at all.

*   *   *

"Be warned, Jamie, me boy, there's odd happenings afoot." Hampton shook a finger at the butler. "Master Nick would be a bit frightening for a lesser soul, to be sure."

"Balderdash," Jamieson pronounced, straightening his already impeccable coat.

Hampton scowled up at his nemesis. "It'll take more than you leaning over like that to unnerve me, you pompous bag of bones."

The nostrils on Jamieson's aquiline nose flared. "Does this conversation have a purpose, or are you simply speaking to hear your own blathering?"

"I'm trying to tell you about Master Nick."

"That he has become frightful?" Jamieson crossed his arms. "Rubbish."

"Rubbish! Rubbish, you say!" Hampton raised up onto the tips of his toes, trying to glare back at Jamieson. "Then tell me, you old fool, why Lady Andrea quit the room after Master Nick arrived and why Lord Thomas stood stiff as a post while Master Nick gave him the evil eye? Can you answer me that?"

Disapproval lengthened the grooves upon Jamieson's face. "Were you spying on the Master, Hampton?"

Hampton bristled. "Now there's a rotten term. Spying! Indeed. I was merely going about my business. Is it my fault that I chance upon the family?" He shook his head fiercely. "No, it is not, I tell you."

"A proper servant would have vacated the room," Jamieson returned.

"Not everyone is a wiggy ninny like you, Jamie!" Hampton leaned forward. "Besides, how else is a body going to learn what's happening? Everyone's bloody closed-lipped about Leighaven."

"It is not your place to—"

"Saw it off, Jamie," groused Hampton, cutting off the butler's reprimand. "They belong to us, don't you know? And as such, it's up to us to make sure that all runs smoothly."

Jamieson shifted, his expression grim.

"Ah, it pains you to agree with me, doesn't it, Jamie?" Hampton laughed, slapping Jamieson's arm. "But this time you know I'm right."

"While I am exceedingly pleased with the Master's return, I will concede that perhaps it will disrupt the daily schedule."

Hampton howled in amusement at the stiff concession. "I vow it will do a sight more than disrupt our schedule."

Jamieson straightened, tugging down the edge of his coat. "I shall keep a close vigil."

"And I'll keep an eye upon them."

"That is what I just said, Hampton."

Hampton swatted Jamieson on the arm again. "If you'd knock off those fancy phrases of yours, mayhap I'd have a chance to understand you."

Hampton's eyes widened when he saw a smile play upon Jamieson's lips. "I doubt you will ever understand me," Jamieson announced.

"Just as well," Hampton agreed. "I'd begin to worry about myself if I agreed with an arrogant blowhard like you."

Jamieson's sniff of disapproval was drowned out by Hampton's laughter.

Hampton wiped the tears from the corners of his eyes. "If we're working together to keep an eye on the family, I'm thinking this makes us comrades, doesn't it?"

"Lord help me now."

"He already has, Jamie boy." Hampton beamed at the butler. "He sent me to assist you."

Jamieson's only response was a loud groan.

* * *

33

The hall clock chimed the predawn hour as Andrea made her way up the winding staircase, her steps slow and measured. Exhaustion weighed her down, making it a Herculean effort to reach her chamber.

After she'd fled the drawing room, or, more to the point, Nicholas, she had headed to her one sanctuary: the stables. Once there, she had begun to check on the horses. While it was true that they could now afford more trainers and stable hands, she enjoyed working with them far too much to turn over their care to someone else. Besides which, the members of society were paying for her expertise, not that of her staff.

The beautiful gown that Thomas had admired earlier was stained, and hinted at the unappealing aroma of manure. If she hadn't been so tired, she would have laughed out loud when she imagined her mother's reaction to the gown's present condition.

The door to her chamber swung silently inward when Andrea pushed it open. Unfortunately, she would have to ring for a maid to assist her with the long line of closures on her gown. Her hand was curved around the bellpull when a voice reached out of the darkness.

"No need for that, Andrea. I would be delighted to serve as your maid."

She whirled about, her gaze going unerringly to where Nicholas sat in the chair next to her bed. Her exhaustion fled as awareness kicked through her veins. Every nerve ending seemed to spark when Nicholas arose, strolling toward her. With only inches separating them, he finally came to a halt, reaching behind her to push the door closed.

His gaze held hers, the intensity making her heart race. Finally, she looked away. Nicholas seemed so different, so changed . . . so fascinating. There was no denying her attraction to him still, but he also aroused a spark of fear. She didn't know this Nicholas. He was nothing like the smiling, teasing man she'd married.

She watched him move around her, but she was unable to stop herself from flinching when he began to unfasten her gown.

"I owe you an apology."

Nicholas's warm breath rushed over the sensitized flesh at the back of her neck, making it difficult to concentrate on his words.

"While there is no justification for my earlier behavior, I am asking for your forgiveness. I can only say that I now know the aspersions I cast upon you were completely unfounded. It was badly done of me."

Andrea struggled to focus on the words, trying to ignore the rising hunger of her body. For so long she'd gone without a husband's touch and her physical senses were clamoring for satisfaction.

Her emotions, on the other hand, were swiftly withdrawing.

On their wedding night, she had surrendered herself to him heart and soul, only to be left hurt and bewildered. Could she allow herself to become that vulnerable again? Would he take her hard-won confidence and wound it as he had once done to her feelings?

This man was a stranger. She didn't know him, wouldn't even know what to say to him once their passion was spent. Would she look over at him, their bodies glistening with sweat, and inquire after his well-being? A nervous laugh nearly escaped her.

Nicholas had completely unhooked her gown, his hands resting on her shoulders to push the material downward, when she broke away from him. She held her arms crossed over her chest, her dress hanging loosely about her as she spun to face him. His stunned expression swiftly changed, hardened.

It only strengthened her resolve.

"I can't do this, Nicholas."

" 'This' being, I presume, to make love."

"Would it be?" she asked softly. "Truly? Do you love me now or would we just be . . ."

"Sharing the expected relations between a husband and wife?"

"Please, Nicholas. Try to understand." She kept her gaze fixed firmly on his closed face. "You return after seven years, your first words to me those of accusation . . ."

"For which I've already apologized," he inserted stiffly.

"But that doesn't alter the fact that our reunion has been less than ideal," she said softly. "I have changed so much from the girl you married and I am quite certain that the years separating us have not left you untouched."

His rigid stance did little to relieve her taut nerves, but Andrea pushed forward regardless. "What I want is to take the time to reacquaint ourselves."

"I have already apologized for my error."

She felt like shouting in frustration. "That is not the issue, not truly. Your mistake earlier merely emphasizes my point that we don't know each other anymore. If you knew me, you would never have doubted my integrity."

"So you are, in essence, asking for a reprieve from your intimate duties as my wife."

Phrased in that manner, it sounded just dreadful. Andrea straightened. "I'm requesting a chance for us to renew our affection in an emotional sense before we do so in a physical one." She stretched a hand out to him. "Please don't ask me to open myself up so quickly, not after all that's gone before us. Give us the time to learn of each other, to grow to appreciate who we have become, not who we left behind."

Nicholas looked at her steadily. "Andrea, you do realize, don't you, that I have been in prison for seven years?"

The question softened her as she thought of his suffering once more. "Of course."

"Do you comprehend the physical aspects of that imprisonment which would cause me to hesitate in granting you this boon?"

It was her turn to stiffen. "It has been an equal amount of time for me, my lord."

"Then I suggest that we develop both sides of our marriage simultaneously," Nicholas stated with a firm nod.

The man was totally inconsiderate.

"I refuse to satisfy my physical urges with no regard given to my heart."

He took a half step forward. "And what of me? Of my needs?"

Her frustration grew. How could she make him understand that until she could trust him not to trample over her emotions, it was simply impossible for her to give herself to him? They seemed unable to reach an agreeable solution. This only emphasized their differences.

It stunned her to realize that she had been holding on to a tiny, frail hope that one day he would return, beg for her forgiveness, and tell her of his love. Instead, he'd come home, accused her of betraying him, then handed her an apology, expecting her to nod her acceptance and share her body with him.

She felt saddened, mourning the loss of the man she'd thought she loved. Slowly, Andrea shook her head. "I'm sorry, Nicholas. I just cannot become intimate with you now."

"You are my wife."

"I don't feel like one," she whispered, tears welling.

Nicholas's features darkened. "You once did."

"Please try to understand, Nicholas. I simply cannot go back to being the girl I was when you left."

"I'm not asking you to," he insisted, reaching out to grasp her arms. "I've just returned from seven years in Hell and I want to forget it all. It is time to resume my life."

"And I will do everything in my power to aid you," she said quietly. "All but this."

Nicholas's fingers curled inward. "It is my right," he ground out.

She blanched. It was perfectly clear that he cared nothing of her feelings. Her refusal came easier now. "Perhaps," she consented, "but if you exercise it, you do so in force."

For a moment, she thought he would pull her into his arms and do precisely that. The muscles in his arms tightened briefly, then he released her, as if it hurt him to touch her. "When did you become so unfeeling, Andrea?"

"How can you ask that?" Hurt deepened her question.

He tilted his head back, looking up at the ceiling. "What did I ever do in my youth to deserve this?"

She gazed at his distant expression. "I've often wondered the same," she whispered softly.

Nicholas appeared to pull himself inward as he walked over to the door. With a hand upon the knob, he turned to face her again. "Since you have refused my advances, I can only presume I am free to seek my, shall we say, *comfort* elsewhere."

If he had slapped her, he couldn't have shocked her more. She drew herself up to her full height. "To humiliate me in that manner will not aid your cause to rekindle my affections."

"Forgive me for being blunt, my dear, but after seven years of abstinence, your affections or the lack thereof wane when measured against more elemental needs."

His crudeness was an insult unto itself. Her chin tipped upward. "Then you must do as you see fit."

"As I shall." He bowed low.

The mockery angered her further. "Does this mean, my lord, that I am also free then to pursue more pleasurable sport elsewhere?"

Fury flashed in his gaze. "Do so and pay a swift justice."

"So should you consider yourself forewarned."

His entire frame shook with rage, and Andrea feared he would storm toward her, but after a few seconds, Nicholas relaxed. His gaze began to wander over her face, onto her shoulders, down her body, and back to her face once again. When their eyes locked, the sadness in his golden gaze made her want to cry. "This is not how I imagined the situation between us, Andrea."

A solitary tear slipped out. "Nor I." The glimpse of vulnerability encouraged her to take a step toward him, her hand reaching out. "Please, Nicholas. I do not care to have anger between us. I merely need a bit of time."

"Time." The pain in his voice was so raw that her tears began to fall in earnest. "I've already lost seven years of my life, Andrea. How long shall I wait before I reclaim what is rightfully mine?"

His expression bleak, Nicholas walked from the room, quietly closing the door behind him.

The moment he was gone, Andrea sank onto her knees, tears rolling down her cheeks. Once again, she was alone.

If only he'd been willing to listen. But he hadn't.

Nicholas had been unable to understand, to truly hear, what she was saying. There was so much she needed to tell him, so very many things he needed to know. Yet he'd been so cold, so distant. . . . How could she tell him? To share with him the years he'd missed would distance them further and make him despair his imprisonment even more.

Yet it had to be done.

Tomorrow she would face him with the truth.

The crisp morning air filled Nicholas's lungs as he walked briskly through the fields surrounding his cherished Leighaven. He had longed for these gentle, sloping hills, for the sweet scent of honeysuckle, for the invigorating pulse of the land.

He'd risen early, too eager to explore what the darkness had kept from his hungry sight the previous night. Thoughts of Andrea had tormented him all evening, making him wonder if perhaps Leighaven didn't hold worse tortures than the Bastille. Knowing that his wife lay in the next room had made it impossible to calm his physical need for her.

Time.

He laughed out loud, remembering her request. Perhaps it took losing one's freedom to make a person truly appreciate the value of time. But he had returned home, and soon he would begin to reclaim his world. First, he needed to reacquaint himself with the life he'd left behind, to rid himself of his nightmares, and return to his normal routine. After he'd taken stock, he would relieve Andrea of her duties running the estate and allow her to resume her life of leisure. She'd been doing far more than she should have for too long. It would, undoubtedly, come as a welcome change for her.

Then, and only then, when he had taken over his

estates, would he turn his attentions to his wife and claim her as his own. He had little doubt that once Andrea was relieved of the burden of running the estate, this contention between them would melt away. She simply needed a bit of guidance.

Invigorated, Nicholas strode through the knee-high grass, heading back toward Leighaven.

A flash of dark blue caught his attention and Nicholas slowed down, keeping his gaze directed toward that spot. There it was again. He headed toward it, curious. A loud yelp right below him made Nicholas step too wide over a ball at his feet. He tumbled down onto the thick grass, barely managing to avoid landing upon a small child lying on his belly.

Nicholas squinted against the blinding sun at the face of the child. Dirt streaked the gamin's face; a worn hat was slung low upon the child's brow. "Good morning."

Nicholas's casual greeting was met with a broad grin. "Same to you, sir."

"Lovely day we're having here, isn't it?"

"It is at that."

Nicholas curved his arms beneath his head, lying back upon the grass. "You've got a wonderful view here."

The boy flipped over, looking up at the blue sky. "That I do."

It was Nicholas's turn to smile. Here they were, lounging about in damp grass, carrying on a conversation better suited to a formal parlor. The silliness of it all struck him.

It was perfect.

"I was walking about," Nicholas said, relaxing further. "What brings you to this field?"

"You."

41

He glanced in surprise at the lad. "I beg your pardon?"

The boy tugged on his cap. "I followed you," he mumbled.

"I see." Nicholas digested this bit of news. "For what purpose?" he finally asked.

The lad shrugged his shoulders. "I don't know. Just because."

"That seems as good a reason as any," Nicholas said, turning his face toward the sun again. "But surely you have better things to do, lad. I'm naught but an old man, strolling about for some fresh air."

The boy crossed his legs, his wool breeches rasping together. "You don't look *too* old."

"You sound far too doubtful of that fact for my comfort," Nicholas laughed. "What's your name, lad?"

"M-Marcus," he finally stuttered.

"M. Marcus, eh?"

"No, sir, just plain Marcus."

"Well, just plain Marcus, I'm Nicholas Leigh and I am honored to make your acquaintance." Nicholas slanted a grin at the boy. "I would shake your hand, but my arms are a tad busy holding up my head at the moment."

The lad folded his arms beneath his head, mimicking Nicholas's position. "It's right nice."

Nicholas closed his eyes against the bright sunlight. "It is at that, Marcus."

Crickets resumed their song, filling Nicholas with a kind of peace he'd longed for these past seven years.

"I can't imagine that even Heaven could be finer than this," Marcus said softly.

"Neither can I," Nicholas returned. Who would know better than a man who'd already been to Hell? The sleepless night began to catch up with Nicholas;

the sun warming his body, the company soothing his soul. "Just like Heaven."

"You have wonderful hands, Andrea."
"Thank you, Harry."
"You know just the perfect spot to touch."
"Practice, lots and lots of practice."
"I love the way you—"
"Am I interrupting, Lady Leigh?"
Andrea jumped at Nicholas's question, bumping her head against Lord Harry Hartnell's chin. She slipped from her place between Harry's horse and the man himself, uncomfortably aware of their closeness. Why did Nicholas always come upon her in seemingly compromising positions?

"Nicholas, you startled me."

"Apparently."

A flush stained her cheeks. "We were, that is, I was showing Harry, rather, Lord Hartnell the bruising on his mare's foreleg." She paused, taking a deep breath in an attempt to keep her voice from wavering. "You remember Lord Hartnell, don't you, Nicholas?"

Nicholas glanced at the shorter, heavyset man. "Hartnell."

Andrea smiled tentatively at Nicholas. "I looked for you this morning, but you had already left the house."

"I was taking a stroll around. I wanted to tour *my* estate, get reacquainted with the lands."

"It's a lovely morning for it." His pronounced phrasing didn't lose its impact on her, but she held her temper. There were far more important issues they needed to discuss this morning. As soon as Harry left the stables, she would talk to Nicholas.

"I found it so," Nicholas agreed. "As did a likable lad named Marcus."

A frown formed. "Marcus? I'm not sure I know of a boy by that name."

"His cleanliness left something to be desired, but he seemed a clever child."

"And how did you and your friend Marcus pass the time?"

To her surprise, Nicholas's cheeks darkened to a dull red. He mumbled something.

"What was that?" His reaction made her only more curious.

"Napping."

"Excuse me?"

Nicholas gave her a glare. "You know good and well what I said, Andrea. There's no need to force me into repeating it."

"I'm sorry, Nicholas, but I must be mistaken. Did you indeed say you were napping?"

"And if I was?"

The wary note in his question helped to hold back her laughter. She allowed a small smile to play upon her lips when she murmured, "It is of no consequence." She cleared her throat softly. "How was your tour of the estate? Is all as you remembered?"

His considering look made her catch her breath, robbing her of humor as swiftly as it had come upon her. The words spoken in the early hours hung between them. Finally, Nicholas murmured, "For the most part. I am just glad to be home."

"It must have been simply dreadful for you." Harry reached over, lightly touching Andrea's arm. "For both of you."

Under Nicholas's intent gaze, Harry's hand felt like a shackle. "I'm just so thankful that it is over and my husband has returned safe and whole to us." She shifted out from underneath Harry's touch and moved closer to Nicholas.

"If you would excuse us, Hartnell, I'd like to have a word with my wife."

"Certainly." Harry nodded to her. "With your leave, I will converse with you regarding my mare, Wildstar here, later this evening."

Andrea held her breath, praying that Nicholas wouldn't catch Harry's reference. At the morning repast, Lady Miriam had informed her of Nicholas's request for privacy within his own home. Since their guests were all due to leave today, it wouldn't be a problem. However, Harry had requested to stay on a bit longer to ensure the welfare of his mare. Andrea knew Nicholas wouldn't be happy about that bit of news, and it was too much for her to hope that he hadn't heard Harry.

"This evening? Are you staying on then?"

No one could ever accuse Harry of being a stupid man. He glanced back and forth from her to Nicholas, the tension gathering between them clearly discernible. "I've been invited by your wife to stay on for a few days."

"I see."

"Only until we can uncover what is wrong with my girl's stride . . . Wildstar, I'm referring to."

Andrea looked up at Nicholas in time to catch his lips twitching. "Don't concern yourself, Hartnell. I never imagined you were referring to Lady Leigh."

"I say not," blustered Harry, drawing himself upward. "I am a gentleman, my lord."

"Clearly."

That took the steam out of Harry. He nodded once, his pale blond hair falling into his eyes. "My lady." He bowed his head briefly. "Trent."

The minute Harry left the stable, Andrea began to smile. "I venture to say you nearly made dear Harry suffer an apoplexy with your teasing."

"Never," Nicholas countered. "He *is* a gentleman, after all."

Andrea's laughter was so loud it caused a stable hand to peek out from the tack room. "Everything is fine. John, go back to your work." She waved the stable boy off, wiping at her eyes. "Truly, Lord Hartnell is a lovely person."

"I remember Harry quite well from our days at Oxford, and he never missed a chance to boast of his stellar character traits. So, I am confident that if presented with the opportunity to expound upon his nature, Harry wouldn't have been shied from informing me himself."

"Oh, Nicholas." She looked up at him and felt her heart trip. With his eyes crinkling in the corners and the hint of humor playing upon his lips, he seemed like the old Nicholas, *her* Nicholas.

The laughter in his eyes slowly died, heat taking its place within the golden depths. Then, as quickly as it had begun to burn, it cooled.

"So this is the saving grace of Leighaven." He made a thorough check of the well-ordered stables. "Very impressive, Andrea. I must commend you on your extraordinary efforts."

Pleasure sizzled through her. "Thank you, Nicholas. I have endeavored to build the finest stables in England."

"That is apparent."

She didn't know how to respond. She could have handled his anger, but when he praised her, it was difficult to keep her heart from leaping.

His gaze roved over her features, caressing each curve, sliding over every line. Nicholas shook himself, clearing his throat. "Fine then, I'll be off and leave you to your duties."

With her head spinning from Nicholas's words of

praise and smoldering gaze, Andrea was momentarily put off course. She chided herself for not speaking with him when she had the chance. Some things could wait no longer.

Gathering her courage, Andrea hurried out after him.

Three

$\mathcal{N}$icholas paused at the foot of the stairs, thinking of his morning.

He'd fallen asleep.

The sun, the peace, the boy had all combined to lull him into a drowsy state, before he'd slipped from resting into napping. Not that it mattered, he conceded silently. It wasn't as if he was urgently needed elsewhere. Everything was running so smoothly here at Leighaven, he doubted he'd been missed during the past seven years. He shifted beneath that painful realization as he made his way up the stairs.

He was halfway down the corridor when he caught a flash of a dirty cap wink around the corner. Marcus. Curious, Nicholas passed by his chamber and followed the boy. What was Marcus doing in the house, not to mention on the second floor? The lad disappeared into one of the rooms off the main corridor.

The door stood open, allowing Nicholas a clear view into the room. Lavender ruffles lined a petite bed, strewn with dolls. His brow drew downward. Whose room was this? Finding the answer to that question would have to wait, for amidst the feminine setting stood Marcus, glancing around him, completely out of place. Nicholas leaned against the doorjamb, his mouth tilting upward.

"A bit intimidating, isn't it?"

Marcus spun around, startled. His face had been scrubbed clean, but before Nicholas could get a good look at him, Marcus tipped his head down.

Staring at the top of the child's hat, Nicholas said, "Fret not, Marcus. I will remain mum about this foray of yours."

The boy shook his head, his body still stiff. Nicholas moved closer to the child. He'd obviously scared the lad with his unexpected appearance. Why, Marcus was undoubtedly terrified that he would be punished for entering one of the upstairs rooms.

"Come now, lad. Where's that smile you were sporting just this morning?" Nicholas curved a hand beneath the boy's chin, reaching for the filthy cap with the other. "Let's remove this bit of dirt and—"

"No!"

The protest came too late. Even as Marcus's shout echoed in the room, Nicholas pulled the cap from the lad's head.

A wealth of silky black hair fell from beneath the cover, swinging to the child's waist.

"Marcus?"

Nicholas's bewildered whisper lifted the child's gaze. This morning with the sun blinding him, he hadn't gotten a good look at the boy, but now he could see the child in perfect detail.

Nicholas forgot to breathe.

It was like looking in a mirror, only the features were more delicate, a feminine version of himself. Nicholas dropped to his knees before the child, his hand moving from her chin onto her cheekbones, feathering across her nose, skimming over her fore-head. Finally, his hand dropped to his side, his mind unable to comprehend what his senses were telling him.

"Marcus?" This time his whisper was harsh, filled with raw emotion.

The little girl shook her head. "Marissa."

"Marissa," he repeated slowly, savoring it on his lips. Was she . . . could she possibly be . . .

She gifted him with a shy smile. "Hello, Papa."

Papa. The single word rocked him back onto his heels. She was his daughter. The thought was almost too powerful to comprehend. Seven years ago, he must have created this miracle with Andrea . . . but why had she not told him? Why keep it a secret?

"You must be six now," Nicholas said tenderly.

"And a half."

Her lopsided grin brought a matching one to his face. "That grown up, are we?"

Marissa inched closer. "I've always wanted a papa."

"That's splendid, for you have one." His voice, so thick with emotion, sounded odd to his own ears.

"Forever?"

The soft, hopeful lilt to her question tugged at his heart. "And ever."

Marissa launched herself into his arms and Nicholas savored the sweetness of her innocent embrace, find-ing within it a joy he'd never before experienced.

"Oh, my little girl." He clasped her close. "Why didn't you tell me this morning? Why did you tell me your name was Marcus?"

Marissa leaned back in his arms. "I didn't think you would want me."

The pain took him aback. "Not want you?" He couldn't believe it. "Of course I want you, angel. You're my daughter."

The little girl wrinkled her nose. "No one wants a girl."

He didn't know how to reply for a moment. "That's not true. I want you to be my little girl very much."

Marissa's hair brushed against his arm as she shook her head. "I heard Grandmama telling Mother that it was a shame I wasn't a boy."

Anger filled him at the thoughtless words that had hurt his daughter. "Well, she was wrong. I adore having a daughter."

Marissa smiled at him brightly. "Will you have time to play with me? Mother is always so busy. She almost never has time." Her expression sparkled. "Will you play with me?"

He could as soon cut out his own heart as deny her. "Of course, Marissa. I'll show you all the secret passageways in Leighaven, I'll take you to my favorite fishing hole, and I'll even teach you to dance."

Displeasure darkened the eyes so like his own. "Do I have to?"

"Have to what?"

"The last part."

He thought back. "Learn to dance?"

At her nod, he continued, "I thought all little girls loved to dance."

"Not me."

He widened his eyes. "Wouldn't you love to twirl about the grand ballroom in a pretty gown?"

Marissa wrinkled her nose at him. "No, and I don't have to do nonsense like that if I don't want to. I heard Mother telling Grandmama that."

At the mention of Andrea, fury flared within him. Andrea's deceit was unpardonable, her cruelty in keeping Marissa from him unconscionable. Nicholas tamped down his anger; he'd have time to deal with his wife later. At this moment there was nothing more important than his daughter. "But, angel, every little girl must learn to dance."

"I don't want to."

He struggled to keep from laughing at the mutinous expression on his daughter's face. "Sometimes we all have to do things we don't particularly care to do."

"Not me," Marissa announced proudly. "Mother says that if I don't want to wear dresses, I don't have to, and if I don't want to learn how to set a perfect table, then that's fine too. Grandmother Anne and Mother had an argument about that just three days ago." With the ease of a child, she shifted topics. "I can count by threes. Three, six, nine, twelve . . ." Marissa's voice trailed off and she began to frown. "I think sixteen comes next, but I'm not sure."

"Fifteen," Nicholas supplied.

Marissa smiled at him. "Oh. Three, six, nine, twelve, fifteen!" she finished with a flourish.

Tenderly, Nicholas wrapped his hand around his daughter's, bringing her fingertips to his lips for a kiss. "What a bright girl you are."

Marissa lifted her chin, her expression so like her mother's it made Nicholas catch his breath. "I know all my numbers," Marissa said. "Grandmama and I are working on my letters."

He couldn't keep his gaze from roving Marissa's animated features. The immediate rush of love for this child, his child, filled him close to bursting.

"Marissa, have you seen . . ." Andrea's voice trailed off.

Slowly, Nicholas rose to his feet, lifting Marissa within his strong embrace, before turning to face his wife. "Has she seen whom, Andrea? Her father, perhaps?"

All color drained from Andrea's face. "Nicholas, I can explain—"

"Not here," he cut her off, a spark of anger seeping through his control. Nicholas turned his attention back toward his daughter. "Marissa, love, I need to speak with your mother."

"But I thought you were going to play with me," Marissa protested.

"And I will," he promised, bending to put her down. "But at present, I need a word with your mother."

"But—"

Nicholas pressed a finger to Marissa's lips, breaking off her protest. "What do you say to a walk in an hour?"

Immediately her face brightened. "In our field?"

Who could have imagined that the word "our" would invoke such a rush of pleasure? Nicholas nodded. "If you like."

Marissa tipped her head to the side. "No napping this time, though."

"Agreed," he laughed.

Her slender arms wrapped about his legs as Marissa pressed against him tightly. "I'm glad you're home, Papa."

His hand shook as he stroked her dark hair. "So am I, love. So am I."

"Why did you have to go away for so long?" Her words were mumbled into his leg.

Nicholas knelt down again, holding his daughter by her shoulders. "Trust me, Marissa. I didn't want to stay away. Some bad men locked me into a room and I couldn't get away. I wanted to, but they wouldn't let me."

She seemed to consider this a moment. "Will they come and take you away again?"

"Absolutely not." He smiled at her. "I won't go away again."

"Good." The single word filled him with joy. His daughter needed him. He hugged her close. After a minute, he gently moved Marissa away from him and rose to his feet.

"One hour."

Marissa nodded brightly. "I'll be waiting right next to the stable." Suddenly, her brow creased. "You won't forget, will you?"

Nicholas grinned. "Don't worry. I won't forget, my impudent miss," he replied, tapping the end of her nose with his knuckle. He then turned toward Andrea, who stood in the doorway, her fingertips pressed to her lips.

Nicholas approached Andrea and grasped her elbow, steering her out of the room and down the hallway, unable to say a word for fear of loosing his fury. With every step, his joy at discovering he had a daughter drained away. How could Andrea have kept his own child from him? He increased his pace until they reached his chamber. Not giving her a choice, he pulled her into his room, shutting the door behind them.

Nicholas propelled Andrea away from him, unable to touch her any longer. "Why?" Anger made his voice vibrate. "Why did you keep my daughter from me?"

"I didn't!" Andrea's denial faltered. "Not intentionally."

Her protest fell upon deaf ears. "I've been home an entire day, not even to mention last evening, yet not once did you feel compelled to inform me that I had a daughter."

She shook her head. "I've been so off balance since your return, Nicholas. It was not my intent to withhold her from you."

"Then why did you remain silent when I came to

your room last night? Why didn't you find me first thing this morning?"

"Last night, I was overwrought because of our conversation—"

"What of this morning?" he demanded.

Andrea drew herself up. "Stop reproving me, Nicholas. I tried to speak with you before the morning meal, but you'd already left the house. I haven't done anything wrong."

"I believed that to be true up until I discovered I had a daughter." He slammed a fist against the closed door. "Damn it, Andrea. I had a right to know immediately!"

The flash of guilt upon her face did little to ease his anger. "I'm sorry, Nicholas."

"Is that pitiful little phrase supposed to make everything dandy?"

Her eyes narrowed. "When you apologized to me last night for your dreadful accusations, did I toss it back? I think not."

"One hardly compares to the other."

"Was my mistake so unforgivable then?" Andrea took a step closer. "Think on it, Nicholas. You come home after seven years, completely unexpectedly, and begin to intimate that I'd been unfaithful. I didn't know how to react, what to do."

"That much was made evident last evening," Nicholas said, thinking of her rejection.

"Your insistence that we resume our romantic relationship immediately only made matters worse." She placed a hand upon his arm. "When was the right moment to tell you of Marissa? When you were accusing me of infidelity? Or perhaps when you were trying to bed me?"

He refused to acknowledge her reasons, preferring to ignore her logic and hold on to his anger.

"I can only apologize for my lack of judgment, Nicholas. There just didn't seem to be an opportunity to tell you."

He stepped away, allowing her hand to fall from his arm. "Don't expect your pretty apology to sway me."

Her face grew flushed. "You are being unreasonable. There was never a good opportunity to tell you about Marissa."

"I know I was out early this morning, but did it ever occur to you to locate me?"

He didn't even give her a chance to respond. "No. You were far too busy with your beloved stables. For all your cries of protest, you were amazingly able to squeeze in time with Hartnell."

"That was work!"

"And this is family!" Nicholas shouted. "It is perfectly clear that our daughter garners little attention from you."

Andrea's head snapped back.

"She runs about Leighaven in torn breeches and a filthy cap better suited a beggar's daughter than an Earl's."

Andrea lifted her chin. "What our daughter wears is her choice."

"Since when have six-year-old children decided upon their wardrobe?"

"I became a woman beneath the rigid dictates of society and I will not allow my daughter to suffer that fate."

"And what horrendous fate has met you?" Nicholas waved one hand in a wide sweep. "You suffer greatly here in this humble abode, for truth."

"Do not sneer at me, Nicholas."

"I would not dare," he returned smartly, making a mockery of the four words. "From this moment forth,

I will guide Marissa into fulfilling her proper place in society."

"She needs no guidance in being a child."

"She is swiftly becoming a young lady, though, and how prepared is she to meet her future? Not overly, I'll wager."

"I will not allow you to force my daughter into speaking a certain way or dressing just so, in order for you to parade her about." Andrea shook under the force of her convictions.

"*Your* daughter? So that's the way of it." Nicholas tilted his head to the side, quiet, his gaze fixed upon Andrea's heated features. "You truly wish I'd remained in that hellish prison, don't you, Andrea?"

She took a step back. "How can you say such a thing to me?"

His short laugh held not an ounce of amusement. "Even before we wed, you were always chafing under your parents' guidance. How you must have gloried when I left and you were able to control your own life; to gain the ultimate freedom. Everyone in the whole of England seems to know that you've spent the last seven years running the entire Leigh estate."

"I did so only in order to save your wretched holdings," Andrea returned.

"Ah, but what freedom you have enjoyed in the doing of it." He walked around her, stalking her. "You have everything, you control everything . . ." He paused behind her, leaning in for the kill. "In essence, you have become me, the lord of this estate."

She whirled away from him. "Don't be absurd."

"Hardly," he scoffed. "Who would be managing the estates if I hadn't been imprisoned? Me. Who would be guiding our financial situation? Me again. Who would the staff look to for final judgment? Why, that would be me once more." He spread his hands wide, palms up. "But here I am, unwanted, unneeded, a mere figurehead on my own estate while my wife, brave, undaunted, rules on."

"What was I to do, Nicholas? Allow everything to fall to pieces about me?" She faced him boldly. "What is your intent with these foolish accusations?"

He ignored her demand. "You would have preferred if I had never returned."

"Ridiculous."

"Is it?" His voice had softened to a silky murmur. "You deny me my husbandly rights, you bid me no welcome this morning, you continue onward as if nothing had happened to ripple your empire, and you deny me my daughter, seeking control in even this, the most personal of matters. It seems perfectly clear that you never wanted me to return." He lifted his eyebrows at her. "So, tell me, Andrea, are my suspicions truly so unfounded?"

"Unfounded?" She shook her head. "No, they're preposterous!"

"No rebuttal, Andrea? No words of explanation?"

"These accusations don't even warrant the attempt."

Nicholas walked to the door. "Rest assured, my lady. I have returned and it is time to reclaim my place as Earl."

He nearly smiled over the wary glare she gave him. "What are you insinuating?"

"Insinuating?" he murmured, grabbing hold of the doorknob. "How very dramatic, Andrea. I'm not *insinuating* anything; I'm stating bluntly that the Leigh estate will once again be run by the Earl of Trent . . . *not* his wife. I'd thought to give myself time to acclimate, but I can see now that it is imperative that I resume my duties immediately. Time is a luxury I can ill afford."

Andrea flushed a brilliant red. "I have forsaken my personal concerns in order to keep this family from becoming beggars, and this is the thanks I receive?"

"I believe I have already expressed my gratitude for all your efforts, Andrea, but that doesn't affect my actions now. I have returned and am ready to resume responsibility for what is mine."

Her hand flew to her throat. "And am I so readily placed into that lot?"

"As mine?" Nicholas smiled, a cold twist of his lips. "Most certainly. You are *my* wife, are you not?"

"Just as you are *my* husband," she retorted.

"True, but in the eyes of the law I am considered . . . what is that lovely phrase . . . ah, yes," he paused, savoring the look of anger upon her face. "Your master."

Her gasp filled his ears as he pulled the door open and left the room, ignoring Andrea's loud demand for his return. His path was set.

For the first time since his return, his purpose was clear.

Andrea sank into a chair. Pain pulsated through her, Nicholas's words still piercing her heart. All her hard work, all of her successes, all of her sacrifices . . . and this was her reward.

On her wedding night he'd dismissed her, treating her like a traditional wife instead of like the partner she longed to be. During his absence she had changed, grown, taken pride in her accomplishments. She'd overcome scorn from the men who doubted her abilities and overlooked the snickers from their wives, who ridiculed her efforts. Despite it all, she'd succeeded. She'd made a success of her business and saved Leighaven.

But now Nicholas had returned and with a flick of

his hand, she was relegated to the role of wife; to speak only when spoken to, to blithely hand over all responsibilities and begin to concern herself only with her appearance.

Anger seared through her, strength flowing into her limbs. She had proven herself over these past years and she would receive proper acknowledgment. It wasn't too much to ask from Nicholas. She fully understood all the suffering he had born these past years, but her life hadn't been easy either. She deserved his respect.

What would happen to her when Nicholas resumed the running of the estate? No longer would she be in control of her own life, but neither would she be burdened with the enormous responsibilities. The extra time would allow her to spend more hours with her daughter. When she thought of all the picnics she'd missed, how often she was too late to even kiss her daughter good night, or even to read her a story, it made her heart ache. Her intentions had always been the best, but the unending duties had often waylaid her plans to spend time with Marissa.

Now, time could begin to slow, enabling her to enjoy life more, to spend leisurely moments with her daughter. She could teach Marissa to ride, see how her reading was coming along, brush her dark hair, finally go on a picnic with her.

Her emotions were jumbled; a riot of fear, anger, and even a touch of joy at the thought of turning over all she'd worked to rebuild. It had never been her intention to deny Nicholas his rightful place or responsibilities, but one question plagued her: Would this world she'd created still hold a place for her?

* * *

"In here, Jamie." Hampton tugged Jamieson into the library, glancing around quickly before shutting the door. "Something just happened."

"This is hardly the place to discuss—"

"It can't wait!"

"Nothing ever can, with you."

Hampton waved his hands. "Master Nick and Lady Andrea were just arguing. It seems Master Nick only now found out about the little miss."

"Then I presume he was delighted."

"With little Marissa, yes. With Lady Andrea, no."

"You must be mistaken. She is the mother of his child," Jamieson asserted. "Why wouldn't he be pleased with her?"

"Because she didn't tell him right off!"

Jamieson stumbled backward, his elbow rapping sharply upon the wooden bookcase behind him. "Didn't tell him?"

Hampton's eyes gleamed at Jamieson's shock. "Managed to stun you, didn't I, you silly flummadiddle?" Hampton's chin lifted as Jamieson straightened.

"Precisely how did you gain this information?"

Hampton rolled his eyes. "I pressed my ear to their door. How else would I overhear them?"

Jamieson blinked once before cuffing Hampton on the shoulder. "You fool, you! They are the lord and lady of this household, and your behavior is abominable."

Indignant, Hampton replied, "Well! It seems that I'm the only one who is concerned about what goes on here! If it weren't for my quick thinking, I would have been caught for sure when Master Nick unexpectedly yanked open the door."

"Dear God." Jamieson braced himself with one hand.

"Yes, indeed. The Lord was smiling down upon me

from Heaven, I can tell you," Hampton continued. "When Master Nick opened the door, I jumped to the side and pretended to be dusting a portrait."

"And the Master didn't find this unusual?"

Hampton lifted a shoulder. "He didn't even notice me. Which was probably a good thing," Hampton added. "Seeing how I didn't even have a duster with me. I think Master Nick might have caught on if he saw me using the cuff of my sleeve to dust."

Jamieson groaned.

"Anyhow, Master Nick was fierce with Lady Andrea for not telling him about the little miss, and he shouted at our lady, said some nasty business, too." Hampton shook his head sadly. "It wasn't right, I tell you, Jamie."

"It would appear that your suspicions were correct," Jamieson acknowledged reluctantly. "Master Nick and Lady Andrea are infelicitous with each other."

"Infel-ish-what? Will you speak in English, old man?"

Jamieson rolled his eyes. "It means incompatible."

"How's that?"

"Unhappy, you dolt!"

"Well, that's right now," Hampton agreed, finding Jamieson's reddened face thoroughly entertaining. "And didn't I tell you this very thing yesterday?"

Jamieson's silence made Hampton smile.

"Now who's the dolt?"

"I do so appreciate your graciousness," Jamieson said dryly.

"You're very welcome."

"At this point, we should merely keep watch." The butler pointed a finger at Hampton. "Not *too* close, mind you, Hampton. If you are caught, you will be dismissed." Jamieson thought for a moment, then smiled. "On the other hand . . ."

"Go on with you, Jamie," Hampton scoffed. "You're all blow and you know it. You and me both know we're chums. And if not for me, who else would befriend you?"

"Bedevil me is more to the point."

Hampton laughed, nudging Jamieson's shoulder. "You do love to tease. I never knew you could be so amusing, Jamie."

"A true jester," Jamieson replied.

Hampton was still chuckling as the two men left the library, neither noticing the silent figure perched in the chair near the fireplace.

Lady Miriam peeked out from around the wing of the chair where she'd been concealed, a considering look upon her face.

Nicholas's spirits were still soaring as he stood in the field where he was to meet Marissa. For the first time since his release, he felt almost like his old self again.

The tall trees on the edge of the forest that bordered the large field shaded him from the heat of the afternoon sun. Bright daisies grew in the tall grass catching Nicholas's gaze. A smile played upon his lips as he imagined the flower tucked into his daughter's dark hair.

As he bent to pick a bloom, a whirling object rushed over him, narrowly missing his shoulder. He raised his head, shock striking him when he saw an arrow protruding from the ground. Instinctively he dropped to the grass, twisting to face the direction from which the arrow had come.

Through the dense forest he could see a dark shadow running deep into the woods, bringing a curse to Nicholas's lips. His first thought was to run after the poacher, but he stilled the idea. He'd been away for so long he was unfamiliar with the woods and there'd be no catching the man. Rage swelled within him as he pulled the arrow free. His daughter played in these fields, making this threat of injury intolerable.

He fingered the deadly point, realizing how close it had come to piercing his body. How ironic it would have been to have survived years in prison, years of torture, only to return to his personal haven and be killed by a poacher's stray arrow.

Nicholas rose to his feet. And why was the man forced to hunt so close to Leighaven? He'd yet to tour the entire estate and meet with his tenants, but surely the situation wasn't so grim that it warranted poaching. In his father's reign, the farmers were a valued part of their lands and always had enough to eat, living quite well under Leighaven's guardianship. Were the tenants completely destitute, forced to hunt for food?

It was intolerable that his people might live under those conditions, and he resolved to assess the situation after his walk with Marissa. It was yet another example that all was not as it should be at Leighaven. Perhaps his leadership had been missed more than he'd realized. A grim smile darkened his expression as he snapped the wooden staff of the arrow in two.

"Dinner last evening was a horrid affair." Lady Anne set her teacup down with a pronounced *clink*.

Miriam followed suit. "It is quite obvious that the situation between our children is less than ideal."

"You speak far too lightly," Anne disagreed. "The air between them is verily taut."

"True." Miriam sat back against the plump cushions on the settee. "It is far worse than I'd imagined."

Anne delicately brushed some errant crumbs off her

skirt. "Their public display of emotions is unseemly, most especially in front of our guest, Lord Hartnell."

"They are not unpleasant with each other," Miriam said slowly, hesitant to reveal the information she'd overheard from Hampton.

"Come now, Miriam. If we both perceived the strained nature of their relationship, then it is apparent that they make no effort to curb their emotions."

"Perhaps they cannot help themselves." Miriam shifted, once again in the unenviable position of defending members of the family from Anne's rigid sense of propriety.

"My daughter was trained far better than her indecorous behavior reflects."

"I believe our efforts would be of more use if we help them appreciate each other."

"Surely you are not implying that we attempt something as vulgar as matchmaking."

Anne's patrician tones made Miriam wince. She smiled weakly at Andrea's mother. "Not exactly, as they are already matched, but I was thinking of something along that course."

Anne shook her head, taking a sip of tea. "Marital relations should remain private between a husband and wife."

"But what if they haven't a clue as to how to come to a mutual agreement?" Miriam sat upright.

"Ridiculous," Anne pronounced. "It comes naturally. A husband and wife must reach their own understanding."

"It's not always that simple." Miriam paused. "It wasn't for me."

"You, Miriam? I thought your marriage perfectly suitable."

"Most of the time I found it so." Miriam smiled, memories flooding her. "My husband was ofttimes overbearing and judgmental, yet I knew beneath his somewhat harsh exterior he was a fine man. Still, there were times when I didn't know how to speak with my husband."

"I hardly see the need for me to hear this, Miriam."

"It is not my wish to make you uncomfortable, Anne; I'm merely pointing out how difficult it can be for a husband and wife to clearly understand a situation when they are so deeply entangled."

"And how will learning the intimate details of your marriage aid your son and my daughter?"

This time, Anne's sharp tones fueled Miriam's explanation. "By understanding that I was once in your daughter's position, and how some assistance would have been so very welcome."

"I do not wish to continue this discussion," Anne announced with a firm nod.

"Then I am sorry to offend you, Anne, but I fear I must press on for the welfare of our children." Miriam leaned forward. "If my mother hadn't been so rigid, perhaps she could have directed me on how to break through my husband's austere nature. Perhaps if she had given me one word of advice, I could have had a marriage of love instead of one of polite decorum."

"You had a solid match."

"But it could have been so much more, Anne. It could have been so very much more," Miriam ended on a whisper, blinking back tears.

Confusion tightened Anne's expression. "Why would you have wanted more? Don't you comprehend how much you had?"

"I yearned for him to love me."

"He provided for you," Anne insisted. "At least he fulfilled his part of the marriage contract."

"But that was all."

She was stunned when Anne thrust to her feet.

"That is enough!" Miriam blinked at Anne's unusual display of temper. "You never had to worry about losing your home, your name, your dignity. My husband frittered away every last farthing he possessed. We were on the verge of begging for crumbs off relations when he inherited the title and, thankfully, a fortune along with it."

"I had no idea you suffered financial constraints," Miriam whispered.

Anne sank upon the settee again. "Which is the way I would have preferred that it remain." She laid her hands in her lap, her expression calm. "I am quite well set now. While my husband managed to go through his inheritance before he passed on, my daughter has admirably regained all we had lost."

Miriam smiled. "She is a wonderful girl and that's why she deserves our help. We need to guide her, to assist her in making the right choices, and keep her from suffering from the mistakes we once made."

Anne shifted, obviously uncomfortable with the discussion. "I understand why you wish to help my daughter, but I cannot agree with your suggestions. She should be allowed to find her own way."

"And what of my son? Should I stand and watch as he allows the chance for true happiness to slip through his fingers?"

Anne stood, straightening her skirts. "I am firm in my decision, Miriam." She walked toward the door. With one hand on the knob, she turned back. "I would prefer that the intimacies we shared here today not be repeated."

"By my honor," Miriam said.

"And I would appreciate restraint regarding any future discussions of this nature."

The delicately coached question made Miriam sigh. There would be no changing Anne. "Granted."

Anne smiled at her before slipping from the room. Miriam slowly picked up her teacup. Nothing Anne had said changed her intentions. Miriam allowed herself a smile. Her son deserved happiness, as did her daughter-in-law, and if they needed a little nudge to find it, she was up to pushing.

With a bit of help from Thomas. After all, matchmaking was a tricky business, and she could use all the help she could get!

How the devil had he allowed Thomas to talk him into a game of whist?

Nicholas looked across the table at his partner. If Andrea's expression were any indication, she was no more eager for this game than he. Then what was he doing playing cards in the parlor with her?

True, his anger had abated, but his sense of betrayal had not. For the past two days, he had managed, quite successfully, to avoid close contact with her, seeing her only at meals. It was, to him, a perfectly acceptable pattern for their future.

He had a lovely daughter, and was quite content with one child. Marissa was proving to be as headstrong as her mother, though. For the past few days, he'd been trying to get her to wear a dress, but hadn't been successful as of yet. Every time he mentioned it, she would balk, become upset, yell, or even worse, cry. Unwilling to disrupt their growing rapport, he had backed down, vowing to bring her around as soon as he secured a place in her heart. After all, it was for Marissa's own well-being.

"You've been busy these past few days, Nick."

Nicholas nodded to his brother, who was partnering their mother. "I've been reacquainting myself with the books."

Thomas shivered. "Nasty business."

"Hardly." He had already taken over control of the daily running of the estate. His tour of the surrounding properties had confused him. The farms all looked prosperous and well-tended, so he didn't know why anyone would be forced to poach. Perhaps someone had gotten lost while hunting and hadn't realized how close to Leighaven they'd come. He took little comfort from the explanation though, for it didn't alter the fact that he'd nearly been shot with an arrow.

With a few more days studying the books, he would have a hold on the financial situation. Then he could see to it that Andrea cut back her hours in the stables. Not that he was concerned about her, he assured himself. His main focus was to see that she have more time to spend with their daughter. No, it didn't bother him at all that he frequently heard his wife return to the house from those damn stables in the early morning hours. Nor did he concern himself with the fact that she often appeared exhausted. The idea that he might worry about Andrea was positively absurd.

"It's your play, Nicholas."

He glanced at his mother, pulling himself from his thoughts. "Sorry." He tossed a card on top of the pile.

"As I was saying, Tilwood then asked Lady Harrow if she were in a delicate condition because he'd noticed she'd begun to fill out a bit." Thomas delivered the sentence with savory expectation.

Lady Miriam tried not to smile. "Poor Lady Harrow. It must have been mortifying for her to have a gentleman remark on her increased size."

"Poor Lady Harrow indeed," Thomas said, folding his cards. "It's Tilwood I feel sorry for. All he received from his kind inquiry was a whack on the head with her fan."

This time Miriam laughed. "Yes, poor Lord Tilwood. He is forever suffering from his own unintended gaffes."

"If he minded his tongue as much as he does his attire, perhaps he wouldn't make so many blunders," Andrea said, smiling.

"Ah, but that would rob the gossips of much fodder." Nicholas captured his wife's gaze for the first time that evening.

One glance was enough for him to remember why he had been avoiding her.

The sparkle in her green eyes set him aflame.

"Dear me, we wouldn't want that grievous event to occur."

He almost smiled over her dry wit. "Indeed not, for then they would search out new targets for their vicious attentions."

"The mere thought sets me aquiver."

"As well it should." His cards lay forgotten as Nicholas began to enjoy the repartee. "The prospect would prove daunting to even the bravest of souls."

"A reputation to which I cannot lay claim," Andrea returned.

Nicholas gazed at his smiling wife and felt himself tense.

Desire gnawed at him, destroying any response he might have made, leaving him awash in his hunger. His gaze roamed over her face. Her smile began to fade, only to be replaced by a look of expectant awareness.

The cards began to crumple between his tightening fingers.

The sound of Thomas clearing his throat made him jump. As the haze of passion cleared, Nicholas became aware of his blatant display of desire. He flushed beneath his brother's amused stare.

Nicholas glanced down at his hopelessly crushed

cards, his embarrassment only increasing. "It, that is, I would—" He paused in his stammerings. Tamping down his simmering desires, Nicholas straightened, dropping his cards upon the table. "My apologies, Mother, Thomas . . ." He dared to glance at Andrea, but the heat still flickering in her gaze was too much for him to withstand. Nicholas looked away quickly. "Andrea," he finished, his voice tight. "I am more fatigued than I had realized. If you will excuse me, I will fetch myself a glass of port and retire for the evening."

He didn't miss the look his mother exchanged with his brother, nor the significance of their matching expressions of smug satisfaction. How could he begrudge them their amusement? He had played the fool, fairly panting over his own wife in front of them.

Miriam laid her cards on the table. "Good night, Nicholas."

Nicholas nodded to his brother, before bracing himself to look at Andrea again. Her gaze, bold and direct, captured his.

"Enjoy your port, Nicholas."

The way his name whispered over her lips . . . ah, the things he could do with those lips. *Enjoy your port,* indeed. Nicholas allowed himself one glance at her luscious mouth. Oh, the delights he would rather enjoy! Her mouth, the soft nape of her neck, the sweet curve of . . .

Nicholas stood up abruptly, careful to keep his hands clasped tightly in front of his nether regions. He bowed slightly before turning and walking from the room. The moment the door closed behind him, Nicholas exhaled deeply, aware of his narrow escape. His steps were firm as he headed toward the study to pour himself a glass of port.

Damn *that* idea! He would need an entire bottle of brandy to drown the lust raging in him now.

"The joys of married life," he muttered to himself as he slammed the study door behind him.

Andrea sat, stunned. After having taken great measures to avoid her, Nicholas had gazed upon her with potent desire. Her heart still raced within her breast. His witty rejoinder captivated her attention, bringing to mind the carefree days of their courtship. With memories of their love swirling in her mind, he had bestowed upon her a look of heated measure, entrancing her. That golden gaze had liquified her, causing her to melt into trembling awareness of never-forgotten intimacies. For that moment, he'd made her forget all the anger between them. Their discord since his return was overshadowed by the memory of their passion. Confusion filled her. How could she be furious at him, yet still desire him?

She floundered to regain her composure. "It is rather warm in here," she murmured, fanning herself with her hand.

Thomas had the audacity to laugh out loud. "I imagine more so for you."

It was clear that there would be no graceful dismissal of her reaction to Nicholas. "You are undoubtedly correct, nevertheless it is not something a gentleman should remark upon."

"A gentleman, no, but a family member is a different issue altogether," Thomas answered with a grin.

Even Miriam smiled over that response. Andrea knew when she was defeated. As graciously as possible, given the circumstances, she rose to her feet. "I believe I shall retire."

"Feeling a bit fatigued, are we, Andrea?"

She shook her head at Thomas, a smile playing

upon her lips. "The affection I bear for you astounds me."

Thomas stood in deference. "As I am such an unlovable creature, I am quite sure that more than one person has questioned that very matter."

"Why do I find that so very easy to believe?" Andrea jested, before pressing a kiss upon Thomas's cheek. She leaned down to repeat the gesture with Miriam.

"You always were an impertinent wench, Andrea," Thomas said smoothly.

Andrea merely laughed as she walked from the room.

Miriam lingered in the foyer with Thomas. "This evening went splendidly, don't you think?"

"Indeed." Thomas's eyes were bright with laughter. "Nick practically ran from the parlor."

"An excellent beginning."

"He couldn't keep his eyes off her."

"Nor she him."

Thomas grinned. "Our first attempt at matchmaking was successful. Congratulations, madam."

"We didn't do much," Miriam fretted.

"We got them into the same room, didn't we? That's something they haven't managed to do on their own in days."

"True," she acknowledged. "Still, I believe next time we should prompt a more intimate conversation."

"Next time?"

Miriam smiled over the wary note in her son's voice. "Of course next time. Your assistance is invaluable."

Thomas shook his head. "I'm not sure if we . . ."

"I couldn't have accomplished this evening without you," Miriam said, not feeling the least bit guilty for manipulating her son's affection.

A sigh broke from Thomas. "What is our next plan of action?"

"You are a wonderful son." Miriam hugged Thomas before responding to his question. "As to our next course, I'm not quite sure as of yet, but it is obvious that forcing them to spend time together will garner the best results." She nodded succinctly. "I shall think on it."

"Perhaps we could plan an outing of some sort."

Miriam heard the spark of interest in Thomas's words. "That sounds delightful."

"We can include Marissa too," he said, warming to the topic.

"Perfect."

"Then, if we wander off with Marissa, it will leave the two of them alone."

"Brilliant."

Thomas smiled down at her. "I must admit that I was not too keen on this plotting of yours a few moments ago, but it is beginning to hold more appeal now."

Miriam melted at her younger son's concern. "You do so want your brother to be happy, don't you?"

"There is that," Thomas conceded, before gracing his mother with a wicked grin. "That and the fact that I so dearly love to see him tied up in knots."

Miriam laughed. "You always were an impossible child," she said, presenting him with her arm.

As Thomas escorted his mother upstairs to her bedchamber, Jamieson stepped out from the alcove where he'd been standing, unobserved. He glanced around as Hampton came down the hallway, practically tripping in his haste.

"Jamie, did you hear that?"

Hampton's stage whisper was hardly quiet. "Keep your voice down," Jamieson reprimanded softly. "It wouldn't do for the underservants to hear us gossiping like a pack of old hens."

"Did you hear?" Hampton repeated, not minding Jamieson one wit.

"My ears are functioning properly."

"Quiet, you stiff-necked doodle," Hampton muttered, but he was too distracted to put much heat into it. "We need to assist them."

"Lord, help us now." Jamieson shook his head. "While I will undoubtedly regret inquiring, were there any inspired thoughts whirling about in that confused brain of yours?"

Hampton smiled at Jamieson, too proud of his grand idea to mind the insult. "I was thinking . . . what if we nudged them together like Lady Miriam suggested? You know, help her out a bit. Master Nick and Lady Andrea would have to talk to each other then."

"In the present state, I'd be more afraid they'd inflict bodily harm upon each other."

Jamieson's droll comment brought a frown to Hampton's face. "Go on with you, Jamie boy. You know as well as I do that Master Nick wouldn't hurt a fly, never mind his wife."

"I was merely being satirical."

Hampton frowned at him. "Would you stop worrying about your personal problems and focus in on this?"

Jamieson rolled his eyes. "It doesn't mean . . ." He broke off, shaking his head. "Why do I even bother? Very well, Hampton, what do you propose for our course of action?"

Hampton swatted Jamieson on the arm. "Haven't you been listening? I think we should do what Lady Miriam suggested and try to get Master Nick and Lady Andrea to spend time together."

"And how do you suggest we do that?"

Hampton threw his hands up in the air. "Sweet peas, Jamie, must I handle every wee detail?"

Jamieson looked at Hampton in disbelief. "You are an old fool," he stated succinctly.

"Coming from an overbearing pincushion like yourself, Jamie, I'll take that as a compliment." Hampton smiled at his friend. "So, keep lively tomorrow and we'll see if we can't arrange for Master Nick and Lady Andrea to spend some time together."

Jamieson's gaze followed Hampton as he turned and headed back up the stairs. "We're done for it now!"

The next morning, Miriam sat brushing Marissa's hair, pulling it back into a pretty braid. While a maid could have performed the task, Miriam cherished the quiet time alone with her granddaughter.

"Did you know that one of my favorite games is 'Let's Pretend'?" Miriam asked, a smile coloring her voice.

"Mine too," whispered Marissa, sitting very still. "Do you want to play?"

"That sounds like fun." Miriam continued the rhythmic stroking of Marissa's hair. "What if we invite your mother and father to play with us?"

In her excitement, Marissa twisted her head, yanking her hair out of Miriam's hands. "That's a . . . ouch!" The little girl reached up and rubbed at the sore spot. "That hurt."

Miriam smiled at the accusing tone. "I know, darling, which is why you must sit very still while I'm fixing your hair."

"I forgot. Sometimes it's hard to remember, isn't it?"

"Yes, sometimes it is." Miriam gently turned Marissa

around again and resumed her brushing. "Now, angel, do you think your father and mother would like to play?"

"I know my father will play with me. He told me so," Marissa announced proudly. "But I don't know if Mother will have time. She's very busy."

Miriam continued her steady strokes. "Oh, I'm sure she'll want to play; after all, it might be nice if we all pretended together. You could be the fairy princess . . ."

"Can't I be the evil witch? The princess never does anything except sit around waiting for the prince to come. It's not very fun to just sit there."

Miriam's laugh sparkled. "No, I suppose it isn't. Very well, then, you can be the evil witch and we can pretend to be . . . what?"

"My wicked henchmen," Marissa crowed, bouncing once on her chair.

"Oh, how fun." Miriam secured the end of Marissa's braid with a ribbon. "Then, I could arrange for Cook to prepare a noon repast and we could all picnic near the river."

"Can we, Grandmama?" Marissa turned and launched herself into Miriam's arms.

"If you'd like."

"Very, very, very much."

"I will assume that is a yes," Miriam laughed, hugging her granddaughter close. "And then we shall play a silly trick on your mother and father."

Marissa looked at Miriam, her eyes wide. "What?"

"After our picnic, you can pretend to have a horrid bellyache. Can you do that, darling?"

In response, Marissa began to groan, clutching at her stomach. "It hurts. It hurts." The little girl's writhings almost had Miriam convinced.

"I knew you could do it," Miriam chuckled with glee. "Then, I'll bundle you up in the carriage and take you home. Now, here's the silly part," Miriam said, her eyes glowing. "We leave your mother and father behind."

Marissa's mouth formed a perfect circle. "They'll think we left them there forever!"

"Mm-hmm." Miriam nodded. "They won't know that we'll come back for them after a little while and when we do they'll both think you're the best actress in the world to have fooled them like that."

That was all it took to convince Marissa. "What fun!"

"It will be, sweetling, it will be." Miriam straightened Marissa's shirt. "Now why don't you run along and ask your mother and I'll ask your father?"

Marissa's expression fell. "Mother won't want to play."

"I'm sure she will. Now that your father has returned, your mother has more time."

"Do you truly think so?"

Miriam gave the little girl a quick hug. "With all my heart."

"I'll try," conceded Marissa. "I will even cry if I must."

"I doubt you will be forced to resort to such lengths," Miriam returned with a smile.

Marissa sighed. "I do hope you're right, Grandmama." A look of displeasure crossed her features. "Crying always makes my eyes itch." With that explanation, Marissa headed from the room, leaving Miriam to dissolve into laughter.

Andrea startled when Marissa came into her room and hopped onto her bed. The hairbrush lay forgotten in her hand as she turned to face her daughter.

"Good morning, darling," Andrea murmured, holding out her arms to her daughter.

Marissa hopped off the bed, but came to a halt beside Andrea. "Hello, Mother," she said, kissing Andrea upon the cheek.

Andrea's hands dropped into her lap. "I'm delighted you came to visit me this morning, Marissa," she said brightly, trying to overcome her daughter's subtle rejection.

"You are?"

The innocent surprise in her daughter's voice filled her with guilty regret. "Of course I am, goose."

Marissa gave Andrea a tentative smile. "Then will you come play with me and Grandmama and Father? We're going to go on a picnic and I'm going to pretend to be the evil witch and you can be my wicked henchman. Doesn't that sound like fun?"

"Loads of it."

"Then can you come? Can you?"

There was no withstanding her daughter's plea. Andrea mentally crossed off her list of chores for the day. "I'd be honored to accept your gracious invitation, oh Magnificent One."

Marissa's giggle was her reward. "You're being silly, Mother."

"I believe today just might be a silly kind of day, don't you?"

Marissa's braid bobbed as she nodded.

Andrea glanced down at the breeches that Marissa was wearing. Perhaps Nicholas was right. Maybe she should try to show her daughter both worlds and then give her the right to choose. "I have a splendid idea, angel. Why don't we both wear lovely gowns on this picnic and pretend that we are grand ladies?"

Marissa wrinkled her nose. "Must I?"

"It would be more fun that way," Andrea said. "In fact, you can even pick out the dress you want me to wear."

That caught Marissa's interest as she glanced over at Andrea's large wardrobe. "Any one that I like?"

"Yes."

Marissa was quiet for a minute, her gaze fixed on the white and pastel fabrics spilling out from the wardrobe, her lip caught between her teeth. "All right," she finally said. "We'll both wear dresses." Marissa looked at her mother. "And I want you to wear your hair in a braid just like mine . . . only yours will be red and mine is black . . . and you can put a pretty ribbon on the end like this."

The little girl reached back and grabbed the end of her braid, showing the red ribbon to Andrea. "If you don't know how to tie it on, I'm sure Grandmama would help you."

The solemn tone in Marissa's voice made Andrea ache to hold her. "Thank you, darling, but I'm sure I can manage. Now why don't you decide what you want me to wear today while I braid my hair? After all, I can't very well go to our picnic as your wicked henchman in my dressing gown, now can I?"

"I suppose you . . ."

Andrea smiled as she steered her daughter toward the closet. "We agreed on a dress, now pick one out for me."

Her heart felt fuller than it had in years as Andrea watched her daughter rummage through her dresses. She divided her hair into three thick strands, plaiting it, feeling closer to her daughter. It was time she began to take advantage of Nicholas's return.

It was indeed a perfect day for a picnic.

Four

"Good morning, Harry," Andrea said as she sailed into the parlor, her dress streaming out behind her. "Jamieson told me you asked to see me. I fear we do not have much time to conduct this conversation. I am off on a—" She broke off her explanation when she glimpsed Harry's face. "Harry? Is something the matter?"

"Your dress . . . or, rather, your gown . . . is somewhat, ah, startling for this hour of the day," sputtered Harry, his pale complexion becoming infused with a bright red hue. He glanced around quickly before shutting the door, affording them privacy.

Nonplussed, Andrea glanced down at her gown. Marissa had picked out the frilliest dress she could find. There was nothing alarming about the pale green, sprigged muslin gown with buffonts of lace over the bosom . . . for evening attire, that was. To show so many curves in the morning was somewhat shocking, making Harry's astonishment perfectly understandable.

Andrea smiled at Harry, reaching over her shoulder

to pull her long braid in front. "Look, I even have a ribbon to match." She chuckled as she released her hair, allowing it to fall upon her bodice, a long strand of auburn silk crossing her creamy flesh. Bewildered at Harry's continued silence, she took a step forward.

"Harry?" she asked again, laying a gentle hand upon his shoulder in concern.

He gulped, his throat working, as his face turned a florid color. "Oh, Andrea!" he moaned. In an explosion of movement, Harry grabbed her by the shoulders, pulled her against him, and pressed his moist mouth onto hers.

Shock held her immobile. What was Harry thinking? Andrea shimmied her arms between their bodies and pushed him away, pressing a hand against her mouth. She was too jolted to speak.

"Andrea," he began, stepping forward again to clasp her free hand. "I can bear it no longer. It broke my heart when your husband returned. For so long I thought him dead and I had hoped that you and I were growing closer."

Her eyes widened with each word. She'd never viewed Harry as anything other than a client, and here he was pledging himself to her.

"I've fallen deeply in love with you and I no longer have the strength to hold it within me. I must share my deepest feelings with you." He began to inch his hands up her arm. "Allow me to show you how—"

"Harry!" she exclaimed, freeing herself from his grasp once again. "Please calm yourself."

Oh, Lord, how was she going to handle this delicately? Why hadn't she foreseen this unfortunate turn in Harry's attentions?

"Please allow me to be privy to your thoughts, your heart, Andrea, my love," Harry urged, getting down on one knee. "Tell me that you long to be mine."

"Oh, dear," Andrea whispered, glancing about her, certain that Nicholas, with his impeccable sense of timing, would walk into the room at any moment. "Please do get up, Harry," she urged, tugging at his arm, wondering why she was forever finding herself in these situations. "I expect my husband at any moment," she fibbed, trying to extract herself gracefully from Harry's embarrassing declaration.

"I would defend your honor," Harry pronounced, rising to his feet.

And more than likely get thoroughly trounced in the doing, Andrea thought. "Harry," she began slowly. "I'm sorry if I misled you in any fashion, yet while I hold you in the deepest regard, my heart does not sway in that direction."

"Surely I have not mistaken the way you address me."

Simply by calling him Harry? Had he taken that as an indication of deeper feelings? Surely not. "Harry," she said again, trying desperately to end the scene. "Rather, Lord Hartnell. While I consider you a dear friend of this family, never once did my intentions become more personal in nature. We converse on horses and the like, not on intimate matters."

"If truth, then why was I continually invited to spend time here at Leighaven?"

If she had known where it would lead, the invitations would never have been issued. Andrea shook her head. "Each time you stayed with us, you were concerned about one of your thoroughbreds. As it is a few hours to London, it was only courtesy which led to your invitation to reside here as our guest."

Harry's eyes narrowed as he leaned toward her. "Are you denying your emotions because of your allegiance toward your husband?"

Harry was only now considering the fact that she

was a married woman? Andrea took a step back. "Please, Harry, speak no further. I fear I would be unable to work with your horses if you continue. As it stands now, this situation will make matters extremely awkward between us."

"Not if you acknowledge my pledge." Harry reached out for her, his hands closing over her forearms. "Discretion will be necessary, to be sure, but the joy we shall find will overcome the disadvantages."

Andrea stepped back again, out of his grasp. "I must ask you to stop immediately. This conversation is uncomfortable for—"

A knock on the door interrupted her. Thankful, she hurried over to answer the summons, more than eager to leave the room. Hampton stood on the threshold, a worried expression weathering his normally smiling face. "What's wrong, Hampton?"

"It's Master Nick, my lady. He's been hurt and I need assistance." Hampton hurried away, waving for Andrea to follow him.

"Excuse me," Andrea said to Harry before quickly stepping after the manservant. She ignored Harry's call, focusing on Hampton, who was winding his way down to the basement.

What in the name of Heaven possessed Nicholas to come down here? Besides the wine cellar, there were only little-used rooms for storage. Breathless, Andrea asked, "Is he badly hurt?"

"Master Nick needs your help," Hampton replied over his shoulder, not pausing to answer.

They made their way to the wine cellar and Hampton unbolted the tiny door leading into the vaulted room. "In here, my lady," Hampton urged, signaling Andrea to precede him.

Too worried to question anything, Andrea stepped through the door, bending down to enter the dimly lit room. She had just cleared the entrance when the door swung shut behind her. "Hampton?" she asked, confused, as she turned back toward the door.

She heard the key turn in the lock. *"Hampton!"* she shouted, pounding on the wood. "Open this door immediately!"

"Don't mean to frighten you none, my lady. Just settle in." Hampton's voice was muffled. "I'll be back in a bit to let you out."

"Hampton, I insist you release me now!" she shouted back, once again pounding her fist on the door.

"You will bruise your hand for naught."

Andrea spun to face Nicholas. He stood in the dusky light, leaning against one of the wooden wine racks, his arms crossed over his chest, looking as if he didn't have a care in the world. "What is happening? What in heaven's name prompted Hampton to lock us in here?"

"Haven't you figured it out? It is quite simple, really." Nicholas pushed away from the rack, his arms falling to his sides as he moved toward her. "I'll admit that I too was confused at first, but now that you've been, shall we say, *escorted* to join me, it all makes perfect sense. Apparently our dear old Hampton has decided to do a little matchmaking."

"By locking us in the wine cellar?"

"We're here alone, aren't we? No way out, no one to hear us. Seems like a fairly logical plan to me." Nicholas held up one hand. "With one exception, that is. That wily old man didn't take into account that I will thrash him from one end of this estate to the other when I *do* extricate myself."

The image made Andrea laugh.

"There's no way out other than the door," Nicholas told her. "I was in the back of the room searching for another exit when I heard you shouting for Hampton. It was then that the pieces fell into place."

"I don't know what he hoped to accomplish by this." Andrea was suddenly exhausted. First her confrontation with Harry and now this. "I wonder how long he's determined to keep us in here?"

"I'm more concerned that the old fool will pass on unexpectedly and we will be left here to rot."

Nicholas's disgruntled rumblings made her smile. "Of course, his demise would not affect you in any other fashion."

"I stand here locked in my own cellar and you feel compelled to even ask?" Nicholas shook his head, his lips tilting upward. "Come now, Andrea."

"How imprudent of me." She shifted away from the wall, toward the middle of the room, wrapping her arms about her. "It is chilly down here, isn't it?"

Nicholas came closer, shrugging out of his jacket. "I should have realized, what with your interesting choice of attire, that you would feel the cold."

He slipped the coat about her shoulders, sliding his hands along the collar to secure it in place. "It was remiss of me . . ." Nicholas's words trailed off as Andrea tilted her head up, her gaze meeting his. Silence entwined them, a dusky bond of awareness.

"Thank you," she finally murmured, glancing away from the heat of his gaze. "You even warmed the jacket for me."

His fingers curled into the coat, the small movement bringing her closer to him. "My pleasure."

His words rushed over her, bringing forth all her lost dreams of love and passion. It was difficult to resist him when he was holding her against his lean body, igniting longings within her. "Thank you," she said again, trying to shift away.

He didn't let go.

Involuntarily, she glanced upward—and realized her mistake an instant later.

On her wedding night, he'd looked at her like this, with fire in his eyes, hunger flushing his features, and passion parting his lips. Memories of the way his mouth had run over her breasts and how his hands had stroked down her length burst to life within her.

Denial was impossible. The reasons why she needed to remain firm in her resistance, the reasons that had been so clear to her the other night, seemed immaterial at this moment.

"Andrea."

His whisper feathered across her parted lips. As his head dipped, she rose to greet him. His mouth brushed against hers once, twice, before lingering upon the softness. Gently, he tasted each curve, moving his mouth over hers in a sensual exploration.

Andrea moaned, winding her arms about his neck, shifting into him, so close that even air could not lie between them. For so long, her senses had lain dormant, hungering for this one man, craving his ardor. With the touch of his lips, her passions sprang forth, making her more than eager to follow him down the path of desire.

Lightning exploded between them as Nicholas moved his lips upon her parted mouth, his tongue smoothing the softness.

Lessons learned long ago urged Andrea to accept his kiss, giving welcome to Nicholas's deeper taste. Their heads tilted in unison as the kiss became hotter, fusing them together in a lock of passion. Nicholas's hands roamed over the length of her back, his fingers sinking into the fabric to reach the curved flesh below, pressing her into him, arching her against his hardness, creating an ache deep within her for utter completion.

Memories of their wedding night bound them together in reignited passion as Andrea tilted her hips forward, brushing against Nicholas's straining manhood, bringing a groan from him and a renewed fervor to their kiss. Andrea allowed herself to be swept away by the passion, clinging to Nicholas, the only man who could ease her hunger.

She gave herself up to the dark embrace of desire.

"Jamieson, have you seen either Nicholas or Andrea? They were to join Marissa and me on our picnic, but I can't find them anywhere." Miriam stood in the foyer, her hand wrapped firmly around Marissa's little one. The morning hadn't started off as she'd hoped. First Thomas had been unable to accompany them on their picnic as planned. A tenant had required some assistance, and instead of taking Nicholas away he had decided to handle the matter himself. And now the guests of honor seemed to have gone missing.

Miriam glanced back at the butler. "I don't know where they are."

"I'm afraid I haven't seen them, my lady," he replied. "Shall I check on the grounds?"

A small frown furrowed Miriam's brow. "I believe that's the only place left to—"

"Excuse me, Lady Miriam, but they're not outside," interrupted Hampton, coming toward them from the kitchen, a wide grin on his face. "No, indeed, they are not."

Jamieson's eyes narrowed. "And how do you know that?"

"Because not only do I know where they *aren't*, I know where they *are*."

"Where can we find them, Hampton?" Miriam took a step forward, bringing Marissa with her. "We should leave soon if we're going to catch the best part of the day."

Hampton rocked back on his heels. "I'm willing to lay odds that they're catching some fine time right now, my lady. Indeed, I am."

Jamieson paled. "What have you done?"

"Oh, I've done something, all right, Jamie boy. I've done something just right this time."

Miriam looked in confusion at both men, not understanding why Hampton was looking like a crowing rooster while Jamieson appeared to be ill, a greenish cast draining him. "What is going on? Where are Nicholas and Andrea?"

"In the wine cellar," announced Hampton, lifting his chin for an exaggerated nod.

"The wine cellar?" It still made no sense to Miriam. "Why are they down there?"

"Probably because they're locked in."

That bit of information brought an explosion from Jamieson. *"Are you befogged, man?"* Both of his hands clenched at his sides. "Do not tell me that you've taken leave of your senses and locked the Earl and his wife in the wine cellar?"

"Indeed I have."

Miriam placed a calming hand on Jamieson's arm when it appeared he was going to step forward and strangle Hampton where he stood. "There's no sense in arguing about this now," she said in a smooth voice, trying not to reveal how shocked she was by Hampton's actions. "The important thing is to release them right away before Nicholas's ire is raised any further."

"It wasn't his ire I was hoping would rise," grumbled Hampton, obviously disgruntled that no one else appreciated his efforts.

Miriam wasn't fast enough to stop Jamieson from clouting Hampton on the back of the head, sending the smaller man stumbling forward a step. "You dolt!

Do not dare to speak in such a vulgar manner before the dowager countess and Lady Marissa."

Hampton mumbled an apology, rubbing at the back of his head as he glared at Jamieson. "There was no call for hitting me so hard."

"I was hoping it might scramble your brains into some semblance of order," Jamieson retorted.

"Gentlemen, please!" Miriam said, trying to hold back a smile. "We must remember that Nicholas and Andrea are still locked in the wine cellar." She glanced down at her granddaughter. "Come along, Marissa, shall we go fetch your parents?" Miriam led the way, holding on to Marissa's hand, with Hampton and Jamieson trailing close behind.

At the threshold of the wine cellar, Miriam stood to the side, allowing Hampton to step forward and unlock the door. Miriam placed Marissa in front of her, in clear view, hoping that Nicholas would see her first and it would calm him a bit. Miriam leaned forward to peer into the room, curious as to the outcome of Hampton's attempt at matchmaking.

The sight of Nicholas and Andrea wrapped in a passionate embrace shocked everyone into silence.

Everyone, that is, but Marissa.

"Why is Papa trying to eat Mother?"

Nicholas pulled away from Andrea so quickly she stumbled backward. It was painfully obvious, though, to everyone over the age of six that he was having trouble orienting himself. His chest sawed in and out, his eyes glaring at them in disbelief. Andrea, in the meantime, was shifting her bodice back into place and smoothing her hopelessly wrinkled skirts.

"I don't understand, Grandmama," Marissa stated, looking up at Miriam. "Why was Papa trying to eat Mother? Didn't he have any breakfast?"

It was all Miriam could do to keep from bursting

out in laughter. "Of course he did, darling. He was only kissing your mother."

Her nose wrinkled. "That's not how people kiss. You kiss me all the time and you've never done it like that."

Hampton's snort of amusement came close to making Miriam lose her composure. "No, sweetling, that is how fathers kiss mothers."

"Ooohhhh." Marissa turned back around to look at her mother. "Can I see you kiss Papa again? It happened so quick that I didn't get a good enough look."

That did it for Miriam. She began to laugh, her shoulders shaking with mirth.

Marissa glanced first at Hampton, who was doubled over in laughter, to Jamieson, who was chuckling discreetly behind his hand, then up at Miriam. "Why is everyone laughing?"

Andrea moved forward to claim her daughter. "Come with me, Marissa, we'll head back up to the foyer. Everyone can join us there."

Clearing his throat, Nicholas turned around and walked to the door, pausing in front of Hampton who, by this time, had gained control on his amusement. "Dare to do something like this again, Hampton, and I vow I'll release you without any references."

The older man waved a hand at him. "Go on with you, Master Nick. You've been threatening to do that very thing for nigh on twenty years now."

"Then perhaps he'll take mercy on the rest of us and actually do it one day," murmured Jamieson.

"Why, you old blowhard," groused Hampton, apparently unwilling to take grief from both Nicholas and Jamieson at the same time.

"Come on, Nicholas, we'll miss the sun if we delay any further," Miriam interrupted, afraid that the conversation would begin to deteriorate. "Jamieson, would you please fetch the picnic basket from Cook and put it in our carriage?"

A dull flush stained Jamieson's cheeks. "Right away, my lady. My apologies for the delay."

"Growing a bit remiss in your duties there, aren't you, Jamie boy?" taunted Hampton as Jamieson hurried up the long staircase.

"I can only surmise that he has been spending too much time with you, then," Nicholas said before he followed Jamieson back to the main house, Hampton's sputtering protests echoing up the staircase.

Miriam waited until the sound of Nicholas's footsteps had died down before she moved forward, placed a hand on each of Hampton's shoulders, and graced him with two kisses, one on each cheek. "I don't care what anyone says, Hampton. I think you're a genius."

His cocky grin reappeared on his lined face. "I *knew* someone would appreciate my efforts."

Miriam squeezed his shoulders before she began her ascent, Hampton following along behind her.

"It was right brilliant of me, I think."

Miriam paused on the steps, glancing back at the manservant. "We're about to enter the main house, Hampton. Why don't we keep our appreciation of your cleverness between us?"

"Oh, right, Lady Miriam." Hampton nodded sagely. "Not too many people can appreciate the delicacies of my plan."

"So true," she agreed with a smile before resuming her climb up the stairs. After all, she was the only one who knew that Hampton's little plan was simply the appetizer.

Nicholas and Andrea had yet to dine upon her scheme.

A brilliant smile curved upon Miriam's lips as she followed her family out to their carriage.

Nicholas lay upon the blanket, his hands folded beneath his head, his stomach pleasantly full, as he watched his wife and daughter wade through the stream. Both of them had taken off their slippers and stockings and were wading barefoot in the cold water, shrieking as they slipped over the moss-covered stones.

Andrea looked utterly ridiculous standing in the middle of the stream in her evening gown with her skirts hiked up to her knees.

Yet, for the life of him, he couldn't ever remember seeing a more enchanting sight.

Marissa had finally relented and donned a dress, but it too was crumpled around her hips as she made her way across the rocky bottom of the stream. Andrea took another step forward, nearly losing her balance in the process, her skirts dipping into the water. As his wife smiled at their daughter, Nicholas felt his heart constrict.

And the sight of her shapely legs made another region tighten.

The fresh memory of their kiss tantalized him. Down in the darkness of the wine cellar, he'd looked at her in that silly dress with the long braid dangling down her back in a childish fashion, and he'd wanted to taste her again so badly he would have given up seven more years to the devil for it. There he'd been, locked in a room so like his prison cell, yet it hadn't bothered him at all. All he'd been able to think about was Andrea and how luscious her mouth looked.

Foolishly, he'd played the gallant, offering her his coat, moving so near that he could feel her warmth. It had been his undoing. He hadn't been able to turn her loose. Instead, he'd pulled her close and satisfied his fantasy, delving into her like the starving man he was.

Her response had inflamed him, making him lose all reason. If his family hadn't interrupted, he would have lowered her to the floor and eased his aching body, his hungry soul, within her warmth. The thought gave him pause. Andrea was his wife. She deserved better than a dirty basement.

The problem lay in the fact that up until today she had been withholding herself from him, claiming she needed time. Would she be so willing the next time? If only he could be certain she would respond to him again . . .

Nicholas almost shouted in triumph. That was the answer! Seduction. When he'd tried to make love with her before, he'd grown angry at her refusal, lashing her with scornful words. How could he have forgotten what had won her heart so long ago? His laughter.

Instead of getting annoyed with her, he would smile at her refusals. He would touch her, whisper to her, entice her until her body overruled her mind. After her tempting response to him this morning, he doubted that he would be able to wait for her much longer.

His eyes followed Andrea and Marissa as they abandoned the stream for the sunshine of the grassy meadow. Andrea's gown puddled around her as she began to unbraid Marissa's hair, taking the ribbon and tying it around the little girl's neck. A smile slid unbidden onto his face when Andrea began to place buttercups in Marissa's dark hair.

Love for his daughter swelled within his heart. What a gift she was to a man who'd long ago lost his soul. Just the sight of her, the sound of her voice, warmed him . . . and he'd been so very cold for so very long. His gaze slipped to his wife.

Andrea. With a warm smile and a quick hug, she had apparently reclaimed Marissa's affections. The distance of which his daughter had spoken was no more. The two of them, mother and child, sat in the middle of the field and played without a care.

Why must everything be so difficult for her?

Andrea sat behind Marissa, weaving flowers into her daughter's hair and listening to her chatter on about her papa and grandmama with nary a mention of the time they'd spent together the previous day.

". . . then Grandmama said that the pretty lavender flowers attract bees, so it wouldn't do to place them next to the terrace."

"No, I wouldn't care to have a swarm about me the next time I stepped out for a breath of air." Andrea plucked up another buttercup. "Do you remember when we played dominoes yesterday?"

"Yes. Oh, did I tell you of the red fox Papa and I saw when we were taking our walk?"

When compared to grand adventures with Nicholas and digging expeditions with Miriam, Andrea doubted that the occasional game she played with her daughter held any fascination.

"Yes, angel. You told me of that interesting fox." *And about the bullfrog, the hawk, and the ducks.* Andrea pressed a hand against her temple. It was becoming increasingly clear that she still wasn't spending enough time with her daughter. How did one make up for lost ground? Perhaps as with her horses, it took gentle words, soft strokes, and attention over time to regain trust and affection. Perhaps right here, in this field, was a beginning.

Andrea entwined the last buttercup into Marissa's

glistening hair. "Finished." She peeked over her daughter's shoulder to capture her gaze. "You look beautiful."

"Thank you."

She smiled at Marissa. "Would you care to do my hair now?"

Her daughter's hesitation tore at her heart, but Andrea kept her smile firmly in place.

"All right."

Warmth flooded Andrea as she turned, presenting her braid to Marissa. Tears moistened her eyes when she felt little hands working on her hair. It wasn't an overly enthusiastic response to the suggestion, but it was something.

It was a start.

As was her kiss with Nicholas. She'd begun to see the old Nicholas, her Nicholas, peeking out from beneath the stranger's mask. His wit, his laughter, the devilish gleam in his eye, all belonged to the man she had once loved. One kiss. One taste to refresh memories that had grown dusty with time.

It had been unwise to allow herself to give in to her desires so soon, before Nicholas conceded her worth, her value to the family. Yet hadn't she already begun to see changes in him? Positive reactions to her work in the stables, acknowledgment of her expert handling of this account or that? At this rate, he was bound to come around; to see her as the valuable asset she knew herself to be, not just as a wife to warm his bed at night. Though warming his bed was becoming more and more of a delightful idea.

The thought made her smile.

Certainly not more than a few more days would he suffer the constraints of continued celibacy.

He lay back upon the blankets they had spread for

the picnic, confident of his wife's desire. His mother had gone for a stroll, leaving him alone with his wife and child.

Nicholas watched as Marissa loosened her mother's hair, until a river of molten lava flowed down Andrea's back, capturing the brightness of the sun within its fiery depths. Nicholas had to swallow. Hard. The urge to sink his hands in Andrea's hair, to bury his face into the wealth, flowed strong and fierce through him, but he resisted, comforting himself with thoughts of how soon he would be able to fulfill these yearnings.

"She is a beautiful woman, Nicholas."

His mother's quiet voice jolted him as she sat down upon the blanket next to him, having just returned from her walk.

"Hmmm," he murmured, closing his eyes to the enticing picture of his wife, hoping to calm his body. However, behind his closed lids, an image of Andrea sitting amidst a field of flowers wearing nothing but a smile and her cloak of fiery hair burned itself into the darkness. His lashes flew upward as he tried to focus in on the tree before him. A dull tree. Nothing exciting about that . . . unless one pictured Andrea sitting in it, naked, an apple in her hand, tempting him in the age-old ways of women.

Nicholas sat up abruptly, rubbing his hands over his face, trying to erase the erotic images.

"Andrea is also one of the most intelligent women I know. And she's wonderful with the servants." Miriam folded her hands on her lap. "Why, just the other day—"

"You can cease in your praise, Mother. I have already wed the woman." He slanted an amused glance at his mother.

97

Miriam shifted beneath it. "I just want to ensure that you realize just how fortunate you are."

"Me? Fortunate?" Bitterness speared him. "You are quite mistaken."

"How can you say so?"

"Oh, I don't know," Nicholas said dryly. "I wager seven years rotting in a prison would be enough to convince even the thickest of men."

"I wasn't speaking of that," Miriam said softly.

"How can you not?" Nicholas faced his mother. "How can you dismiss something that shaped me so greatly?"

"I do not dismiss it, I am merely pointing out all that you have at present."

"Do you speak of this?" he asked, splaying a hand over the sun-drenched meadow where his wife sat with his daughter. "None of this is real. It's like a picture of what my life would have been if I hadn't spent seven years rotting in jail."

"Now, Nicholas—" began Miriam before he cut off her words.

"There's the loving wife with my daughter. We can even make Andrea expecting the birth of our second child if you like. And here I am, replete and satisfied, lounging upon the blanket, watching them frolic in the grass. As far as fantasies, this one would be difficult to improve upon."

"But this isn't a fantasy, Nicholas. This is reality. That *is* your wife over there playing with your child."

Miriam's protest made him smile. "Ah, but Mother, nothing is as it seems." He had called Andrea a loving wife, which was far from the truth. He'd also said replete and satisfied. He could count the replete portion as the fullness in his belly, but satisfied? Absolutely not. The constant ache in his loins in no way qualified him.

"But it can be, Nicholas. If you mold your future, it can be all of which you dream."

"Was it that way for you, Mother?"

Miriam raised a hand to her throat.

"Knowing Father as I did, I find it difficult to believe that he fulfilled your dreams."

"Then you must learn from my mistakes," she returned quietly.

"The years apart have changed Andrea and me, Mother. We are no longer the young innocents who wed." Nicholas reached over to squeeze his mother's hands. "Do not concern yourself so, Mother. Andrea and I have come to terms and have forged an arrangement that is mutually satisfactory," he explained, forgiving himself the lie for his mother's ease.

"But—"

"I must ask you to refrain from any further, shall we say, *aid* on my behalf," Nicholas interrupted.

"Aid?" Miriam's eyes rounded. "I'm not sure I comprehend your meaning."

A corner of his mouth quirked upward. "The rousing game of whist? This picnic itself?"

"Perfectly innocent outings."

"Perfectly aimed toward matchmaking, I wager."

"Nicholas," Miriam murmured, looking down. "How could you imagine that to be true?"

Nicholas laughed at his mother's inculpable expression. "I scarcely know."

His caustic tone brought a flash of a smile from Miriam. "You always were an irrepressible child."

"And have only perfected the ability as an adult." Nicholas rose to his feet, brushing at his breeches, before turning to offer his hand to his mother. "Shall we collect the other ladies and depart?"

"I suppose," Miriam replied, accepting his assistance.

"Marissa, Andrea, it's time we headed back," Nicholas called. They started toward him.

Suddenly, Marissa stopped in her tracks. She wrapped her arms about her stomach and began to moan loudly that her belly hurt. So loudly, in fact, that it made the horse stamp his feet nervously.

"What's wrong, Marissa?" Andrea asked, leaning over the child.

"My belly hurts and I want only Grandmama to take me home," Marissa moaned.

Nicholas tilted a look at his mother, who smiled weakly and raised her shoulders. He returned his attention to his daughter. "Come on, Marissa, into the carriage with you and we'll take you home."

"No, I only want Grandmama to take me back to Leighaven," she repeated. "You and Mother stay here and we'll send the carriage back for you."

Nicholas squatted down on his haunches to look his daughter in the eye. "You're really that ill, are you?"

"Oh, yes, Papa." Just to emphasize the point, another loud moan escaped Marissa. "It hurts terribly, but I don't want to spoil your day with Mother. You can stay here. I'm sure I'll be fine."

Nicholas touched the back of his hand to Marissa's forehead. "This seems very serious, Marissa. I think it's best if your mother and I accompany you and your grandmother."

"No, Papa. You stay here."

The spark of annoyance in her reply made Nicholas smile, but he quickly hid it from Marissa. "I'm afraid I can't, love. You see I'm the only one who knows how to mix up the special potion."

"Special potion?" Marissa asked, hesitant.

"Yes," he returned, his face serious. "Whenever someone suffers from something this badly, they need to take the special potion." Nicholas tucked a strand of hair behind Marissa's ear. "And I wouldn't want anything bad to happen to you. So, as soon as we get back to Leighaven, I'll have Cook round up some cod liver oil and a few fish scales and some mashed up bugs. Then I'll be able to make the potion."

Marissa's eyes had grown wider with each ingredient until she looked downright panicked. "You know, Papa, I'm starting to feel a little bit better."

"Only a little?" A sigh broke from him. "That's still not good, since you were so very, very ill just a moment ago. I think we still need to fix the potion when we get home."

Marissa's little arms flew out from her body, spread wide, as she announced, "I was wrong, Papa. I'm all better. In fact," she added, leaning in close to him to add to the effect, "I'm feeling better than before we *came* here."

Nicholas allowed a smile to touch his lips before he leaned forward to press a kiss on the tip of his daughter's nose. "What a miracle."

"It certainly is," Marissa agreed, eagerly stepping into Nicholas's arms as he held them out, picking her up off the grass. "Up you go, young lady." He turned to his mother. "You're next, Madam Busybody."

Miriam accepted his outstretched hand as he assisted her into the carriage. "Thank you."

"What's a busybody?"

Nicholas nodded toward his mother. "You need to ask your grandmama, Marissa. For she is the queen of the busybodies."

"Oh, hush," Miriam reprimanded with a laugh.

Nicholas turned toward his wife, who was grinning at him, admiration shining in her eyes. "Well done, Nicholas," Andrea murmured.

His eyes rolled. "Not at all. Good God, if she could

outsmart me at six, I'd be in trouble when she reaches ten, wouldn't I?"

Andrea's laughter skimmed down him like a fingertip, bringing his loins to awareness again. Nicholas helped her climb into the carriage, trying his best to ignore the curved flesh of her bottom.

Only a few more days. He'd have her seduced and in his bed. He contented himself with the thought, taking up the reins and clicking to the horses.

"Papa, must I still take the medicine?"

The hitch in Marissa's question made Nicholas smile. "Not if you're fully recovered."

"I am," she rushed to tell him. "Truly I am."

"I suspected as much," he returned, his eyes sparkling. "Though, I believe your grandmama is looking a bit peaked. Perhaps she could benefit from a dose."

"Nicholas, this isn't—" Miriam began.

"Do you think so?" Marissa cut into her grandmother's protest.

"Most definitely," Nicholas replied.

"Nicholas, I don't believe—" Miriam tried again.

"Perhaps she could do with a double dose at that," he added, cutting off Miriam's protest.

"A double one?" Marissa asked in a whisper.

"Most certainly," he pronounced.

Marissa looked at Miriam, pity in her expression. "It shan't be too awful, Grandmama."

Miriam shook her head, a smile playing about her lips. "Did I say irrepressible? Perhaps I misspoke. I believe I should have said incorrigible."

"Inkarigable?" Marissa tipped her head to the side. "What is that?"

Miriam laughed, hugging Marissa. "I daresay you should ask your papa this time, for he is the expert in *that* area."

"Amusing, Mother. Very amusing."

Andrea's laughter joined Miriam's as the carriage swayed homeward.

"I don't believe this is one of your better ideas, Nick."

Nicholas continued to roll up the sleeves on his shirt. "Come now, Thomas. I promise not to go too hard on you."

Thomas slowly removed his jacket, casting a wary eye upon Nicholas. "So you say, but you appear ready to tear the very flesh from my body." Carefully, he draped the coat over the fence. "Are you positive it must be fisticuffs? A challenging match of archery has greater appeal."

"Archery? Have you become an old maid then, Thomas?" His grin flashed white in the twilight. "We have often practiced together before going a few rounds at Minton's."

"True enough, but you never before wore such a look of wild eagerness. Whatever has happened to warrant it?"

More to the point, what *hadn't* happened. He'd spent all day with his wife. First their kiss, then the picnic, followed by dinner, where he'd been the perfect, attentive gentleman. He'd helped her into her chair, making sure his fingers brushed against her arms, then he'd escorted her to her room, his hand pressing against hers where it lay upon his sleeve. There was a roar in his blood that needed to be given release. Release that his wife wasn't willing to offer him. A good, healthy bout of boxing would exhaust him enough where he'd finally be able to get a good night's rest. Still, he couldn't very well admit such a thing to his brother. "Nothing."

"Ho, Nick, do you think me the fool? You're near

to boiling over and I'm not particularly fond of being burned."

Nicholas continued to pull on his gloves. "I vow it will be a mere singe, Thomas."

"Still a bit too close." Thomas propped an elbow on the fence, not making a move to ready himself for the fight.

"Don't exaggerate," Nicholas said, glancing at his brother. "I'm just in the mood for a bit of sport."

"So now you find sport in punching your brother?"

Nicholas slapped his gloved hand upon his thigh. "You are only lessening my resolve to be gentle, Thomas."

"Gentle?" Thomas's laugh rang out. "At present, you'd be more likely to rip my bloody head off than box in a civilized fashion."

Nicholas paused, then slumped against the fence. "My assurances that it wouldn't be on purpose undoubtedly would not help, would they?"

Thomas ran a hand over his throat. "I've grown rather fond of my head. Perhaps it would serve better use if I helped you sort out your troubles."

Nicholas thought of the desire plaguing him and of the confusion Andrea aroused in equal measure. He shook his head. "I'm fine. I'm merely finding my ground within the family."

"Ahhhh."

"What the devil do you mean by that?" Nicholas asked.

Thomas turned and rested both arms on the fence. "Nothing more than that I understand your struggle, have fought the same demons myself."

The desire to ask for his brother's advice warred with the need to appear in control. It didn't take much reasoning to decide that the latter was fairly impossible this far in the game. "Have you reached any truths in doing so?"

"Only that perhaps Father had the way of it."

"Father? Our father?"

"Are there so many from which to choose?"

Nicholas frowned. "What could we possibly learn from him? How to set impossible demands upon everyone around us? Or perhaps we should model ourselves after him and become cool and distant with each other?"

Thomas laughed, nodding. "He was a tough buzzard, to be sure, and he certainly lacked skills of a personal nature, but he also ran this estate in an admirable manner."

Nicholas remained silent, allowing his brother to say his piece.

"He managed the properties with an ease I've envied for some time now and, while he was ofttimes too harsh, he did instill in us a sense of purpose and direction."

"By continually hounding us to better ourselves," Nicholas retorted.

"At least he cared."

"If that was his brand of affection, I could have done very well without it."

"Could you really?" Thomas shifted to face Nicholas. "How many of our chums had fathers who acted as if they didn't even exist, never mind matter? If our father was too stern, it was far preferable to an utter lack of concern. Think on it, Nick. Did you ever once doubt Father's interest in our welfare?"

"No, but . . ."

Thomas put out his hand. "Leave it at that, Nick, and allow the remainder to be forgotten. Look upon the man as a whole and learn from his mistakes."

"Utilize the areas in which he exceeded and discard those in which he failed," Nicholas finished.

"Precisely."

It was worth consideration. Filing away the thought, Nicholas tapped Thomas on the shoulder with a gloved hand. "For such an intelligent man, you can certainly prattle on, Thomas, but I do believe it's time to knock each other senseless."

Thomas groaned. "I was hoping you would become too embroiled in our conversation and forget about this silly boxing idea."

"Silly?" Nicholas rapped Thomas on the arm, this time harder. "Afraid, are we?"

Thomas rolled his eyes. "Do you still believe your ridiculous taunts can incite me as they used to when we were boys?"

"Starting to feel your years?" Nicholas ducked down, jabbing his brother in the ribs.

"Ouch," Thomas protested, rubbing at the area. "Cut it out, Nick. I'm heading into London tomorrow for an overnight trip and I've much to accomplish."

"With the ladies, Thomas?" Nicholas knocked his fist against his brother's stomach. "Afraid I'll damage your pretty face?"

Thomas shoved Nicholas's hand away. "Run along now, old man, and find someone else to indulge you."

Nicholas grinned at his brother, lightly pushing at Thomas's jaw. "Quite all right, Thomas. It was always far too easy to best you anyway."

"Hold on," Thomas retorted, his eyes beginning to flash. "My memory serves victory more often to me."

Nicholas assumed a pugilist stance. "Lost your physique and now your mind is on the blink, too?" He shook his head. "Poor fellow. It's only fitting I take pity upon you."

"Pity?" Thomas pushed away from the fence, snapping up the pair of gloves lying on the ground. "I'll gladly prove which one of us is the more pitiful creature."

"Just like old times, right, Thomas?"

The first thing Thomas did was punch the grin off Nicholas's face.

Five

Nicholas fingered his sore jaw as he waited patiently in the field for his daughter. It had quickly become their habit to take walks every midday. As they strolled, they discussed anything—notwithstanding the nonsensical—that struck their fancy. These past few days had been some of the best in his life.

Lord only knew, his time with Andrea wasn't half so satisfying. The beguiling female had taken to smiling at him, then turning away. He wanted to pull her into his arms, kiss her senseless, and make her see how foolish she was being by denying him. He had some marital rights due him and by God, he was aching for them.

But he was a gentleman, above all. He was an Earl and, as such, would not beggar himself to her—regardless of how much he craved surcease within her sweet body. No, his plan to seduce his wife was beginning to bear fruit, though far slower than he cared to admit.

Nicholas's thoughts skittered to a halt when he heard Marissa call to him. A broad smile covered her face as she raced over the grass. Suddenly she stumbled, fear twisting her features.

What the devil was wrong with the girl? But before he could call out to her, a shot rang out, echoing across the field a second before the bullet shook his body, hitting his left shoulder and driving him to his knees. A second bullet grazed his temple, throwing him to the ground. Nicholas rolled toward his daughter, calling out a warning.

"Get down!"

His head lifted slightly, just in time to see her drop to the ground. His eyelids closed. He was losing too much blood, he knew, his fingers lightly feeling his shoulder where the first bullet had gone straight through, leaving gaping holes on both sides.

Nicholas was dimly aware of Marissa screaming his name, but a warm haze was enveloping him. Weakly, he tried to reassure her, but his muscles would not respond. His vision was beginning to sparkle with white lights, blinding him to all.

His eyes closed and willingly Nicholas gave himself up to the peaceful oblivion that awaited him.

"Andrea, might I have a moment of your time?"

Lady Anne's bidding caused Andrea to pause in the middle of the foyer. Though couched as a question, Andrea knew from her mother's tone that she would not be denied. Still, Andrea tried.

"I'm quite pressed this morning, Mother. Perhaps we can speak later today."

"This matter is of the utmost importance and cannot wait," Lady Anne said, moving forward to clasp her daughter's arm.

Andrea held back a sigh as she allowed her mother to guide her into the library. Comfortable settees were placed about the fireplace, forming a semicircle to catch the warmth, and a few overstuffed chairs were set around the rest of the room, giving the air of privacy.

Lady Miriam sat reading quietly in the settee nearest the window, a cup of tea cradled in one hand. Her face lit up when she saw Andrea. "Hello, dear, what a pleasant surprise."

"Do not speak so swiftly," Andrea murmured.

Miriam's eyes clouded in confusion at Andrea's words, but cleared with dawning comprehension when she caught sight of Lady Anne's determined expression. "Oh. I see. Let me gather my things together and I will be out of your way." She set the china teacup onto the saucer and shut her book.

"No, Miriam, please stay. I believe your input might be useful. After all, he is your son."

"To whom do you refer? Thomas or Nicholas?"

"Which one is creating an uproar within our household?"

Miriam laughed lightly. "I can only presume you speak of my eldest."

"None other."

"I doubt if I can offer any insight."

"Mother," Andrea interrupted, aware of time slipping past.

"We have a very serious problem," Lady Anne stated firmly, smoothing back the elegant twist in her hair.

"We?"

"Precisely. We. After all, I am a member of your family, am I not?"

Andrea felt a wave of regret sweep over her. Her relationship with her mother had deteriorated over the years into one of polite restraint. "What is the problem?" Andrea questioned quietly.

Lady Anne sat down on the settee opposite Miriam.

"My problem is your husband or, more succinctly, his threats."

"Threats?" Andrea was amazed. Why would Nicholas be threatening her mother?

"Yes, blatant ones issued earlier this morning."

"What happened?" Andrea asked.

"Why, he threatened to cut me off dry! There I am tending to personal matters when he comes barging into the study making all sorts of wild accusations and uncalled-for—"

"The study?" Andrea interrupted, positive that she had heard incorrectly. The study had always been considered her private domain, one which she had now relinquished to Nicholas. To her knowledge, her mother had never before ventured into it.

A light flush crept over Lady Anne's alabaster skin. "I just happened along with—"

"Please, Mother, I find it difficult to believe that you could just 'happen' along into the study. If I am to sort through this mess, I need to know your true reasons and actions."

Lady Anne's flush grew to a dull red as she lifted her chin and boldly announced, "Very well, then. I deliberately went into your study."

Andrea sank into a chair. "For what purpose?"

"I simply wanted to understand our financial situation in more detail." Lady Anne fingered a ribbon on the front of her gown. "Since you blithely handed everything over to him without a thought."

She couldn't have been more shocked if her mother had declared she was joining a nunnery. "But, Mother, is that not what a good wife should do? Simply hand the reins over to her husband with nary a word? You've lectured me on this issue quite often. A wife is to bow to her husband's wishes."

"Not at the cost of her family," countered Lady Anne.

"You have hardly been made to suffer," Andrea stated firmly.

"While that is true, it is of concern that you are no longer involved with our finances. Did your experience with Thomas teach you nothing?" Lady Anne shifted upon her seat. "It was in our best interest that I decided to investigate the matter myself."

"What exactly do you mean by 'investigate'?" Andrea asked quietly.

Lady Anne squared her shoulders, clasping her hands at her waist. "Naturally, I wished to ascertain my position, so I took a look at the accounts."

"You didn't," exclaimed Miriam, speaking for the first time.

"So what if I did?" Lady Anne challenged. "It is my right to ensure my financial security. It is quite obvious that in her attempts to placate her husband, Andrea has thrown my fate to the winds. Thus, I decided it was time to see to my own future."

"I assume that Nicholas came upon you while you were, ah, 'investigating' the accounting ledgers," Miriam said softly.

Lady Anne's coiffure barely moved as she nodded her agreement. "But not before I saw his notes. Apparently he is planning on cutting back my monthly stipend to a quarter of what I now receive."

"Mother, you must admit that your allotment is more generous than most."

"Generous?" Lady Anne stiffened. "It is nothing less than I deserve."

Andrea rubbed at her forehead. "Shall I presume you would like me to speak with Nicholas regarding this matter?"

"Of course," Lady Anne insisted. "I would greatly appreciate your immediate attention to this issue."

Andrea simply wanted the conversation finished. "As you wish, Mother. I shall ask Nicholas of his future financial plans. Now, if you would excuse me—"

"Lady Andrea!"

Jamieson's voice was raised to a frantic shout. Andrea rushed forward, brushing past her mother, a feeling of dread filling her.

Andrea skidded to a halt when she came out of the library into the foyer and caught her first glimpse of Nicholas, unconscious and bleeding, held up by Jamieson and two stable hands. A weeping Marissa stood beside them, clutching Nicholas's limp hand. Disbelief flooded her at the sight.

"What happened?" Andrea gasped, racing forward to Nicholas's side, her hands skimming lightly over his body.

"Someone shot Papa," sobbed Marissa. "Someone came out of the woods and shot him."

All the blood drained from Andrea's face when she saw the wide red stain spreading on Nicholas's shirt. "We need to stop the bleeding," she said, finding the wounds on Nicholas's shoulder and head.

"Master Nick!" shouted Hampton, tripping down the stairs in his haste. "What's happened to Master Nick?"

Andrea fought back her panic and took charge of her emotions. Nicholas needed her help. She had to pull herself together. "Hampton, send someone to fetch the doctor and the constable immediately. After that, bring hot water and fresh bandaging to my chamber. Jamieson, bring him upstairs so I can try to stop the flow of blood."

At the top of the stairs, Andrea directed the trio of men to the closest bedroom . . . her bedroom. Gently,

Nicholas's body was laid down on top of Andrea's coverlet. At the door, Andrea turned to her still sobbing daughter, who had followed them. She enfolded her child with her arms. "I need for you to be very brave now, angel."

"I want Papa," she cried, tucking her head into Andrea's neck.

Aware of Nicholas's seeping wound, Andrea squeezed her daughter once more before releasing her. "I know you do, Marissa, but I need you to be a big girl and help me."

Marissa wiped at the tears on her cheeks. "What shall I do?"

"I'm very concerned about your grandmama. She is distraught and very much needs hugs and attention to ease her mind."

Marissa glanced at Miriam who stood, crying, behind the child. "I will see to her. I promise."

"And I will see to your papa." Andrea gave her daughter a kiss on the forehead before turning back toward Nicholas.

Andrea reached into her nightside table and removed a pair of shears. She began to cut away Nicholas's blood-soaked shirt. As the two stable hands left, Hampton rushed in, carrying bandages and a pan of hot water. Jamieson moved forward to assist him.

"We need to act quickly," Andrea said, focused upon Nicholas's wound. "It is imperative we stop the bleeding."

Leaning in closer, she saw a few fibers from his shirt protruding from the wound. She knew from her experience with the horses that cleansing the wound was essential in order to stave off infection. She continued to cut away the shirt as she gave instructions, "Jamieson, I need whiskey and a very, very sharp knife at once."

As Jamieson hurried from the room, Hampton helped Andrea remove Nicholas's shirt, lifting his upper body, enabling Andrea to pull the material out from under him. Andrea smiled her thanks to him before she bent over Nicholas's head to examine the bullet wound at his temple. Luckily, it was only a surface injury. The wound at his shoulder, however, troubled her. The flow of blood had slowed, making her believe that, while serious, it was no longer life threatening.

Her greatest fear was for the fever that always came after a serious injury such as this. With the large amount of blood loss, she knew it would be hard for him to overcome it.

As soon as Jamieson returned, Andrea took the knife, poured whiskey over it, and began to carefully remove all traces of foreign material from the gaping wound. She repeated the procedure on Nicholas's back, where the bullet had entered. Once she was done, Andrea poured whiskey over the entire area, causing Nicholas to arch upward as the intense pain penetrated his unconscious state.

A long needle, threaded with silk, was then run through the whiskey before Andrea cautiously stitched the wound closed. Her bottom lip was caught between her teeth as she slowly pierced the tanned skin at Nicholas's shoulder until the hole was pulled closed. After washing his upper body with the warm water, Andrea fastened a tight bandage around his shoulder, wrapping his left arm against his body to prevent him from flailing it about in the throes of fever and harming himself further.

Releasing a breath of relief, she turned her attention toward the nick at his temple. Cleansing the wound, she simply bandaged it tightly. Gazing at his body, she checked for more damage, but found no other injuries.

"If you want, Jamie and me can take off the rest of Master Nick's clothes and settle him in bed while you see to Marissa and the constable," Hampton offered.

"Thank you both for your help," she murmured, her gaze still focused on her husband. Her hand shook as she reached out to trace his lashes where they lay upon his cheeks.

So beautiful, she thought, her heart catching a little. Slowly, Andrea leaned forward and pressed her lips against his forehead in a sweet, loving kiss before she straightened and walked from the room, unaware of the amazed expressions covering the faces of Hampton and Jamieson.

A loud sigh slipped from Andrea as she sat down in the chair next to where Nicholas lay still and silent, lost in the large bed they had shared one night so long ago. Andrea leaned her head back against the cushion, closing her eyes as she relaxed for the first time since seeing Nicholas helpless in the foyer. Her thoughts wandered over the events of the day. As soon as Nicholas had slipped into sleep, she had left him for a moment to check on their daughter. Marissa had been hysterical with worry, somehow blaming herself for not warning her father of impending danger, sobbing over and over about how she had seen a masked figure step from the woods. Marissa had cried when she told of how she'd seen the man point a gun at her father. But instead of yelling a warning at him, she'd frozen in fear. Andrea had done her best to comfort the child, repeating over and over that it was not Marissa's fault.

The doctor had arrived with his bag and a harried expression and, upon examination, announced that Andrea had done stellar work on the Earl and that he was now in God's hands. The constable had arrived a short while later and, after speaking with everyone in the household, promised to investigate the matter. The constable had then ventured to say that it was undoubtedly a poacher whose shot had gone astray, and he would speak with the tenants to see if they knew anything.

Andrea leaned forward to stroke her husband's arm, the soft gauze of her nightgown brushing against her bare legs when she shifted. He seemed so vulnerable, so helpless. She longed for an arrogant grin, an amused glance, or even a frustrated demand. To have him silent, weakened, made her heart ache.

The white of the bandage stood out, stark, against his skin. Drawn to him, Andrea slipped quietly from the chair to perch on the edge of the bed, her hip pressing against his where it lay under the covers.

Her gaze fluttered over his chest, noting the small nicks and cuts, now healed, that were scattered across his sculpted flesh. She reached out to gently touch the tiny marks. No wonder he was so bitter, Andrea acknowledged, only now getting insight to the hell that had been his existence for the past seven years.

So much pain, so much suffering, Andrea thought, tears slipping over her cheeks. He had already been through so much and now here he was, once more fighting for his life. Her chin lifted stubbornly as she realized that at least this time, he would not be fighting alone. She was with him now.

Nicholas was hers.

Her heart skipped a beat at that thought. When had she begun to think of him as hers again? Had it been when they'd been locked in the wine cellar and he'd reawakened her desire? Or perhaps from all the gentle touches and soft glances he'd been giving her lately? It could have been as she witnessed all the tenderness he offered their daughter.

The reason really was immaterial, because it did not alter the end result: the heady feeling of falling in love. Wonder filled her as she brought both hands up to stroke Nicholas's broad chest. A smattering of dark curls grew across the silken hills and valleys of his chest, catching Andrea's fingers, enticing her for a more intimate look. Nicholas's dark head twisted against the pillow, turning to bury the right side of his face into the soft down.

She was a fool.

Today Nicholas had almost been lost to her. He could have been killed and, all the while, she had stubbornly refused to accept him as her husband. Since his return he had teased her, enticed her, angered her. Was that not the role of a husband? Her senses hungered for him, craving the magic of his embrace, but still she had denied him until he recognized her true worth. But if they bonded physically, would it not bring them closer emotionally? Would it not be easier for him to see her as an equal if he saw her through the eyes of love?

Now he lay caught in the throes of a fever, while she could only watch, unsure if he would survive. That thought was too painful to bear. After he'd left her, she had struggled so hard to save her family, never realizing how much she'd given up. Then Nicholas had returned, breathing new life into their existence, challenging her, pushing her into examining her life. Because of him, she had seen her mistakes with Marissa, had begun to reevaluate her priorities, and had been reawakened as a woman.

If he left her now, it would devastate her.

Determination filled her as Andrea reached for the washcloth. Wringing out the water, she pressed the cool, damp material against Nicholas's burning forehead, crooning softly to him in comfort. She would fight the devil himself for her husband.

He belonged to her.

The pain radiating from his shoulder penetrated Nicholas's consciousness. He slanted open his eyes, the late-afternoon sun bothering him.

"So, you have awakened."

Nicholas blinked, watching Thomas stride into the room. "Nicholas—Lord, old man, you gave us all a fright. I got back from London as soon as I received word." Thomas shook his head, concern etched within the light words. "I'm gone only three days and look at you."

"I assure you, it was not intentional," Nicholas replied, rubbing a hand over his shoulder.

"You've been feverish for a full day," Thomas informed him. "It broke only a few hours ago."

Hazy memories of sweet hands stroking his heated flesh made him pause. Had that loving touch belonged to his wife? Highly doubtful, Nicholas scoffed silently. More than likely it was the product of his overheated imagination. He forced himself to concentrate on his injury. "What happened? All I remember is seeing Marissa's distress before I felt the bullet hit me. Did anyone see who shot me?" *Other than his daughter.* The grim thought disturbed him greatly.

Thomas eased himself into a chair. "Marissa said a person dressed in a black shirt and pants and wearing a mask stepped out of the forest and shot at you. One of the stable hands heard Marissa screaming, and he sent someone to the house to fetch Jamieson. They carried you here."

"What about the constable? Was he notified?"

Thomas nodded. "Our constable, Mr. Bridgeton, does not inspire confidence in his abilities. He looked around, but he didn't find anything. Bridgeton believes it was a hunter who shot you by accident. He's been questioning the locals, but hasn't turned up anything yet."

Disbelief crossed Nicholas's face. "My daughter tells the constable that she saw a man step out of the woods, point a gun, and shoot at me, and the fool thinks it was an accident?"

"The incompetent Bridgeton feels that Marissa is too young to give an accurate account. He believes that she was so upset that she doesn't remember what truly happened."

"Did he speak with everyone else regarding their whereabouts?"

"As I said, he's been talking with—"

"I mean here at Leighaven."

Thomas's brows raised. "Leighaven? Surely you don't suspect . . ."

"It's always best to begin looking around you first; eliminate the ones closest to you, then widen the search."

Thomas paused for a moment before he began to check off people on his fingers. "Harry was in the stables . . ."

"Alone?"

"No."

"Can anyone verify it?"

"Yes. A stable hand, a fellow by the name of John . . ." Thomas paused. "Have you met the lad?"

Nicholas shook his head.

Thomas shrugged. "Anyhow, John was laying fresh hay in the barn when Harry entered. The boy was working in the main area of the stable until a servant from the house came to fetch him for his meeting with the constable."

"And what of Hartnell?"

"Harry left the stables at the same time as John."

Nicholas lay quiet, concentrating on the various possibilities. "Perhaps this fellow, John, wasn't at the doors to the stables the entire time. He could have been fetching another bale of hay from the loft and simply missed him."

Thomas shook his head. "I already thought of that possibility and ruled it out after the hand said he brought down six bales before starting in order to avoid running about. He was at the entrance to the stables the entire time Harry was inside."

"So, that eliminates Harry."

"I told you, Nick, the constable spoke with everyone."

"He didn't speak with me." Nicholas looked at Thomas. "You see, I would have told him that this was the second time this type of 'accident' has occurred."

Thomas's entire body tensed. "The second time? What on earth are you talking about?"

"A number of days ago, someone shot at me with an arrow. At the time, I assumed it was a poacher whose shot had gone astray." He lightly touched the bandage on his forehead. "However, when the two incidents are combined, they seem to form a deadly pattern. . . ."

Thomas sank back into the chair. "But who? Why?"

"I haven't a clue."

"But it makes no sense," Thomas protested. "Why would someone want to murder you? You've only just returned home."

"Which only adds another interesting angle to the situation, don't you think?"

"So, where do we begin?"

Nicholas rubbed a finger against his temple. "I believe our only recourse is to try to find possible motivation."

"Find the reason, find the assassin."

"Precisely."

Thomas looked at Nicholas, his expression thoughtful. "And what about me, Nick? I'm the one who inherits the title. Am I a suspect, too?"

A laugh rumbled in Nicholas's chest. "Hell, no, Thomas. I know you too well. You view the responsibility of the title as a burden, something which you've managed to avoid with amazing success."

"I am relieved to be out of the running."

Nicholas levered himself up onto one elbow. "I need your help, Thomas."

"Always," he answered immediately.

The quick response made Nicholas smile. He'd known he could count on his brother. "Look at the two of us. Did you ever imagine yourself searching for a murderer?"

"Never. And the stakes are far too high for me."

"If we lose, I'm dead."

Nicholas's statement made Thomas pale. "Don't worry. I plan on watching my back here on out. Together we'll catch the bastard."

If anything, Thomas grew whiter. "I've got to confess, Nick, I'm a bit unsure of how to go about it."

"Carefully, Thomas," Nicholas replied, lowering himself back onto the sheets. "Very carefully."

Six

A soft hand stroking the side of his face was the first sensation to awaken Nicholas. Instinctively, like a flower turning to the sun, he moved toward the softness, his eyes still closed, rubbing against the warm contact. Awareness began to filter through his sleep-colored thoughts, causing his body to jerk in reaction, his eyes shooting open.

Andrea's lips curled into a welcoming smile as his bewildered eyes focused on her face. Nicholas lay rigid under her touch as she stroked the hair off his forehead.

"So, you finally decided to rejoin the world of the living," she murmured softly. "I've brought you some dinner."

His stomach growled in response. "Thank you," he said, acutely aware of her fingertips skimming over his hair.

"Some delicious broth."

"I thought you mentioned *dinner,*" he returned dryly.

Andrea's laugh feathered over him. " 'Tis all you can handle at present."

The aching throb from his shoulder radiated outward, lending credence to her statement. "Unfortunately."

She skimmed her fingers lightly over the bandage on his shoulder, her nails scraping across his chest, before she leaned forward to assist him into a sitting position. Under any other circumstances, he would have accepted her touch as an invitation for additional intimacies. He was sure, however, that only concern for his well-being inspired it.

Nicholas winced as he propped himself upright against the pillows.

Andrea perched on the edge of his bed, her hip tantalizingly near his thigh. Even in pain, his desire for this woman could tempt him. "Here we are," she said, lifting a spoon to his lips.

Obediently, he swallowed the broth, hardly tasting it. His level of fatigue after having slept all day amazed him.

"You had us worried last evening." Andrea gave him another spoonful. "Your fever was very high."

A side of his mouth tilted upward. "I do seem to inconvenience you, don't I?"

"Most greatly," Andrea responded pertly with a smile of her own. "Shall you forever be a burden in my life?"

Her teasing words made his grin waver. *A burden in her life.* The few sips of broth he'd managed soured in his stomach, everything within him rejecting his own thoughts. They were too strong to be denied. Did she truly think him a burden? He knew she hadn't wanted him to return, but did she still feel that way?

Andrea had unwittingly given him one possible motivation for wanting him gone.

Unknowingly, she had cast suspicion upon herself.

He refused to believe it to be true. She might argue with him, disagree with his decisions, but never would she stoop to such depths. Never.

Trustingly, he opened his mouth for the next spoonful of broth.

"Marissa peeked in on you today, but you were sleeping." Andrea's eyes sparkled as she continued. "In fact, she seemed greatly relieved to see you asleep. According to our daughter, you frequently nap when you lie about in the field, and it reassured her to find you enjoying your favorite pastime."

Andrea smiled at Nicholas, but no witty rejoinder was forthcoming.

"How is she?"

Compassion flowed through Andrea. "Marissa is fine, Nicholas," she reassured him, giving him another taste of broth. "I cannot deny she was exceedingly distraught over your injury, but once she saw for herself that you would get well, it eased her worries."

Relief softened the lines upon his face. "I'm thankful."

"As am I," Andrea agreed. Her heart melted at the weariness she saw in him. He'd been through so much already. His scars bore testament to that fact. Would they ever find peace together? Gently, she laid a hand upon Nicholas's cheek. "I'm also thankful for you."

He started beneath her palm, confusion darkening his gaze. "Are you?"

She leaned forward. "Positively."

Nicholas said not a word, his expression suddenly wary. They took measure of each other before Nicholas finally looked away.

Andrea slid her palm down the line of his jaw, aware that her display of affection surprised Nicholas. She bit back a smile. After he was fully recovered, she would tell him of her decision to become his wife again in truth.

But for now, she needed to concentrate on returning him to health. "Would you care for more to eat?"

He cleared his throat, pausing, before replying, "Don't you mean *drink?*"

"Must you be so literal, Nicholas?"

"No," he said. "But I do try my best."

Her laughter made him smile.

"Take that swill away," groaned Nicholas, waving off Hampton.

Some of the watery porridge sloshed over the edge of the bowl as Hampton offered it to Nicholas. "But . . . but, Master Nick, you have to eat in order to get back your strength."

"That refuse will only sap what strength I have left, not add to it. I need some real food. It is time everyone stop treating me like an invalid." Nicholas swung his legs out from under the covers, moving to sit upright, keeping the blanket wrapped around his frame.

"Oh, no," worried Hampton, his gray head shaking in distress as he moved to place the tray on a nearby table. "Lady Andrea will be most— It is not the best thing— I don't know if—" Hampton's muttering ceased while he hurried to the door, opening it wide to bellow, *"Jamieson!"*

"Fetch me some clothes, Hampton."

Once more he shook his head. "I don't think I should do— *Jamieson!*" Hampton roared again.

"What, what, you old fool," Jamieson snapped out as he marched into the bedroom. "Fine way to bellow in a convalescent's room, you—"

"Not now, fussbudget. We don't have time to bicker. Look!" Hampton pointed a long finger at Nicholas.

Jamieson started at the sight of Nicholas sitting upright. "Why, my lord, you must lie back down and rest. You need—"

"Jamieson, I assure you that I have long since outgrown the need for you to tell me what I should and should not do. Now either someone fetch some clothes for me or I will be forced to parade down the hall in my natural state with only this blanket to assist me."

"Master Nick, I would never presume to tell you what—"

"Then don't," Nicholas interrupted Jamieson's stilted argument.

"It is just that Lady Andrea—"

"Yes, that's right. Lady Andrea," Hampton cut in, drowning out Jamieson's voice.

The interruption earned him a glare from Jamieson before the butler continued, "What I was attempting to say before I was so rudely interrupted—"

"Well, pip, pip to you, too," muttered Hampton under his breath.

Jamieson calmly ignored Hampton's comment. "—was that Lady Andrea has been taking care of you, so I feel it would be best to consult her before we do anything rash."

Nicholas looked from Hampton, who was wringing his hands, to Jamieson, who stood erect, certain his logic would prevail. Silence deadened the room for a long moment before Nicholas spoke very softly, causing both men to lean closer in order to catch every word. "Listen carefully, both of you, for I am only going to say this once. First, I am an adult with all the privileges entitled to me as such. Second, and more important, I, not Lady Andrea, happen to be the master of this house and if my wishes are not met, I will send you both packing and find staff who will be more than willing to follow orders."

"Oh, go on with you," Hampton laughed, waving a hand at Nicholas. "You could no more release us than you could your dear lady mother."

Jamieson nodded in agreement, aligning himself with the manservant.

"Nicholas, are you badgering poor Hampton and Jamieson again?"

The two elderly men turned to Andrea, who stood in the open doorway. "Lady Andrea," Jamieson murmured, relief coloring his greeting.

"Here's Lady Andrea now to set things straight." Hampton rocked back on his heels, a smug smile set upon his face.

Nicholas's gaze swung to his wife. Her warm, dare he say loving, attitude toward him during his convalescence confused him. He was unsure of how to handle the swift change. On guard, he retreated behind humor. "So, the mother hen has come to check on her baby chick."

A throaty laugh spilled from her. "Lord, Nicholas, I would never refer to you as an innocent 'baby chick,' even in your wounded condition. I am not mad, you know."

"You are certainly driving me there with your orders to these two gentlemen."

Andrea sent a sparkling smile toward Jamieson and Hampton. "Thank you for your help with your cantankerous lord. I know it is difficult to listen to these outbursts of petulance."

"Andrea," Nicholas said warningly.

Another chuckle escaped her. "Don't be so touchy, Nicholas. After all, even you must admit that your behavior these past two weeks has left something to be desired. You have been irritable, querulous, and altogether unpleasant to be around."

"Surely not that terrible," he argued.

"Deny it if you want, Nicholas, but every member of this household knows it to be the truth. Now, if you are feeling well enough to be up and about, I see no reason why you cannot dress and join us for the noon repast. Naturally, your activities should remain limited for another few weeks."

"I would prefer to discuss this in more depth after I have dressed." Nicholas pulled at the blanket, keeping it wrapped tightly about him.

"Certainly," she agreed.

The laughter he saw on her face brought a frown to his own.

"Hampton, would you mind fetching some clean clothes for the Earl?" Andrea's question did little to appease his annoyance.

The elderly man was quick to respond. "Not at all, my lady. That is my job."

"With the way you perform it, no wonder Lady Andrea was forced to question it," muttered Jamieson out of the side of his mouth, his face remaining set.

Hampton's amicable round face screwed up. "Why, you old—"

"My clothes, Hampton."

At the sound of Nicholas's dangerously calm voice, Hampton's insults died in his throat. A fierce glare was all he gave Jamieson before he marched from the room.

"The crisis is over, Jamieson. You may go now and I will see you downstairs."

"Very good, sir," Jamieson said, bowing slightly before he withdrew from the room.

"Well, now that this little incident is over, I believe I shall remove myself as well and afford you some privacy," Andrea said, smiling at Nicholas.

He appeared nonplussed for an instant, before a

familiar expression slid onto his face. "You are certainly welcome to stay and assist me."

Oh, how his decidedly sensual invitation cut her. Although it shouldn't, she acknowledged silently, as she'd been receiving them since his return. But she was disappointed. After all she had done for him, it seemed that he still viewed her as nothing more than a convenient bedmate. "I highly doubt you are physically capable of much at this moment, Nicholas, even if I were to assist you."

His smile was utterly cocky. "I would be more than willing to try."

Was that to be her prize for helping him? Here she'd gone and tumbled in love with him again and he simply wanted her body. She prayed that once they became intimate again, it would allow him to focus on her other attributes. "I know," she murmured, before slipping out the door, wishing that he could have said two simple words.

Thank you.

The sun shone directly on Lady Miriam where she knelt in the garden, casting a shadow onto the moist soil she was tilling.

"Here you are, Miriam. I have been looking all over for you." Andrea's brows drew together as she watched her mother-in-law wipe dirt from her gloves while turning to face her. "Really, Miriam, there is no longer a need for you to tend the gardens by yourself. I greatly appreciate your efforts in maintaining the grounds while we were conserving our funds, but now we are certainly capable of hiring additional staff to take over this chore."

"Oh, gracious no," laughed Miriam as she rose to her feet, her hand raised to adjust her wide-brimmed sunbonnet. "While it is true that my original reason for tending the garden was to help you in my own small way, the fact is that I have grown to love working with the flowers. There is something so rewarding in tilling the soil, sowing the seeds, and tending the blooms. I do not wish to give up this feeling."

Andrea's gaze roamed over Miriam's earnest visage. "As long as you enjoy the work, then consider it yours. But if it ever becomes a burden, please tell me immediately so that I can hire someone to take it over from you."

"A burden?" asked Miriam. "It is a joy, not a hardship. This garden is like my own child now."

"Your child? I understand the pleasure you gain from it, but surely you exaggerate."

"Oh no, my dear, not at all. After all, I give life to the flowers. It is my nurturing that gives them health, my care that lends them their splendor." A dark shadow covered Miriam's clear gaze as she twisted her head to gaze down at the flowers she had been planting. "But, unlike children, if a stem breaks you can simply plant another. With children, it's not so simple."

"I know," whispered Andrea, thinking of the distance between her and Marissa that still needed to be breached.

"You spend time with your daughter," Miriam said quickly.

Andrea's pain filled her expression. "Time, but not attention." She shook her head to stave off Miriam's protest. "It's true, Miriam. The day of the picnic, all Marissa could talk about was you and Nicholas. 'My grandmama does this. My papa does that.' It was then that I realized how little attention I'd paid her over the past few years."

"At least you were consistent," Miriam said.

"An hour a day does not a close relationship make,

and I should know better than most." The smile she gave Miriam held no joy. "How do you imagine my childhood?"

"You and Nicholas both," Miriam whispered, shaking her head.

"Are you speaking of his father?"

Miriam closed her eyes briefly. "Yes." A breath shuddered out of her. "My Jonathan was a good man, truly, but with Nicholas he was often harsh. He loved both of our boys. He simply wanted them to have the best, to be the best."

"My parents were the same," Andrea admitted, laying a comforting hand upon Miriam's forearm.

"With Thomas, his father's stern attitude didn't seem to affect him overly. Nicholas was impacted far greater. He always looked to his father for approval, and, while Jonathan was proud of Nicholas, he never expressed it. I can't remember him ever clasping Nicholas on the shoulder and telling him he did a good job. Instead of giving him praise, Jonathan would tell Nicholas how he could improve, and I would watch as my son's excitement and pride withered."

Andrea shifted closer.

"My failure lay in that I never intervened, never insisted that Jonathan ease up on his sons." Miriam tilted her quivering chin upward. "For that I shall always have regret."

"Do not judge yourself harshly, Miriam. We all flounder with fulfilling our child's needs." Guilt filled Andrea before resolution swept it away. "I am attempting to correct the mistakes I have made with Marissa."

"I'm happy for both of you." Miriam looked at Andrea. "Would it offend you dreadfully if I were to meddle a bit?"

Andrea lifted one eyebrow. "Wouldn't it be more accurate to say 'a bit more'?"

A pretty flush brightened Miriam's cheeks. "Perhaps," she conceded.

Andrea smiled at her mother-in-law who, over the years, had given her the love she had once so craved from her own mother. "I always welcome advice from you."

"Do not allow your marriage to settle into a comfortable routine of polite exchanges. Nicholas has great warmth inside of him and is capable of true love."

Andrea fought back the fresh wave of hurt. "I fear the needs Nicholas has of me are far more, shall we say, elemental."

"He has grown so like his father." Miriam shook her head. "Oh, he's witty, attentive, but he is careful not to expose his true emotions."

"His notion of marriage and mine differ greatly."

"Then convince him otherwise."

Andrea gazed at her mother-in-law. "How does one go about that?"

"Seduce him."

Her jaw dropped open.

Miriam laughed at Andrea's expression. "I have shocked you, haven't I?"

"Quite," Andrea acknowledged, blinking once.

"For truth, Andrea, I do believe that's the answer. With my husband, I allowed him to dictate the terms of our marriage. I calmly fulfilled my part, acting the proper hostess, tending to the children, deferring to his every need and wish, but never once did I demand more. I should have shaken Jonathan up every so often, made him respect *my* thoughts. I truly believe the way to reach Nicholas is to break down his wall of reserve, force him to acknowledge you. Not just when he wants to, but even when he doesn't. Bother him, torment him, argue with him. Make him crazed until all he can think of is you. Show him that he cannot be allowed to dismiss you, that you are a part of his life and he needs to allow you to stand by his side, not behind his back."

"So you believe that if I challenge Nicholas's ideals, perhaps he will come to love me for all I am, not for what I represent." Long forgotten dreams of marriage began to shimmer with life again.

Miriam graced Andrea with a brilliant smile. "That's correct, Andrea. Fight for Nicholas—even if what you're fighting is Nicholas himself."

The chime of silver forks against china plates sounded in the dining room where the family had gathered to partake of the midday meal. Nicholas sat at one end of the long table, flanked by his mother and brother, with Andrea at the opposite end, her mother and Hartnell on either side of her.

Nicholas eyed the man who was trying to capture his wife's attentions. There was an odd tension about Andrea and she was stiff toward Hartnell, not looking at him. It was so unlike his wife to treat a guest in that fashion. Not that it bothered him overly. He was not, to put it mildly, fond of Hartnell. "How long shall we be graced with your company, Hartnell?"

Harry's thinning blond hair fluttered about as he turned toward Nicholas. "You have been most welcoming, Leigh, and I shan't impose on your good nature for much longer."

Hartnell's fawning moved him little. Nicholas sliced into his meat. "Then Lady Leigh has healed your mare?"

"Brilliantly. She is an angel of miracles, a seraph of mercy."

Andrea flushed under Harry's effusive praise. "Wildstar suffered from an overextended muscle. It was an easy matter to reduce the swelling with ice packs and rest."

"Animals, then people," Nicholas began, touching his shoulder. "I am suitably impressed, Andrea."

"Thank you," she murmured, gazing at him.

Nicholas allowed himself to drown in the warmth of her look for a moment before glancing away, all too aware of the people observing them.

"I was wondering, Nicholas, if we might not all return to London . . . after you have fully recovered, that is," Miriam inquired.

"I do so love London," Lady Anne added. "It's such an embarrassment to remain in the country during the Season."

Nicholas thought of all the friends he would like to see again. "Agreed." Aware of fatigue rapidly setting in, he added, "We shall move our residence in a few weeks." He glanced at his wife. "Will that be enough time for you to put the stables in order for your absence?"

Andrea's smile was blinding. "Ample. Thank you for your consideration."

He tipped his head. "You are most welcome."

"I believe I shall return tomorrow, Nick." Thomas laid down his fork. "When I rushed back here, I left a bit of unfinished business in London."

Nicholas nodded to Thomas. The two of them had been storming their thoughts to come up with a possible motive for the attacks upon him. So far, they hadn't discovered a single one. Together, they had agreed to hire a Bow Street runner to see if they could turn up something.

"Were you planning on paying a visit to our, er,

Bow associates and see about the possibility of future employment?"

"Most definitely," Thomas assured him.

"What is this, Nicholas? Who were you thinking of arranging for hire?" Andrea peered around the flower arrangement in the center of the table.

"No need to be concerned," Nicholas assured her. "It is just tiresome business."

For the life of him, he couldn't understand why Andrea blanched at that statement. He was merely trying to save her from worry as any considerate husband would. "Andrea, are you all right?"

"Fine," she replied softly.

He nodded, before redirecting his attention to Harry. "I've a wonderful idea, Hartnell. Why don't you keep my brother company on the journey to London? Especially since your mare is on the mend, I'm sure that you're positively bored being stuck here in the country for such a long while."

"I've quite enjoyed it, actually," Harry returned, shifting in his chair.

"All the same, I vow you'll find it more agreeable to accompany Thomas to London." Nicholas added the final touch. "And I would consider it a personal favor."

Phrased as such, he'd allowed Hartnell no graceful way to decline the offer. As expected, Harry swallowed, glancing briefly at Andrea, before agreeing. "It would be my honor."

"Then it's settled. We shall join you in London in a few weeks." Nicholas felt elated. Not only was he going to begin an investigation into the attacks, but he was also getting rid of Hartnell. He took a hearty bite of his meal.

"If I might impose, Andrea?"

Andrea looked at her mother-in-law. "Certainly."

"I thought it might be appropriate for us to host a dinner party once in London."

Miriam's request confused Andrea. They often hosted parties here at Leighaven. "You have no need to seek my permission for such an event, Miriam."

"Then I might go forward and plan it."

"With my blessings." Andrea smiled reassuringly at her mother-in-law. Their exchange in the garden remained fresh in Andrea's mind as she turned her gaze upon Nicholas. When he had complimented her healing ability, Andrea had been pleasantly surprised. Then, just as quickly, her hopes had been dashed when he had dismissed her inquiry, undoubtedly believing his business matter too confusing for her. Clearly she wasn't making the headway with him that she'd believed.

Perhaps it was wrong of her to feel so downhearted. After all, he had given her a compliment along with the disheartening comment—and one was far better than none at all.

Comforted, Andrea smiled at Miriam. "Would you like assistance assembling the guest list?"

"Oh, no, dear," she replied, waving her hand. "I adore arranging these affairs."

"We will need new gowns, of course," Lady Anne remarked, "and I shall help to consult with you, Andrea, on your choices."

"Thank you, Mother."

"Nothing too revealing, mind you," Nicholas interjected, pointing at Lady Anne.

Before her mother could respond, Andrea said, "I was of the impression that choosing one's wardrobe was a personal matter."

"As it is," Nicholas agreed. "A personal matter between a husband and his wife."

Andrea was stunned. "I beg to differ, my lord. Never once have I been consulted on your attire."

"Do not be absurd, Andrea."

"I'm not. If anything, I am affronted."

Nicholas set down his knife. "Affronted? Why?"

"I take objection to your dictates in this most intimate of matters." Andrea felt all eyes upon her, but she was too upset to care.

"This discussion is at an end," Nicholas announced, tossing his napkin onto the table.

She gasped at his dismissal. "I think not."

Nicholas pushed himself to his feet. "If you find my request that you clothe yourself in a manner befitting a Countess offensive, I apologize, but I insist that you respect my wishes." As he walked from the room, he added, "In the future, all conversations of this nature will be afforded the privacy they deserve. Understood, Andrea?"

Her thoughts flew back to Miriam's words of advice. Fight for him. If she allowed him to blithely issue orders without consideration of her feelings, their marriage would never be one of equality. Her love would ultimately be crushed beneath his dominance. No; if she was ever to forge a true marriage with Nicholas, they needed to go forward as they intended to continue.

"Do you understand me, Andrea?" he asked again, standing at the door, waiting for her answer.

"Perfectly."

He nodded, assured that he had made his point.

She nodded back, certain that he would regret his arrogant demand. In fact, she would make sure of it.

Seven

She was going to drive him mad.

Nicholas tried to concentrate on the ledgers open before him, but his thoughts wouldn't focus on anything other than his wife's disturbing behavior. He'd thought he was growing to understand her, but she'd shocked him yet again. Now she took obvious pleasure at countering nearly all he said. If he requested her presence in the study at 2 P.M., she would knock at the door either early or late, but never on time. When he'd offered to purchase four new gowns for her, she smiled at him and sweetly told him she'd already ordered six. Even when he announced they could return to London in three days, she told him she needed five.

His wife's behavior was completely unpredictable. Andrea had never been more frustrating, more annoying . . . more appealing. It was hard to push her from his thoughts. He was consumed by his plans of teasing her into his bed, if only to end the tension between them. Surely once she'd succumbed to him— to passion—she would become more pliable, more manageable, and he could concentrate on his business

matters without thoughts of her constantly tormenting him.

The knock on the door was a welcome interruption
from his musings. "Enter."

Thomas strolled into the study. "Hello, Nick.
Thought you might like to know that I've hired a Bow
Street runner to look into Harry's background as
you requested. Chester Wiley comes highly recommended." Thomas poured himself a drink.

Nicholas tossed his pen onto the desk and leaned
back in his chair. He rubbed at his eyes. They'd returned to London two days before and he'd been
keeping long hours to compensate for the days lost to
his injury. His distracting thoughts of Andrea did little
to aid the matter. "Did he indicate how they would
progress into the investigation?"

Thomas sat down. "Wiley said he would head for
Leighaven. Once there, he'd question the servants and
try to find any gaps left by our constable."

Nicholas tapped his fingers against his thigh. "And
from that point?"

"If nothing further is uncovered, Wiley will then
begin investigating into the backgrounds of all parties
present at the time of the shooting."

"Including the family members?"

"Yes."

Nicholas was still for a moment. "Sound judgment,"
he finally acknowledged, but it didn't alter the fact
that he didn't like the idea of his family being sub-
jected to an investigation. The implications in such
actions were unpleasant, to say the least.

"I agree," Thomas said, taking a sip of his drink.
"Though I must admit there are things in my past I'd
rather have forgotten."

"Then ask to be excluded from the investigation."

Thomas's smile was so wide it crinkled the corners

of his eyes. "Thanks for your confidence in my innocence, Nick, but I shall not ask to be overlooked. I'll stand with the rest of the family."

Nicholas nodded, not liking this nasty business one whit. What would his father have said if he'd known his family was under criminal investigation? Nicholas rose to his feet. "I see no other way than to pursue this matter to the fullest." He began to pace. "Think on it, Thomas. My daughter was mere feet from where I was struck down. What if the bullet had gone astray and hit her instead?" He shook his head. "This entire situation is intolerable, and the assailant must be found—not just for my safety, but for the well-being of the entire family."

Thomas stood and went to Nicholas, laying a reassuring hand upon his shoulder. "I agree wholeheartedly with you, Nick, as would everyone else who knew of the particulars. Don't go so hard on yourself."

Nicholas calmed beneath the contact. "It goes against my grain to—" A loud crash followed by muted laughter interrupted him. "What the devil was that?"

Nicholas strode from the study, Thomas following on his heels. It was easy to find the source of the noise; all he had to do was follow the laughter.

The doors to the ballroom stood open. Nicholas hesitated at the threshold, too taken with the picture of his wife collapsed upon a chair in laughter, holding his giggling daughter on her lap. There were two rows of chairs lined in the center of the room, three on each side, with one lying on its back upon the parquet floor.

He was unable to keep the grin from easing onto his face. Nicholas strolled forward, leaving Thomas leaning against the doorjamb. "What have we here?"

Andrea wiped the tears from the corners of her

eyes. "Nicholas," she said, out of breath. "We were dancing."

Marissa nodded, her smile wide. "With the chairs." She giggled happily. "All except that one," she added, pointing to the overturned chair. "He decided to sit out this set."

That was all it took to send Andrea and Marissa into another fit of laughter.

Nicholas righted the offending chair. "It is much simpler to dance with people, Marissa." He patted the back of the seat. "They have the tendency to move."

Andrea regained control of her composure. "We are aware of that fact, Nicholas, but we did not have anyone to join us."

He smiled down at his wife, appreciating the lovely picture she made, all warm and mussed from her laughter. Desire for her, never forgotten, began to simmer within him. Soon, she would willingly come into his bed and he could ease himself within her warmth.

It took tremendous effort to pull his gaze from his wife, shifting it onto Marissa. Nicholas bowed to his daughter, offering her a hand. "Might I have the pleasure of this dance?"

Before she could accept, Thomas strode forward. "Oh, no, Nick. Marissa shall be my partner, isn't that right, love?"

Thomas scooped the girl off her mother's lap, hugging her before he set her down. He grinned at Nicholas. "See to your wife, old man."

Nicholas lifted an eyebrow at his brother's less than subtle machinations. He looked toward Andrea, bowing low again, this time offering the homage to his wife. "Would you do me the honor of gracing me with this dance?"

Her delicate flush tightened the muscles in his stomach. "It would be a pleasure," Andrea murmured, accepting his outstretched hand.

The two couples moved a few steps from the chairs. Nicholas retained his clasp upon Andrea's hand. "What dance were you practicing?"

"The Roger de Coverley," she said, smiling up at him. "I was demonstrating to Marissa how we would be dancing this evening at your mother's dinner party."

"There will be dancing?" Nicholas hadn't been involved in any of the planning.

"Before and after we dine," Andrea informed him.

Nicholas looked at her. "Has there been enough time for the seamstress to complete the new gowns you ordered?"

"No," Andrea replied, "but fear not, for I was able to arrange for a gown to be altered."

"Then all is settled." He bestowed a smile upon her, confident that they were finding their way.

"Yes," she answered briefly. "Now, shall we begin our dance? I will hum a few strains of music to accompany us."

Nicholas released her hand and stepped back, facing her in the proper position of the dance. Thomas and Marissa followed suit. "Shall we demonstrate for Marissa first before we teach her the steps?"

"By all means." Andrea began to hum.

Nicholas stepped forward, clasping Andrea about the waist and spinning her once, then releasing her to step back to his place.

As Nicholas walked smoothly around Andrea, he inhaled her unique scent, promising himself it wouldn't be much longer before he could drown in her essence.

Soon.

* * *

The music swelled, filling the elegant room, but the guests had yet to take the dance floor. Instead, they milled about, partaking of the refreshments. Miriam stood on the edge of the dance floor, flanked by Nicholas and Thomas, while Lady Anne sat across the room, chatting with a large collection of ladies.

Nicholas bent down to whisper into his mother's ear. "Have you caught sight of Andrea?"

Miriam shook her head. "No."

"I wonder what's keeping her," he responded, straightening. "Pardon me, Mother. I believe I'll check on her."

"Certainly," Miriam excused him.

Nicholas wove his way through the guests, pausing to shake a hand or exchange greetings with friends and acquaintances on his way to the staircase. He had nearly reached the first step when gasps broke out around him from each person in the room, old and young alike. Following their gazes, Nicholas looked up the stairs.

Andrea.

The sight he beheld froze him to the step. Aware of people seeking his reaction, Nicholas forced his features into an expression of welcome, successfully hiding the shock ricocheting through him.

His wife stood at the top of the stairs, her arms spread wide, posed, fully aware of the outrageousness of her outfit. Her lips were curved in a satisfied smile, her chin lifted proudly, as if feeling the censure radiating toward her and reveling in it.

"Dear God," yelped Lady Anne, voicing the thought echoing through everyone in the room.

Nicholas allowed his gaze to roam over Andrea's body. Her hair was brushed until it flew away in wild abandon, flowing over, but not concealing, the lush curves revealed by the low neckline of her dress. Her bodice was tight to just below the bosom. It was from this point that Andrea's outfit became truly shocking.

Gone was the entire front of her skirt, leaving only a long flow of pale blue silk to curve over her hips into a sweep of material behind her. In place of the skirt, Andrea's legs were encased in tight, form-hugging pants that outlined each sweet curve.

Nicholas's gaze slid down their length with hungry eyes. Desire roared through him, hot and searing, as erotic images flashed before him, images of his hand curving around her full breast, his lips exploring her pinched waist, his hips driving into her while her long, slender legs wrapped about him, urging him into her welcoming warmth. The pants stopped above her ankles, leaving their pale fragility naked to everyone's wandering eyes. Her slender feet were encased in pale blue slippers.

The music trailed off and silence filled the room, much as the shocked gasps had a few moments ago. The tension was so taut, it seemed to be a physical force in the wide expanse of the room.

Andrea lifted her chin higher, emerald fire flashing from her eyes as her voice rang out. "Welcome to our home." Her long, slender legs began to carry her down the stairs, each muscle delineated with the movement, causing the ladies present to gasp in horrified shock and the men to swallow in rising excitement.

"I apologize for my delay, but it was unavoidable. I am afraid my maid had a bit of trouble assisting me." A husky laugh broke from Andrea, sending shivers of seductive promise down Nicholas's spine. "Please, everyone, return to your pleasures. Maestro," Andrea directed, waving her hand at the conductor of the string ensemble, who was struggling to keep his eyes on her face.

When her delicate feet stepped onto the floor, Andrea turned toward Nicholas, a satisfied gleam shimmering in her gaze.

Andrea boldly challenged him, ignoring the scandalized glares from the other occupants of the room. "Does this gown befit a Countess?"

Emotions scorched through him: fury, admiration, frustration, amusement. He had not a clue as to how to respond to his wife's blatant disregard for conventions. It was the sparkle in her eyes that reached him.

His humor won the battle.

Nicholas began to chuckle, the sound growing until he was laughing outright. "Lord, I was a fool to forget even for a moment how you tormented your parents with your headstrong ways. I should have known better than to issue a bold edict to someone of your nature."

She glowed beneath his amusement. "Thank you, Nicholas."

He lifted her hand to his lips, turning it over to press a kiss into her soft palm. "I fear I am easily swayed into forgiving you anything."

"What a lovely thought," she returned, curling her fingers over his kiss.

"For this evening, my dear wife, I shall indulge you." Nicholas offered her his arm. "Shall we lead off the first dance?"

She accepted graciously. "Most certainly, my lord," she replied sedately, slanting a look up at him. "And we shall later ascertain who shall be indulged."

He could not miss the invitation in her words. The gaze he turned upon her was heated. "At your pleasure."

"We shall see," she murmured, curving her fingers into the muscles of his forearm.

"Indeed." Nicholas concentrated on keeping his

heart from racing at the lascivious thoughts she invoked. "We shall indeed."

Andrea's outrageous act required all of her fortitude to brazen it out to completion. Stepping into a private alcove off the main ballroom, she took a few minutes to compose herself. She had danced with Nicholas and then a crush of gentlemen who all begged for a turn. Her feet ached from the attentions of the men and her head pounded from the glares and hushed whispers of the ladies. Her mother's gaze had burned her more than once this evening, and it took little imagination to conjure her mother's fury.

None of this, however, could dim her pleasure at Nicholas's reaction. She'd always known, all those long years ago when they'd first met, that he was unique; a gentleman strong enough not to be threatened by a confident woman. He had not disappointed her this evening.

His warning that he would indulge her this once was merely to save face, to be sure. His laughter had once more won her heart.

At the sound of voices, Andrea pressed further into the alcove, the pale blue of her dress blending with the large plant shielding the archway.

"Good to have you back, Trent."

"Glad to be here, Abernathy," Nicholas replied warmly.

Andrea decided to emerge and greet Lord Centire, Marquis of Abernathy, but his next words stopped her.

"Not a moment too soon, Leigh. Appears your wife needs to be taken in hand."

Nicholas's voice iced over. "Certainly you aren't insulting my wife, sir."

"No, no," the older man was quick to assure Nicholas. "Meant no insult. I merely wanted to compliment you on your forbearance."

Andrea couldn't see Nicholas's face, but there was no mistaking the anger in his clipped tones. "None is required, Abernathy. Lady Leigh is the Countess of Trent and, as such, has my respect and admiration. She need account to no one, save me." There was a loaded pause. "And I would find great displeasure if I was to hear any vicious gossip to the contrary."

"Understood." The edge of panic in Abernathy's voice made her smile.

"Excellent." The plant rustled as Abernathy brushed past it. "And you might want to share my reaction to our discussion with the others."

Andrea listened, overwhelmed by Nicholas's support, as Abernathy moved away. Her heart swelled within her breast.

"You can come out from behind the bush now, Andrea."

She jumped at the sound of Nicholas's voice, causing the plant to rock precariously on its planter.

"Careful, my dear. We wouldn't want the foliage crashing onto an innocent passerby."

She peeked around the leaves. "How did you know I was back here?"

"It's been my observation that plants don't tend to shake without a breeze."

"I was trying to remain still."

Nicholas smiled at her, his amusement obvious. "There are some talents—not many, granted, but a few—to which you cannot lay claim."

"Are you implying that I am not exceedingly patient?" she asked pertly, taking great sport in their exchange.

"No, Andrea, I'm not implying anything of the sort." Nicholas reached out to clasp her elbow, guiding her from the alcove. "I am, however, stating in blunt terms that you lack the qualities necessary for a successful eavesdropper."

She considered that for a moment. "I believe I can accept that failing."

His smile slipped. "I can only offer my apologies that you were forced to overhear such hurtful gossip and—"

"Think nothing of it, Nicholas," Andrea said. "You handled the entire situation with nothing short of brilliance, and I quite admire your statesmanship."

"Hell," Nicholas muttered. "What I wanted to do was bash him in his condescending mouth."

"You showed great restraint." The depth of his concern melted her inside.

He lightly caressed the inside of her elbow. "I've told you before, Andrea. You belong to me, and I care for what is mine."

The last time he had told her that, she had balked at his arrogant pronouncement. But now, still warm from his defense of her, she wasn't upset one bit.

After all, didn't he belong to her in return?

"Besides, Andrea," Nicholas added smoothly, "I consider the right to criticize your wicked attire one of the pleasures afforded me as your husband."

Andrea's laughter rang out as she allowed her husband to escort her into dinner.

Nicholas secured the belt of his robe. Hampton had been dismissed for the evening, and quiet reigned over the household. Everywhere, that was, but inside him.

A torment of intense emotions twisted within Nicholas as he paced the confines of his bedchamber.

This evening, when Andrea had appeared in all her glory—bold, confident—he'd wanted nothing more than to sweep her in his arms and carry her back up the stairs where he could release the passion she aroused. After which, he admitted with a wry smile, he would have spent an hour lecturing her on proper conduct. Once was amusing and made him admire the spirit that had first captured his interest, but further episodes of this type of outrageous behavior could not occur.

Still, the look of her long legs encased in the light blue silk had been worth the shock of their guests. The image, still fresh and alive, drove him to pace faster. Oh, how he wanted to open the door connecting their chambers and secure his marital rights. But he could do no such thing. He'd promised himself that she would come to him; willingly, openly.

It was only right that she seek him out. Nicholas strengthened his resolve.

It did nothing, however, to ease his hunger for her.

Andrea tossed down her hairbrush, too energized to sit for any longer. Her nightgown swirled about her legs as she walked over to the connecting door to Nicholas's room. She pressed a hand upon the smooth wood, her fingers spread wide, desire pulsating within her. Dare she open the door?

The urge to do so was strong. Tonight, when Nicholas had been amused at her challenge, had even defended her against one who had criticized, any last vestiges of restraint were destroyed. He had proven that she was important to him.

Tonight she wanted to belong to him; heart, body, and soul.

Slowly, she moved her hand down to the silver-plated door handle. Not giving herself time to change her mind, Andrea pressed down the handle and pushed open the door.

"Ouch!"

The wood vibrated beneath her hands as it slammed to a halt.

"Nicholas?" Andrea peered around the door to see Nicholas standing a few feet away, rubbing his forehead. The disgruntled look he gave her set off her already jangling nerves, causing a chuckle to break free.

He continued to soothe the injured spot. "So delighted to provide entertainment."

"Oh, Nicholas," she said, gasping to control her giggles. "I had no idea you were standing on the other side of the door."

"I should hope not."

Andrea pushed open the door the rest of the way and stepped into his room. "I almost knocked," she offered.

"Little consolation at this point," Nicholas returned, before allowing his hand to fall to his side. "Luckily, I have an unbelievably hard head and it would take far greater a blow to knock it in."

Her smile widened. "I'll keep that in mind."

He shook his head, a wry twist to his lips. "Charming, Andrea. Simply charming." Suddenly, his motions stilled, his gaze flicking toward the door, as if he just realized the implications of her actions.

He looked back at her, his jaw tight. His gaze dropped downward, roving over her shoulders, down the ribbon flowing over her bodice, and onto her legs, visible through the thin muslin. Every inch his glance touched set her aflame. Finally, he lifted his eyes to capture her gaze, his expression leaving little doubt as to his intentions. "I must say, I heartily approve in the change of attire."

The husky depths of his voice strummed a welcoming chord within her. "I'd hoped you would."

He took a step forward. "Am I correct in assuming

this is for my benefit?" He slipped a finger beneath the strap on her shoulder.

She gasped at the simple touch, her sensitized flesh absorbing the heat from his fingertip. "Who else?"

"Who else indeed," Nicholas murmured, closing the distance between them. He dipped his head to press a moist kiss upon the curve of her shoulder. "Seven years is a long time."

"An eternity," she whispered, tilting her head to the side to allow him greater access. She felt his smile against her skin.

"Day after day I imagined this moment, dreamed of how you'd look." He lightly nipped at the base of her neck. "Nothing could have prepared me for the reality of you."

Her hands slid up his dressing robe as she arched herself against Nicholas's burning hardness. "Make love to me."

He lifted his head, bringing a hand up to sweep the hair away from her face. "No, Andrea, I'm going to make love *with* you."

She melted beneath his tender words. "With me."

He nodded slowly, lowering his head until he brushed his lips against hers.

Intense heat flared within her at the soft touch, bringing a gasp from her. "Please," she whispered, tightening her arms around his neck.

"I plan to." His breath rushed out over her lips. "I plan to please you very much." His mouth moved upon hers, nibbling, tasting, until she thought she'd go mad from want. Finally, he settled his luscious mouth upon hers, his lips enticing hers wide, his tongue delving deep, stoking the fires of her passion higher.

Long-forgotten sensations swept through Andrea, making her feel desperately alive. Nicholas slid his hands down her arm, fingers trailing softly, before wrapping around her waist. Then he eased his mouth off hers, sipping lightly until he'd broken their kiss.

A soft sound of protest slipped from her, bringing a sensual smile of pleasure onto Nicholas's face. The slight tremor in his muscles as he bent, lifting her into the cradle of his arms, brought a smile to her face.

The firelight flickered on the glistening furniture, but Andrea had no notice of anything other than Nicholas's destination—her bed. Wrapped in his arms as he carried her across her chamber, she felt so wanted, so cherished. Gently, he set her onto her feet.

"Let me see you," he urged, sliding his hands along her shoulders, freeing the straps of her nightgown.

As the garment slipped down to her waist, catching upon her slender hips, Andrea stood, proud, beneath Nicholas's impassioned gaze.

"You're more beautiful than I remembered," he whispered, lifting a hand to cup her breast.

Her eyes closed as she arched her back toward the wonderful touch. "Nicholas."

He glossed his hand downward, smoothing the nightgown over her hips, allowing it to drop onto the floor, a forgotten puddle of ivory. Nicholas stepped back, his hands falling to his sides, as he gazed at her in all her glory.

Andrea heated beneath his look, blushing yet remaining still, amazed that she had the power to cause that feverish glow within her husband. She lifted one hand, beckoning. "Please," she said again.

His hands shook as he loosened the tie to his robe, then shrugged out of it, sending it onto the floor. Nicholas stood in the firelight, offering himself to her. Her swift intake of breath caused him to smile, but his expression disappeared into one of heated desire when she stepped forward, placing her outstretched hand upon his chest.

In awe of the raw masculine beauty before her, Andrea feathered her hands over his chest, across the broad shoulders, and down the muscled arms, unable to touch enough of the sculpted form. She melted inside as she touched his virile body.

When her fingertip traced one of the small scarred nicks upon his chest, Nicholas reached up to hold her hand still. "In prison, I was tortured." His harsh rasp brought tears to her eyes. "I am not as you remembered."

"No," she agreed, blinking back the dampness. "You left a youth and have returned to me a man."

He pressed her palm flat against his breastbone, spreading her fingers wide. "I referred to my scars. Do you feel them?"

She nodded, lifting her free hand to cup his cheek. "They are part of you now, Nicholas. They serve as a testament to your courage, your strength."

The blaze of heat in his gaze ignited an inferno within her. "Andrea," he groaned, pulling her to his body, pressing his burning flesh against hers. His hardness fitted in perfect compliment to her softness. Nicholas closed his mouth over her upturned one, their bodies moving against each other, enticing deeper motions as fierce passion descended upon them.

Andrea wrapped her arms tightly about his neck, withholding nothing. Nicholas turned her slightly, lowering her onto the bed, never breaking off their kiss. Mouths melded, bodies writhed, and legs entwined. Their differences were forgotten beneath the blaze of desire.

Nicholas shifted his head, trailing a line of kisses down the vulnerable arch of her neck. Andrea caressed the defined muscles of his back, beyond thought, beyond logic. Powerful needs ruled within her, sensitizing her only to the touch of Nicholas's mouth, his hands, his body.

His meandering kisses led to the slope of her breast, bringing a moan of yearning from her. She arched back, seeking deeper satisfaction, craving the feel of his mouth upon her. His hot breath rushed over her pouting nipple, promising unbidden delights.

A loud gasp broke from her when his lips closed about the aching point of her breast, sending electrical waves of passion shooting through her. Andrea curled her fingers into his hair, holding him to her breast, never wanting the satisfying kisses to end.

She quivered beneath Nicholas's hand as he traced the line of her hips, then inward, onto the soft flesh of her abdomen. Andrea swirled her hips upward, yearning for this, the most intimate of touches. As his fingers feathered through the hair on her mound, she parted her legs, welcoming him, beckoning him. The scent of her arousal filled the heated air, intensifying the fervor of Nicholas's lovemaking.

He drew her nipple deeply into his mouth as he cupped her womanhood, his fingers rubbing against her. Andrea twisted beneath his touch, crying out for more. Slowly, slowly, Nicholas allowed his finger to curve inward, easing into her moisture, causing a shuddering moan to break from Andrea.

A few gentle strokes sent her over the edge, delicious sensations bursting to life within her, as she stiffened beneath him. Shuddering, Andrea lay back on the bed, unable to believe the intensity of her reaction to his caress.

"Beautiful," he murmured against the flesh of her stomach as he moved downward. The excitement began to spark to life within her again. He licked, nipped, and kissed his way down her body, all the while her fingers were captured within his hair.

When Nicholas spread her legs wide and moved between them, Andrea shifted away, embarrassed by the intimacy. "Don't," she said, tugging at him.

He gave her a wicked grin, full of devilish hunger, before lowering his mouth to her most private of places. One touch brought a sharp cry from her, destroying all her protests with a single kiss, shattering all her inhibitions. Her hands fell from his head to lay upon the bed as Andrea allowed herself to be taken into an unknown realm of delight.

Nicholas tormented her with his mouth, bringing her to the heights of ecstasy over and over again. Andrea twisted beneath his clever touch as Nicholas used his hands to stroke her inner thighs, the curve of her buttocks; each brush deepening her arousal.

Her body strained upward, reaching for another peak, this one sharper, needier than all that had come before, when finally Nicholas moved back up her body. He levered himself up on his arms and drove forward, one fierce stroke, into her aching core. A keening cry burst from her at the intense satisfaction of their joining.

Two had become one.

Nicholas moved his hips back, then swiftly forward, in an age-old dance of desire. Pulsating need clawed at Andrea, seeking satiation within her husband's embrace. Nicholas thrust forward again, again, each movement sending her higher, closer.

White-hot sensation splintered through Andrea, a cry of satisfaction bursting from her lips. Another thrust from Nicholas and his shout of repletion joined hers, their cries mingling.

His arms quivered beneath the onslaught of pleasure before he slowly lowered his glistening body onto hers. Andrea wrapped her arms about his back, overwhelmed by love, drifting hazily in a satisfied glow.

"My husband," she murmured, pressing a kiss upon the salty flesh of his shoulder.

Nicholas shifted to the side, bringing her against his chest, his hand stroking the damp tendrils back from her forehead. She snuggled into his heat, at peace with her husband and with herself. The late night and passionate expenditure of energy caught up with her. Sleep beckoned and Andrea closed her eyes, drifting off within her husband's arms.

Nicholas gently touched his lips to her forehead before disentangling himself from her embrace.

"Nicholas?"

He eased from the bed, tucking the blankets around her as she struggled to remain awake. "Thank you," he whispered.

"Where are you going?" Sleep softened her voice.

"It's late," he replied, sliding a finger down her cheek. "You need your rest."

"But—"

"I will see you in the morning," he interrupted, bending to retrieve his robe before leaving her in her bed, softly shutting the door behind him as he left.

If she hadn't been so tired, she would have gone after him and forced the issue, but the thought of leaving the warm bed was too overwhelming. The morning would be soon enough to sort this all through.

Still, she fell asleep with a frown on her face.

Eight

Nicholas's forceful steps faltered when he saw his mother sitting at the breakfast table, calmly sipping her tea. His break in stride was the only outward sign of his reaction. "Good morning, Mother." Nicholas moved forward to sit across from Miriam, gesturing to a servant who hurried off to fetch his meal.

"You look well rested."

Nicholas fought to keep from blushing like an untried schoolboy. "As do you."

Miriam accepted the compliment with a bow of her head. "Did you have an enjoyable evening?"

Again, he could feel the heat rising in his cheeks. "Immeasurably," he said, thankful that she was unable to read his thoughts. The pleasure he'd found within Andrea's embrace had been beyond anything he'd imagined or remembered. The parting years had only served to sweeten his appreciation of her welcoming softness.

"You look well pleased with yourself," Miriam added with a smile.

"I have every reason to be," he returned, thinking

on all he now possessed. A secure financial situation, a solid family, a daughter he adored, and, finally, a wife who shared his bed. What more could a man ask for?

"Andrea created quite a stir last night," Miriam said quietly, taking a sip of her tea. "No one could stop talking about it all evening."

"Bunch of bloody vultures," he grumbled in a low voice, before exhaling deeply. Louder, he said, "Abernathy had the gall to approach me with his criticisms. I assure you that I set him straight. It was intolerable that he insult my wife while a guest in my home."

Miriam nodded firmly. "I could not agree with you more. I was not embarrassed in the least. As a matter of fact, I was rather amused by the entire event." Miriam paused to take another sip. "However, I'm afraid Andrea's mother was not similarly disposed."

Nicholas's response was delayed as he waited until the servant set down his plate of eggs and kippers along with a pot of tea. "In all honesty, her opinion is of little consequence. After all, if she's unhappy residing here, she is free to leave."

"True," Miriam acknowledged. "I understand Anne offers a challenge to one's patience, but she really can be quite interesting."

"My life's been a bit too 'interesting' for me lately. I can use some joyful boredom for a spot."

Miriam's smile turned into a moue of distaste as Nicholas sliced into his kippers. "How can you enjoy those things?"

His eyes crinkled at the corners. "They're delicious, Mother." He held up a forkful. "Are you sure you won't try a bite?"

A shiver ran through Miriam. "You know perfectly well that you are the only one who can abide those dreadful things."

Nicholas laughed as he set down his fork, untouched, to pour himself a cup of tea.

"What are your plans now that our soiree is over?" Miriam asked.

Amusement tilted up one side of Nicholas's mouth. "After last night, I can only assume that Andrea and I are persona non grata here in London."

Miriam's laugh sparkled across the table. "Oh, Nicholas, you have been gone too long, haven't you? Your assumptions couldn't be more off the mark!"

"Excuse me?"

With a small, secretive smile, Miriam pushed back her chair, stood up gracefully, and walked over to the sideboard. Her lavender gown flowed around her as she turned back to Nicholas. At least two dozen cards were gathered in her hand. Lifting them, she stated, "I'm speaking of these, Nicholas."

"What are they? Notes of scorn with perhaps a few letters of condolences mixed in?" His appetite suddenly gone, Nicholas pushed his plate off to the side, leaning back in his chair. The thought of ill-will directed toward his wife set off his stomach.

Miriam glided forward, laughing. "Quite the opposite. Each and every one of these cards is an invitation."

"What?" That certainly wasn't the answer he'd been expecting.

"You heard me quite well. Invitations." The cards spilled over the table as Miriam set them in front of Nicholas. "Some of them are to the most exclusive gatherings."

Nicholas frowned in disbelief. "But why?"

A soft smile curled Miriam's lips as she shrugged lightly. "Society is a fickle crowd, always hungry for new diversions, always seeking the unusual for entertainment."

Nicholas sent a quick look toward his mother before continuing to rifle through the cards.

"May I presume that you were pleased with my attire, then?" Andrea asked, a bright smile on her face as she glided into the room.

"You take far too many liberties if you do." Nicholas stood in deference to his wife. Her radiant features tightened his gut, making him remember how she'd looked when he'd left her last night; her hair flowing about her in wild disarray, her skin creamy against the white sheets, a sated smile upon her face. It had been all he could do to withdraw to his own chambers like a gentleman.

Andrea practically floated toward him, her arms outstretched. Nicholas quickly grasped her hands, leaning forward to press a light kiss upon her brow. It would serve her well to learn that passionate displays had no place outside the bedroom. "You look lovely this morning," he murmured, ignoring the part of him that longed for her embrace. Nicholas stepped back to offer her the chair next to his.

Confusion darkened her gaze. "Thank you, Nicholas."

The polite response was a far cry from her soft whispers last night. He thrust the unbidden thought away, shaken by the depth of his desire for her still. The intensity of his emotions toward Andrea disturbed him. True, she held a position of value within his life, but he should not have to struggle in order to keep her from eclipsing all other thoughts.

Nicholas forced himself to look away from Andrea, redirecting his attention to the invitations. "Why on earth is Whiting inviting us to the derby? Surely he knows we'll be attending."

Miriam returned to her chair. "Of course, but the horse he entered into the race was one Andrea cared for. He undoubtedly wants us to join him in his box."

"Black Thunder has a strong chance of victory," Andrea said, leaning forward to look at the card Nicholas held in his hand.

Nicholas had difficulty swallowing as Andrea pressed her breast against his forearm in order to read the invitation. He wanted to do nothing more than pull her into his arms, sweep the dishes from the table, tear the gown from her body, and—

"Good God!" His own lascivious thoughts had shocked the exclamation from him, earning confused glances from both his wife and mother.

"Nicholas?" Andrea asked uncertainly.

He looked at his wife, praying that his features were devoid of his disgraceful imaginings. "My apologies," he murmured.

Unable to withstand the curious glances from his mother and Andrea, Nicholas tossed down his napkin, rising. "Excuse me, ladies. My day is exceedingly busy and I must be off to the study."

Miriam gestured to his full plate. "You haven't touched a bite."

Another minute of this and he vowed he'd do something rash like pull Andrea into his arms, unfasten her dress and—

"My appetite has waned," Nicholas managed to say in a strangled voice. "Ladies," he said in dismissal, bowing, before walking from the room.

Andrea lifted her eyebrows at Miriam. "That was rather odd."

Miriam beamed a smile back at her. "It would appear our Nicholas is a bit out of sorts."

"I can't possibly imagine why," Andrea said, frowning. Lord knew, their lovemaking should have put a smile on his face.

"I do believe you've confused him, my dear."

"I did nothing of the kind." How could resuming their marital rights confuse him?

"Not intentionally," Miriam asserted, tapping a finger on her saucer, "but there can be little doubt that Nicholas is off balance."

"That is hardly flattering," Andrea replied tartly. After their lovely night together, she'd expected him to welcome her with open arms and loving smiles. She'd never thought he would kiss her politely on the forehead and virtually ignore her at the table. His peculiar expressions hadn't eased her mind any, either. If she hadn't known better, she might have thought him choking.

"Not flattering?" Miriam repeated in an astounded tone. "On the contrary, Andrea, he could pay you no greater compliment."

Andrea looked at her mother-in-law dubiously.

"For someone who values control like Nicholas, his lack of it must have disturbed him. There is little doubt you are the cause." Miriam glanced pointedly at the full plate Nicholas abandoned. "I have never known him to leave kippers untouched."

Slowly, a smile formed on Andrea's face. "He *was* aware of me this morning."

"Of a certainty."

"I am fortunate that I find it disgracefully easy to disturb Nicholas." Andrea laughed, her heart suddenly lighter. "Poor dear."

"Poor Nicholas indeed," scoffed Miriam. "I always said he had the luck of the devil."

"And the devil takes care of his own." Her wicked grin grew. "With a little help."

The two women exchanged glances before they burst into laughter.

* * *

Nicholas had been staring down at the open ledgers on his desk for the past hour, but had yet to focus on the accounts. Again, thoughts of Andrea were running through his head, distracting him.

"Damn it!" He tossed down his pen, leaped to his feet, and strode to the window. Last night had been incredible, but this morning he should have been able to slot it into a corner of his mind and concentrate on other matters. Nothing could have been further from the truth. He needed to refocus on his priorities, was all.

Undoubtedly, once he became accustomed to sharing a bed with his wife, she would likely fade from his every thought, allowing him to proceed with his life as it had once been.

Comforted, Nicholas turned back to his desk to resume tallying his accounts, when a knock sounded on the door. "Come in."

Thomas, Jamieson, and Hampton all entered the study. Nicholas looked at them in surprise. "To what do I owe this visit, gentlemen?"

"It's not good, Nick."

Thomas's grim statement wiped the amused expression off Nicholas's face. "What's happened?"

"Liz Stover, one of the kitchen maids, fell seriously ill an hour ago. Her vomiting was so violent that we called the doctor."

Distressing, but nothing to cause alarm, Nicholas thought, but he urged Thomas to continue. "Is she all right?"

"She'll be fine in a few days," Thomas reassured him. "That's not the problem."

Silence followed as Thomas shifted on his feet, obviously searching for a way to continue.

Nicholas tensed. "What's wrong?" he asked again.

"Are you going to tell him, or what?" Hampton looked at Thomas, clearly exasperated.

Jamieson glared down at Hampton. "Let Master Thomas alone. He'll get around to it in his own fashion."

"Hope I'm still alive to see—"

"Will someone tell me what is going on?" Nicholas shouted, too unsettled by Thomas's odd behavior to put up with the ditherings of two old men.

"The chit was poisoned," Hampton returned in a like manner.

"What?" Nicholas was stunned.

"It's true," Thomas added.

It didn't seem possible that this could happen here in London, especially when he'd been on guard. He'd hired an investigator, interviewed the servants. The realization that someone had been in his house, slipping poison into the food, made him ill. "What happened?"

"Well, this isn't quite as it appears," Thomas began.

"She nipped one of your kippers!"

Nicholas's attention shifted back to Hampton. "She did what?"

"She swiped a kipper off your plate this morning and the next thing, she was cuddling a chamber pot," Hampton explained.

Jamieson rolled his eyes. "Why did I ever agree to allow you to accompany Master Thomas and me?" he mumbled, before addressing Nicholas. "Mistress Stover told the doctor that she had not had anything to eat today except for one of your kippers, left over from your first day meal."

"How do you know it was poison? Could she merely have been suffering from some stomach ailment?"

Thomas shook his head. "The doctor diagnosed it as cowsbane poisoning."

"Apparently, bits of the cowsbane root were found in the cream sauce spread over your kippers. Luckily for the maid, she'd ingested only a tiny amount." Jamieson paled visibly. "If you'd eaten the entire serving, my lord, it would have meant your demise."

Hampton ran a hand down the side of his face. "What are things coming to when a man can't even enjoy a meal without worrying about what kind of new 'spices' have been added to a dish?"

"The poison wasn't found in anything but the kipper sauce?" Nicholas asked.

"No, my lord."

"How did something like this happen, Jamieson?"

The older man looked as if he were going to be ill. "I don't know, Master Nick. I just don't know. There are a number of people on your London staff that are unfamiliar to me, but their references were all checked."

Nicholas looked out the window, trying to quell the wrenching twist of his innards. Someone had invaded his home—his sanctuary—and tried to kill him. What if Marissa had eaten them? Or any member of his family? Raw fury swirled in his heart, nearly blinding him. He fought to regain control of his emotions.

"Can I assume the doctor will keep this information to himself?" There was nothing he could do to keep the anger from deepening his voice.

"He was amply paid to do so," Thomas acknowledged.

"Good. I do not want the rest of the family disturbed by this. Understood?"

All three men nodded in agreement.

Nicholas focused on the immediate problems. "How are we to prevent something like this from occurring in the future?"

Jamieson stepped forward. "I volunteer to personally test all of the family's dishes."

"I volunteer Jamie too," Hampton chipped in earnestly.

"Very generous of you, Hampton," Nicholas said dryly before looking at Jamieson. "I appreciate the offer, but I don't believe that's the solution."

"We could restrict the kitchen to only those people who traveled with us from Leighaven," the butler suggested.

"But the attacker has obviously followed us from Leighaven, so why would we trust those servants?" Thomas asked.

"All were accounted for during the investigation following Master Nick's aggrievous assault," Jamieson pointed out.

It was difficult for Nicholas to sort through the varied implications of the plan; fury colored his perspective. "I think that might be our best option. Jamieson, make sure that the only servants allowed in the kitchen are those who came with us from Leighaven."

"I will see to it immediately, my lord." Jamieson bowed before hurrying from the room.

Hampton turned to follow. "I know he'll have a few troubles organizing this matter, Master Nick, so I'll lend him my assistance."

Nicholas dismissed Hampton with a wave, sending the manservant from the room. Nicholas looked at his brother, some of his fury breaking loose. "This vileness came into my home. Marissa, Andrea, Mother, my mother-in-law; all are at risk." He slammed his hand onto the desk. "The bastard must be caught!"

"I believe it is time to increase the number of runners we've hired. If you remember, Wiley is currently at Leighaven viewing the crime scene."

"And in the meantime, there has been another attempt upon my life. More unforgivable, the attacker has become a threat to my family." Nicholas shook with rage. "I want a minimum of three runners observing this house at all times, along with five working undercover amongst the staff. I want this bastard caught!"

"I'll take care of it immediately." Thomas moved forward, placing a hand on Nicholas's shoulder. "We're lucky, Nick. No one was seriously hurt."

"But they could have been, Thomas." Nicholas shifted out from under his brother's comforting touch. "They could have been."

Thomas remained silent as Nicholas turned from him. There was nothing more to say.

The stakes in this deadly game had just been raised.

Nicholas's muscles quivered as he brought his wife over the peak. Andrea arched up to greet him, a cry bursting from her, her hands clutching at his arms. His entire body shuddered beneath the onslaught of elemental emotions. Satisfaction thundered through him as he looked down upon Andrea's beautiful features and saw the smile of pleasure curving her lips.

Slowly, he lowered himself to the side of her, his breath rasping in and out of his chest. Nicholas threaded his fingers through her tousled hair, watching the firelight captured within the strands.

Finally.

Thoughts of this moment had been tormenting him all day. Foolishly, he'd tried to restrain himself from coming to her tonight, but his need had proved too strong. It was easily justified. After seven long years of abstinence, one night could hardly ease his hunger. The realization that none other than Andrea could satisfy him was easily explained. She was his wife. It was only natural and right that he desire her.

Satisfied, Nicholas continued to finger Andrea's hair. "You are beautiful, Andrea."

Andrea lifted her head to look at Nicholas. "As are you."

"Hardly."

She ran a finger down the slope of his nose. "Do you consider me such a poor judge?"

"Poor? No." He tilted his head to the side. "Blind? Perhaps."

A laugh escaped her as she swatted him playfully on the arm. "You are horrid."

"A monster," he agreed.

"I fear for my life," she gasped in mock horror.

"As you should," he growled, shifting his head to take a nip at her shoulder. "I devour little girls like you for my supper."

The double entendre shaded her cheeks. "I am well aware of that fact," she added in a saucy tone.

Nicholas laughed, a lusty sound that filled the room and brought a smile to her heart. "Would you care for another demonstration—just to reassure yourself?"

"Thank you for your kind offer, Nicholas, but I believe I am in need of a short respite."

"How short?"

His question pleased her. "Am I so tempting that you are unable to control yourself?"

Her teasing words drained Nicholas of his smile, his body stiffening beneath her. "Certainly not," he said, shifting out of the bed.

"Nicholas, I was but teasing," Andrea protested, reaching out for him.

"I understand," he assured her, bending down to kiss her gently. "However, it did serve to remind me that a gentleman shows his wife courtesy above all— even his own, personal desires."

"And what of your wife's desires?" she demanded, sitting up and clutching the sheet to her body.

He glanced down at her bare shoulders. "Have you forgotten our tryst so quickly?"

Andrea shook her head. "You are being obtuse. I want you to stay here with me . . . for the entire night."

"Come now," Nicholas murmured. "You know as well as I that it is impolite for a husband to overstay his welcome. When you sleep, you should do so in privacy and comfort."

"Don't be so rigid, Nicholas."

"Rigid? I prefer to think upon it as courtly." Nicholas tied the belt on his dressing gown.

"Who asked that you be anything other than my husband?" Andrea allowed the sheet to slip an inch.

Nicholas gave no notice to the curve of her breasts. "I ask it of myself."

She was taken aback by the fierceness of his reply. "Why?"

Nicholas thrust both of his hands through his hair, a heavy sigh breaking from him. "Perhaps my habits seem unyielding to you, but for seven years they were all I had to hold on to, all that kept me sane."

The missing piece fell into place with his statement. Comprehension gave way to empathy. "I can only imagine the horrors you faced in prison."

"I am thankful that you will never fully know what I endured during that time." Nicholas spun to face her. "Do not ask for too much of me. Allow us to find peace within each other and to rebuild our lives together."

Tears shimmered in her eyes as Andrea rose to her feet, the sheet covering her lay forgotten upon the bed. She cupped his cheeks. "You have so much to offer, Nicholas, and you've changed, grown, since your return. Don't worry, my husband, I shall never ask for more than you are capable of giving."

"And who shall define what I am able to give?"

A whisper of a laugh shook her. "You are far too smart for me to outwit, Nicholas."

The wariness in his gaze opened her heart. Andrea knew what she must give him. If they were ever to become as one in spirit, the walls between them needed to be destroyed—and she would be the one to start.

"Take comfort in the knowledge that I love you, my husband." A tear slipped down her cheek when she felt him move beneath her touch. "It is true, Nicholas. I love you."

She melted when he leaned forward and gently accepted her pledge with a kiss, its sweetness undeniable.

Nicholas placed his hands over hers where they rested upon his face. "It is right for a wife to love her husband. I accept your troth and shall cherish and protect it forever."

She ached for his pledge of love in return, but knew it was too soon for him to give her the words. That he did, in truth, love her made it far easier to accept the pain now.

"I trust you," she whispered, baring herself.

He kissed her again. Once. A sweet, undemanding gift of true affection.

Andrea accepted it with love.

Nicholas pulled back, slowly sliding their hands from his face. "You should rest," he urged her. Gently, he led her to the bed, helped her lie down, and tucked the blanket around her. He wiped the tears from her cheeks with his thumbs before bending down to give her another kiss. "Sweet dreams," he murmured.

Andrea watched him walk to the door, shutting it behind him. She would dream of the day when he finally admitted that he loved her in return.

Her lips turned upward into a smile as she closed her eyes.

Amusement filled Nicholas as he watched his wife approach, surrounded by a group of animated men. The derby was about to begin, and Andrea had insisted on touring the stables before the race in order to check on Lord Whiting's mount. It was only fair, she'd insisted, since they were his guests.

He couldn't keep his gaze from roaming over her slender body, encased in a stunning white muslin dress. Every night he'd visited her room, filling himself with her love, hoping that his intense craving for her touch would fade. Instead, it had grown until now it pulsated within him, making it difficult to concentrate on anything else.

His hunger for her had now become hard to deny, nearly impossible to contain. He wanted her constantly. His desire for her company was becoming unmanageable, too. He'd caught himself striding from the study to ask her opinion on more than one occasion.

All he knew was that something had to be done. He simply could not continue on like this. He was alarmingly out of control when it came to Andrea.

"Nicholas."

Andrea's call brought him from his thoughts. He turned toward her with a smile. "How are the horses faring?"

"Quite well." She nodded confidently at a beaming Lord Whiting. "I do believe our host will rule the day."

"Lady Leigh is most brilliant in her assessment," asserted Lord Valcourt, standing a shade too close to Andrea for Nicholas's comfort.

One sharp glare took care of the problem. The young dandy backed away quickly. Nicholas hid a smile.

"I merely noted the physical conditions of the other horses competing against Black Thunder," Andrea said, blushing slightly under the praise.

"Your astute observations astound me," added Lord Hartnell.

Nicholas frowned at the fellows surrounding his wife. It seemed whenever they attended a public function, these very gentlemen flocked about Andrea, insistently asking her questions about their thoroughbreds.

He'd had enough of it. Nicholas placed a hand under Andrea's elbow and drew her toward him. "Come stand next to me, darling."

She moved closer without hesitation.

"I say, Lady Leigh, my mare has a slight hitch in her gait and I was—"

"Make an appointment," Nicholas said flatly, cutting Lord Valcourt off midsentence.

The younger man blinked. "Pardon? Did you say make an appointment?"

"Indeed I did, sir." Nicholas gave the dandy one of his coolest glares.

"Well, I . . . that is . . ."

Nicholas watched the young dandy flounder about for a moment, before cutting him off. "I have had quite enough of you gentlemen bombarding my wife with questions, continually hounding her for answers wherever she goes. If you would like her expert advice, you may arrange for an appointment to see her and then pay for the service."

"Come now, Trent, you can't expect us to forgo this opportunity," protested Lord Valcourt. "There is no one else with your wife's eye for horseflesh. Her opinion is invaluable."

"I'm sure we could find a suitable payment for it," Nicholas countered smoothly. "However, the fact remains that she is here as Lady Leigh, not as an adviser to some eager dandies looking to gamble a few quid."

Lord Valcourt grumbled briefly, then fell silent, apparently deciding against arguing further.

Andrea glanced up at Nicholas as they stepped away from the others to the opposite side of the box. "I'm sorry about this," she whispered, thankful that he'd rescued her.

He felt his frown melt away. How could he be annoyed with her when she gazed up at him with solemn eyes? "It's quite all right, Andrea. I'm becoming well versed in these situations."

A sigh broke from Andrea. "I fear I am forever destined to be an original, aren't I, Nicholas?"

"You are indeed, Andrea." He squeezed her hand. "And that's just fine . . . as long as you're *my* original."

"What a lovely thing to say, Nicholas." Pleasure sparkled in Andrea's eyes, before she turned to watch Lord Whiting's horse win the race.

"Papa, may I go see the swans?"

Nicholas placed a hand on his daughter's shoulder as they made their way through the park. "Be careful not to go too close."

"I promise," Marissa sang as she ran quickly toward the duo of swans sitting near the pond.

Nicholas felt pride swell in his chest. His daughter

was a creature of lightness and joy, forever reminding him of all he now had in his life.

"She's a wonder, Nick."

Nicholas glanced at his brother. "Takes after her father."

Thomas crowed at that one. "I wasn't aware you were so fanciful."

Nicholas smiled, his gaze remaining on his daughter as she sang a loud song to the swans. Thoughts of the danger threatening his precious Marissa always loomed in his consciousness.

"I read the reports that Wiley gathered on everyone who was at Leighaven at the time of my injury," Nicholas began.

"Interesting bits of information there."

He nodded at Thomas. "Indeed, but nothing that incriminates anyone."

"No." Thomas kicked at a tuft of grass. "We've no leads at all."

"I made a list of people whom I might have angered or who might hold a grudge toward me, from my days at Eton onward." Nicholas tugged on the lapel of his jacket. "However, I find it highly unlikely that any of them would want to kill me."

Thomas spread his hands. "We must keep searching, regardless of how impossible the idea may seem."

"You're right, of course," Nicholas agreed. "This must end—and soon. It haunts me to know that my daughter, my wife, my family is under threat."

"I myself will rest easier when this business is finished," Thomas concurred.

Nicholas fell quiet for a moment, his gaze following his daughter's path along the edge of the pond as she moved to investigate a patch of cattails. "Until the attacker is caught, I will never be truly free."

Thomas reached out and placed a hand on Nicholas's shoulder. The contact made Nicholas smile. Nothing was more important than his family.

Andrea took a sip of tea, feeling unusually fatigued for early afternoon. "I am afraid I will soon feel the pinch of my gowns if I continue to enjoy these delicious pastries."

Miriam laughed, reaching for another scone. "But how can one resist?"

Lady Anne raised her china cup to her lips. "By picturing the most beautiful gown you own resting, unworn, in your closet."

Andrea smiled at her mother. "I fear that will provide little inspiration."

"Very well, Andrea. Imagine you are too heavy to properly carry yourself in a saddle." Lady Anne nodded confidently. "I'd wager that would convince you to pass on the treats."

"You would win your bet most handsomely." Andrea leaned back upon the settee, leaving the sweets behind.

Miriam tucked her feet beneath her chair. "Oh, yes, Andrea, I've meant to tell you that I signed a few charges while shopping this week. I hope that is all right."

"I daresay there will be no problem," Andrea assured her, "but you will need to mention it to Nicholas. I'm unaware of our current financial situation."

Lady Anne set down her tea. "You've no idea at all?" She smoothed her gown. "Do you think that prudent, Andrea?"

While Andrea understood her mother's concern, she also knew there was no need for it. Her trust in Nicholas's abilities was unflagging. "We've discussed this before, Mother. I'm positive all is well. I have every faith that Nicholas will prove to be a sound investor."

"I do hope so," Lady Anne said. "We all have felt the pinch of poverty, and I don't think I speak alone when I say it is not a comfortable fit."

Miriam nodded in agreement. "Life does seem more enjoyable when one has the money to view it from an affluent abode."

Andrea waved a hand at the two women. "As you shall continue." She sipped at the warm brew. "This is so relaxing."

Miriam glanced about. "Where did everyone get off to?"

"Nicholas and Thomas took a turn in the park with Marissa," Andrea answered.

"Lady Casterling mentioned the other day that her husband had seen Nicholas strolling about with Marissa, and had decided it must be the rage." Miriam shook her head. "Apparently, the park is literally amuck with doting fathers who are spending time with their children."

"Undoubtedly, the greater lot of them don't have the faintest notion as to what to do with their delightful offspring once they've got them out of doors," Lady Anne added.

"The vagarious nature of society never ceases to amaze me," Andrea said. "I wonder if Nicholas is aware he's begun the latest craze."

"Don't undercut your influence, my dear," Miriam declared. "After all, who has made it fashionable to tour the stables before each race?"

Andrea flushed beneath her mother-in-law's gaze. "Perhaps."

"There is no doubt that you began the trend at the derby," Lady Anne interjected.

"That was two months ago," Andrea protested.

"The very fact that it is still the rage only underscores your influence upon society," Miriam pointed out.

If she lived to be a ripe old age, she vowed she would never understand the capricious opinions of her peers. Andrea had to smile, though. Whoever would have imagined that a woman so determined to live life on her terms would one day be viewed as the height of fashion?

Baffled, Andrea sipped at her tea, listening to Miriam and her mother exchange the latest bits of gossip.

Andrea's sigh filled the quiet carriage.

"Is something amiss?"

Her smile was automatic as Andrea placed her hand on Nicholas's. "No, not really."

"Now, why doesn't that enthusiastic response convince me?" Nicholas asked, arching a brow at her.

Andrea laughed lightly. "London is marvelous, truly. It is just that I miss Leighaven."

"I thought as much."

She tilted her head back to look into Nicholas's eyes. "Don't you miss it? The quiet? The peace?"

How was he to find peace when his world was threatened? Instead he answered, "Most certainly. I cannot say I am sorry that this is the final event of the Season."

Another deep sigh rushed from her. "I look forward to being at Leighaven for the Yuletide. I grow weary of all this revelry. Why, just today I was forced to take a nap in order to regain some energy for this evening. I was positively drained before my rest, and, even with it, I remain exhausted."

Nicholas's gaze held a teasing light. "You are getting old, Andrea."

"Posh," she returned easily. "I am but a babe, when compared against your considerable years."

"Not true; for if you were still an innocent, I could not do this." There was a decidedly sensual tilt to Nicholas's mouth as he reached for her.

Before he could touch her, their carriage rocked to a halt. "Blast. We've arrived."

"I thought you were eager to attend this party," Andrea said pertly.

"I would be more than happy to demonstrate what I am truly eager for," he replied, fully prepared to kiss her senseless.

"The residence of the Viscount of Somersworth," announced their footman, opening the door to their carriage.

Nicholas held back the curse that rose to his lips. Instead, he stepped from their conveyance and turned back to assist Andrea's descent.

"Do try to control your wayward impulses this evening," Nicholas murmured as he escorted her into the Viscount's town house.

"And spoil all my fun?" she whispered back, before they were admitted by an austere butler.

Nicholas gave her a warning glance, then turned toward their host and hostess with a cordial smile. After they were announced, Nicholas led the way into the ballroom.

"Did I happen to mention my encounter with our esteemed host the other day in Hyde Park?" Nicholas asked, handing Andrea a glass of punch.

"I don't believe so."

He bent toward Andrea, her alluring scent intoxicating him. It took great control to concentrate on his tale. "When I was taking my daily walk with Marissa, I came upon Somersworth with his young daughter. The man looked immensely relieved to see me and hailed me over."

"I wasn't aware you were intimates," Andrea said, taking a sip.

"We are not," Nicholas confirmed, glancing about them, making sure they would not be overheard. "It seems that I have started a rage by spending time with Marissa, and Somersworth's Viscountess had ordered him to follow suit."

"It will do him naught but good."

Nicholas nodded. "True, but the amusing issue is that the man had literally no idea as to what to do with his daughter once at the park. He stood, looking about with this helpless expression, until he caught sight of me. He was quick to inquire what I did with Marissa."

"And you informed him, I hope." Andrea drained the glass of punch.

"His expression, when I told him to take note of his daughter's interests and hobbies, was quite comical, I assure you." There was a wicked gleam in Nicholas's gaze. "I thought the poor fellow was going to pass out when I suggested he play a game with her."

Andrea smothered a laugh beneath her gloved hand. "Who would have imagined that we would become such paragons of fashion?"

Nicholas considered his wife's observation. Who indeed? His entire life he'd been raised to respect the dictates of society. Surprisingly, it seemed he was now the one to dictate the rules. Did that mean any behavior he deemed proper would be accepted as such? The thought bore consideration.

Unwilling to allow such contemplation to dampen his spirits, Nicholas thrust the thoughts aside, turning to his wife with a smile. "Would you afford me the honor of this dance?"

"With pleasure," she accepted gracefully, handing him her empty glass.

Nicholas escorted his wife onto the dance floor. The lively quadrille began with a merry step. Nicholas grasped Andrea by the waist, swinging her around, then spinning her back to her position.

She stumbled slightly. The unusual movement captured his attention. Nicholas looked at Andrea, growing alarmed at her sudden pallor. The other dancers pulled to a halt as Nicholas grabbed his wife just before she collapsed onto the ground.

Panic clutched at his heart, squeezing tight, as he swept her unconscious form against his chest. One terrifying thought pounded through him.

His wife had been poisoned.

The idea that she could be lying in his arms, dying, tore at him, making him crazed. "Fetch a doctor immediately!" Nicholas barked, his features grim as he strode from the room, Andrea gathered against his chest. "Send a maid with—"

His words broke off at Andrea's whisper. "No, please, Nicholas. Please just take me home."

He shook his head, a fearsome expression on his face. "But you are—"

"Merely tired." She gave him a weak smile of reassurance. "I want to go home."

Logic warred with emotion inside him. Reason dictated that he take her upstairs immediately and ascertain her well-being, ensure her health. If it were poison, wouldn't even the smallest delay be detrimental? His heart bade him fulfill her request and take her home. Nicholas stood still as the battle raged inside him.

She lifted a slender hand to cup his cheek where a tick pulsed. "Please."

His heart won. "Fetch Lady Leigh's cloak," Nicholas snapped at the butler. "Alert the coachman that we are departing."

The crush of people parted for Nicholas as he hurried to the door, his precious wife clutched close to his chest. Pausing only to allow the butler to drape Andrea's fur-lined cloak over her, Nicholas walked into the cool night air toward his carriage, toward home.

"My Lord, might I have a word with you?"

Nicholas's gaze remained on his wife's pale face as he sat on the edge of their bed. He brushed a strand of hair off her forehead as she slept before he stood and headed for the hallway, leaving Andrea in his mother's care. The doctor followed silently.

Nicholas led the doctor down the stairs and into his study, closing the door behind them. "What is wrong with my wife?" Nicholas braced himself for the answer.

"Nothing that six months won't cure," the doctor said with a smile.

"What the devil are you talking about?" He was too distraught to sort through riddles.

"I am talking about a baby, my lord." And just to make sure the obviously stunned man before him understood, the doctor explained again, slowly, "Your wife is expecting. She is approximately three months along."

Nicholas collapsed into his chair. Instead of death, Andrea's weakness had been caused by life. Words failed him. A baby. His baby. Perhaps another little girl like Marissa or even a boy. His arms already ached to hold the precious gift. He would have a chance to experience all the joys he'd missed with his daughter. His happiness was too powerful to contain.

Laughter roared from Nicholas as he grabbed the doctor, hugging him close, patting the man vigorously on the back. "A baby!" he shouted, releasing the smiling man.

"My lord?" Jamieson stood on the threshold of the room, with Hampton not far behind him.

"We're going to have another baby!" Nicholas exclaimed, rushing forward to pull both Jamieson and Hampton into an awkward embrace. Nicholas knew he was acting like a fool—and he didn't care one whit. He pulled away from the two men, grinning broadly. "We're going to have a baby," he said again, warmed to see tears glistening in the eyes of both men.

A thought struck Nicholas, spinning him back around to face the smiling doctor. "My wife? Is she all right?"

"She couldn't be healthier," he assured Nicholas. "I'm afraid she fell back asleep before I could tell her that she was expecting. From her comments, I don't believe she has any idea."

"But this is our second child."

The man nodded at Nicholas's confusion. "It seems impossible to us of the male persuasion, but this happens quite often. According to my patients, each time is different. Or perhaps she just wasn't looking at all the signs."

Nicholas reached out to shake the doctor's hand. "Thank you again." He looked at his butler. "Jamieson will settle our account on your departure."

Nicholas hurried past the three men, bounding up the stairs, unable to wait another moment to hold his wife in his arms.

Miriam sat reading by the light of a single candle, her eyes often lifting from the book to peer at Andrea's sleeping form. The door whispered across the rug as it opened, allowing Nicholas to enter the room. Miriam frowned as she watched her son walk to Andrea's side. "What did the doctor say?" she whispered, her book forgotten in her lap.

Nicholas's face revealed nothing when he turned to look at her. "He said that she would be perfectly fine in another six months."

"Six months?" She was confused. "Why six months? What difference could it possibly— Oh." Miriam breathed as comprehension dawned, widening her eyes. "Oh," she said again, joy beginning to brighten her gaze. "How wonderful for you both."

Another grin spread across Nicholas's face. "Thank you," he whispered. He leaned down to stroke Andrea's hair. "I appreciate your watching over Andrea."

Miriam's thick robe swished against her legs as she walked to the door. "It was an honor," she murmured softly. "I'm so happy for you both." The door clicked shut behind her.

Careful not to disturb Andrea, Nicholas sat on the edge of the bed, enfolding her hand within his. His breath caught in his throat as he gazed down at his wife. He'd been so terrified at the possibility of losing her. In that instant, his feelings for her had crystallized into perfect form.

He loved her.

The realization frightened him. In prison, the only way for him to survive was to shield himself, withdrawing from reality. The idea of love made him feel too vulnerable, unprotected. He felt an odd tension swirl in the pit of his stomach. What if his attentions, his need to have her near him, brought her into peril? The moment when he'd thought Andrea poisoned had nearly killed him yet made him realize something all too important: until his attacker was apprehended, he needed to put distance between himself and Andrea. Her safety was worth any price.

"Nicholas?" Andrea murmured, her lashes lifting to reveal her sleep-filled eyes.

"I didn't mean to wake you."

"I don't mind," Andrea said, moving against her pillow.

Her stretch made him smile. She looked like a silky cat, all warm and cozy.

"I apologize for this evening. I knew I was exhausted, but I never realized just how much."

"You still don't," Nicholas said, a smile playing about his lips.

"Probably not," she yawned. "I fear I shall never become accustomed to the hours we keep in London."

"It is not your schedule. Although your activities have deepened your exhaustion level." Nicholas stroked her hand.

"All the rushing about I do here in town is certainly the reason for my fainting," she insisted. "I assure you, I did not swoon in public merely to provide entertainment."

"Of that I have no doubt," he conceded with a chuckle. "Although I wouldn't be in the least surprised if it became the latest to-do."

She stretched her back. "Highly unlikely."

"But still a possibility." Nicholas shifted closer. "It is more likely that being with child will come of fashion."

"I assure you, that will never come to pass."

He shrugged, allowing some of his elation to shine in his expression. "Perhaps if someone were to blaze forward, others would follow. Haven't you found that to be true, Andrea?"

"In order to accomplish that, I would have to be . . ." Her words trailed off as she pieced together his broad hints. "Am I going to have a baby?" she asked in awe.

Nicholas slowly shook his head. "No, Andrea, *we* are going to have a baby."

A brilliant smile spread across her face. "Yes, we are. Did you speak with the doctor? Is everything all right?"

"Perfectly. He thinks you are about three months along."

"Three months? Then it must have happened that first time we made love."

"The night of our dinner party here in London?"

Andrea nodded silently.

"Well, I must say, we certainly have quite a track record."

"What do you mean?"

Amusement glittered in his golden gaze. "It seems each time we make love, we also create a child. We must be a combustible combination."

"Of that there is no doubt."

Nicholas released her hand, stood, and began to remove his clothes. "Apparently not."

"Nicholas?" Andrea looked up at him, her eyes wide. "What are you doing?"

"I thought it rather obvious."

She shook her head, clutching the sheet to her. "I'm sorry, Nicholas, but I am too tired to make love this evening."

The covers slipped from her fingers when Nicholas pulled them back. He slid in next to her, wrapping his arms around her. "I merely want to hold you."

"All night through?" The wistful note in her voice melted him.

He tightened his hold on her, cradling her into his body. "I've decided to declare it fashionable to spend the entire night with one's wife."

Andrea's gasp was pure pleasure. "A welcome notion, I assure you." She snuggled against his chest. "It shall, undoubtedly, become the most popular rage we've begun to date."

Nicholas chuckled, aware of the deep sense of satisfaction filling him. "Are you usually this talkative in bed?"

She swatted him lightly in response.

Nicholas simply smiled into her hair and closed his eyes, more content than he could ever have imagined.

Nine

~~~~~~~~~~~~~~

"Come sit on my lap, magpie." Nicholas held out his arms to Marissa, who scrambled onto his lap with a smile.

"Will you tell me another story, Papa?"

Andrea reached over to stroke her daughter's hair. "It's not a story, Marissa. This one will be real."

The little girl looked wary. "It's not too scary, is it?"

"No," Andrea said, biting back a smile. "It's a lovely tale about a small family that was blessed with another fairy angel."

Nicholas jostled Marissa on his legs. "You are going to be a big sister in a while. How would you enjoy that?"

Marissa stilled. "Like Uncle Thomas is your brother?"

"Exactly," Nicholas said, hugging her against him. "Won't it be delightful to have another little girl or perhaps a little boy? Imagine that one, Marissa. A little brother scampering about."

"Oh."

Nicholas glanced at Andrea, who wore a matching

expression of concern. "Are you upset, Marissa? Doesn't it sound grand to have a little brother or sister?"

"Yes, Papa." She leaned forward to press a kiss on his cheek. "I need to see Grandmama for my lessons now. Thank you for telling me."

Before he could ask her another question, she hopped off his lap and ran from the room. The gaze he turned upon Andrea was troubled. "Her reaction was less than I'd hoped."

"I venture to say she was displeased by our news," Andrea said, pressing a hand upon her abdomen.

"I must admit I'm surprised. I thought she'd be happy."

"I'm sure she'll be delighted once she's had time to accustom herself to the idea," Andrea said.

"I hope you're right," he replied. Nicholas stood, holding out his hand to Andrea. "Would you care to join me for some tea?"

She glanced up at him, surprised.

"I don't see what good it is doing to dwell on Marissa's disappointment." He shrugged. "Besides, I could use some bolstering from a good cup of tea."

She accepted readily. "As could I." Andrea slipped her hand into his. Warmth flooded her. Their night together had, in many ways, been the most intimate exchange of their marriage. Without the haze of passion the emotions had been soft, tender. She felt cherished this morning.

Amazing what a loving companion throughout the night could do for a person's disposition.

Andrea's steps were light as she followed her husband.

They were just finishing tea when Jamieson burst into the parlor, his impeccable grooming in disarray, his thinning gray hair flying upward in his haste. "My lord, your daughter, Lady Marissa, is missing."

"Missing?" Nicholas asked sharply, shooting to his feet. Dread struck him through, a dark lance in his heart, at the possibility that his beloved daughter had been kidnapped. With the imminent threat to his family, it seemed the logical assumption.

"Are you sure?" Andrea asked, standing tall next to Nicholas.

Automatically, he laid a steadying hand upon Andrea's back. "Has the house been thoroughly checked?"

"Yes, my lord." Jamieson stood wringing his hands, his obvious distress so at odds with his normal reserve.

Nicholas's gaze swung to the clock on the mantel. Half past four. It would be getting dark soon. Time was not in their favor. "Is my brother still here?"

"Yes, he is visiting with your mother."

"Send them both in here immediately," ordered Nicholas before turning his attention to Andrea. Jamieson ran from the room, not even bothering to shut the door in his haste.

Andrea began to pace. "Dear God, Nicholas, where could she be?"

"We'll find her," Nicholas said in comfort. "If we are going to locate her, we need to proceed logically, examining everything before eliminating it as a possibility." A rush of fury swelled up in Nicholas when he thought of the possibility that his daughter was in the hands of kidnappers.

"She must be close by. We left her only an hour ago," Andrea said, straightening her spine.

Nicholas couldn't bear to think of all that could happen in one short hour.

The sound of running feet rang across the room. "Mother and I just heard about Marissa. What can I do to help?" A worried scowl pulled down Thomas's features.

"Yes, anything," agreed Miriam, who was obviously shaken, but struggling to maintain her composure.

Nicholas held up a hand, silencing everyone. "Jamieson, are you sure the house has been thoroughly checked? Each room? Every closet?"

"Yes, my lord. Even the servants' quarters."

"How about the grounds?"

"The rear gardens were deserted."

"And the stables?"

Jamieson nodded. "No trace of her there either."

"Could she be with my mother?" The hopeful note in Andrea's voice struck a similar chord within Nicholas.

His mother crushed that hope. "I was waiting for Marissa to join me for our lesson. She's never even been late before, never mind missing it entirely. Besides which, Anne is visiting with the Duchess of Pendrake, and she would never take Marissa there."

Nicholas raked back his hair, the battle to control his panic intensifying. "Then where the hell could she be?" he ground out in frustration before taking a deep, calming breath. "All right. We need to immediately search her out. Thomas, you check with the magistrate to see if she has been found. Jamieson, you check the nearest infirmary. And I will check . . ." Nicholas's heart was pounding. Where the devil would she have gone? He needed to think like Marissa. Where would he go if . . .

A glimmer of hope sparked to life within him. Nicholas looked at his wife. "You and I will check the park. I think perhaps she went to our special spot. Grab your cloak and we will be off."

"Shall I wait here in case she returns home?" Miriam asked.

"Excellent idea." Nicholas nodded to his family, then they all erupted into action.

"I never knew of this place," Andrea said as she stepped into the clearing. An old sundial sat in the middle of a circular garden, long since forgotten by the official gardeners of Hyde Park. Three moss-covered marble benches faced the sundial, their pristine white hidden by the green velvet of the moss. A weed-laden walkway encircled the garden, further adding to the air of neglect. In the far corner of the garden was a statue of the Virgin Mary gently enfolding a swaddled Jesus in her arms, her stone face softened by a gentle smile.

And beneath the figure lay a small ball of mussed clothes and tangled hair.

Marissa.

"There she is, Nicholas. Is she all right? Has she been hurt?" Andrea began to hurry forward, but her movements were stopped when Nicholas grabbed her arm

"Don't startle her; she's only sleeping," he murmured. "She's fine."

Relief flooded Andrea as she gazed down at her precious daughter. "I need to touch her—just to make sure."

"Let's bring our daughter home," he said in an unsteady voice.

As one, they turned and made their way to Marissa. They knelt down before her, Andrea brushing back the strands of dark hair that lay across her daughter's face. "Marissa," she called softly.

The little girl stirred. "Mama?"

A gasp caught in Andrea's throat.

Mama. It had been a long time since her daughter

had called her that, not the more formal—and infinitely colder—Mother.

Mama. So simple, yet so undeniably sweet. *Mama.* A name that was earned, not merely given. A sign of affection.

Tears gathered in Andrea's eyes as she looked down at her daughter. "Oh, my baby," Andrea whispered brokenly.

Nicholas was visibly moved when he touched his hand to Andrea's shoulder. "We need to get her home. She is probably half frozen after lying on this cold ground."

Wiping at her tears, Andrea nodded, stepping back to give Nicholas room to lift their daughter. Gently, he slid his arms underneath Marissa, cradling her precious form close to his warmth.

The little girl stirred once more in his arms. "Papa?" she murmured, her eyelashes lifting slowly. "Why are we in the park? Did I fall . . ." Memory flooded her golden eyes, so like her father's, and she began to twist against Nicholas's hold. "No, let me go. I am not going back. I am never going back!"

Undaunted, Nicholas's stride never broke as he headed toward their waiting carriage, the need to get his shivering daughter into warmth overriding all other objectives.

"No," Marissa shrieked, kicking out at the air, her arms flailing about and pounding against Nicholas's shoulders. "Let me down!"

The footman blanched at the sight of the Earl holding his screaming daughter, followed by the Countess, who looked close to tears. He rushed to open the carriage door. Nicholas ducked into the warm carriage with his daughter still clasped in his arms. Andrea followed quickly.

As soon as the door shut, Andrea reached forward

to touch their daughter's arm. "Please talk to us, Marissa. What's wrong? Why did you run away?"

Her little face was set in a mutinous cast. A silent glare was her only response.

"Please, sweetheart, let us help you," implored Andrea.

Marissa jerked her arm away from her mother's touch as she turned hot eyes onto Andrea's pale face. "You don't want to help me. You don't even want me around."

What little color remained in Andrea's face drained at her daughter's harsh words.

"Marissa," Nicholas said sternly, obviously torn between the need to comfort his daughter and the urge to protect his wife.

"It is all right, Nicholas," Andrea said, trying to stop her heart from bleeding. "I know I have not always been the most attentive mother, Marissa, and I can only say I regret that more than you can ever realize." Andrea drew in a shaky breath before she continued. "But I have changed. You know that. Think of all we've done together over the past few weeks. We have all changed. Since your father's return, I think we've actually become a family, a true family."

Her bottom lip trembled as Marissa whispered, "You don't want me anymore."

"Of course we do," Andrea hurried to reassure her.

Marissa's dark hair flew, whipping against Nicholas's cheek as she shook her head vigorously. "No, you don't."

"What would make you believe something like that?"

Nicholas's question caused Marissa's tears to spill over. "Because you're going to have a new baby."

"Yes, but that doesn't mean that we don't want you anymore."

Marissa glared at her father. "You might have a boy. That's what you said. And then you won't want me."

"I will always want you," assured Nicholas.

"I don't believe you," she shouted, pushing against his hold once more. "Everyone likes baby boys better. Grandmother Anne told me so a long time ago. If you get a new baby boy, you'll forget all about me." Her sobs began to shake her slight frame and Marissa buried her face against Nicholas's shoulder, unconsciously taking comfort in the very person she thought was causing her pain.

"Shhh, now. It will be fine. You'll see," Nicholas murmured, stroking his daughter's back soothingly. When her crying subsided into sniffles, Nicholas pulled back her head, his hands cupping her swollen face. "Listen to me, young lady, and listen well. You are my daughter. You will always be my daughter. And I will always cherish the time we spend together." His golden eyes blazed into hers as he said slowly, "I love you, Marissa."

Bittersweet tears slid down Andrea's cheeks as the tender words she so longed to hear were given to her daughter. A tremulous smile curved Andrea's mouth when Marissa launched herself deeper into her father's arms.

"I love you, too, Papa," she said softly. After a long hug, she pulled back, her head tilted to the side. "I guess having a baby won't be too bad. Just as long as he remembers that I am the boss."

A smile spread on Nicholas's face. "I am confident that if he forgets you will be only too eager to remind him."

All three of them laughed, the tension gone from

the carriage. Marissa turned toward her mother. "Can we go home, Mama?"

Andrea melted, the sweet feeling of parental love filling her. "We are going home."

Marissa wrinkled her nose. "No, not to that house in town. It is too small and I miss the country. Besides, my room smells funny."

Both Nicholas and Andrea laughed at their precocious child. "We can go home tomorrow," promised Andrea, reaching to stroke her daughter's cheek. "After all, we have so much to do with the fall upon us. Before long it will be time to begin preparing for Father Christmas's visit."

Marissa's eyes grew round. "I almost forgot." Their daughter couldn't get the words out quickly enough. "I want more blocks and a pony with a brand-new white saddle and . . . and I want a puppy with black spots and I want a house for my new puppy and I want . . ."

Nicholas shook his head, an indulgent smile on his face as he murmured to his wife, "What have you started?"

Happy laughter was Andrea's only response.

Hampton nabbed Jamieson, tugging the butler into the alcove off the main foyer at Leighaven. "Jamie, we need to discuss some important business."

Jamieson found it impossible to withhold his groan. Since their return to the country estate a month ago, everything had been running smoothly. "Please, don't even begin with comments on the Master and Lady Andrea."

"There's trouble afoot, I'm telling you."

"They have been managing splendidly," Jamieson insisted, looking down at Hampton. "Master Nick has been most accommodating and displays affection for both his daughter and wife."

"Of course he's wonderful with Marissa." Hampton frowned. "What would make you think that Master Nick had a problem with the little miss?"

"I was merely speculating on what rubbish you might be thinking now."

"But there's no trouble with Miss Marissa. Why would you say there was?"

"I did not say that—" Jamieson broke off his protest. He had been dealing with Hampton long enough to know when the old fool would not listen to logic. It would do little good to point out to the manservant that he had started the conversation. Giving in, he asked, "What do you perceive as the difficulty?"

"Don't you be patronizing me, you old bag of wind."

Jamieson sighed. "I've wasted far too much time on this ridiculous conversation." He took two steps forward, before Hampton grabbed hold of his arm.

"Haven't you noticed how Master Nick spends time with Marissa, but never with Lady Andrea?"

"Of all the fool things." Jamieson shook his head, unable to believe the rot he was hearing from Hampton. "Just yesterday, he strolled the grounds with Lady Andrea."

"And Marissa, not to mention Lady Miriam tagging along to keep things real romantic." Hampton rocked back on his heels. "*Now* what are you thinking of my suspicions?"

"I'm thinking that I'm the greatest of idiots for believing even for a moment that you had something of value to say." Jamieson scowled at Hampton. "You're nothing more than a meddling mumblenews."

"Well, for your information—"

Hampton's tirade was cut short when Andrea

stepped into the alcove. "Pardon me for intruding, gentlemen, but I was wondering if I might ask a favor of Jamieson."

Aghast at having been caught gossiping, Jamieson was mortified, his cheeks aflame.

Andrea touched his arm. "Are you feeling well, Jamieson?"

"Quite." His voice was small and tight, but that could not be helped. He cleared his throat. "It is kind of you to inquire after my health."

Andrea smiled, only making him feel worse for discussing her private affairs. "Would you mind asking Cook to prepare a cake for this evening's dessert? I would normally do it myself, but I'm already late for my lesson with Marissa."

"You've taken over the little miss's lessons?" Hampton asked, his tone perfectly normal. Apparently, being discovered gossiping did not bother him greatly.

"Never would I be so foolish," Andrea said quickly, a laugh accompanying her words. "I've been teaching her to ride since our return to Leighaven."

"She's a quick one, our Marissa." Hampton beamed like a doting grandfather.

"I'm very proud of her," Andrea acknowledged. "The reason I requested a cake was because she's done so very well. I want to celebrate this evening."

"Very well, madam. I will see to it." Jamieson gave Hampton a glare before striding from the alcove.

Hampton looked ill at ease. "I'll just go check on Jamie," he said, hurrying after the butler.

Andrea looked at their departing backs. What had she done to make them so uncomfortable? She couldn't imagine. Matters had been going amazingly smoothly about Leighaven since their return. With the exception of her mother, who adored the London lifestyle, everyone seemed relieved to be back home. Her life was perfect.

Close, she amended. Nicholas had finally begun to spend the nights with her, making her feel loved, but he had yet to say the words. She kept assuring herself that he did indeed love her and that those few words made no difference at all.

But they did.

Each night she gave him her pledge of love and he accepted it with a smile, gifting her a passionate kiss in return. She'd tried to believe that his failure to reciprocate didn't hurt her, but it was no longer possible to ignore the pain in her heart. With all the joy he gave her, why did he so resist admitting to his love? How much longer would she have to believe in blind faith?

She took some comfort in the fact that he seemed to be gaining respect for her. Yet while Nicholas no longer suggested that she abandon her work in the stables, he was clearly pleased that her growing babe was beginning to slow her a bit. And there were still more issues between them that irritated her. Just two days before, she'd been reading in the study when he and Thomas joined her. Nicholas and his brother had begun discussing a land dispute between two of their tenants. Interested, she'd offered an opinion. Nicholas had smiled at her, thanking her for her input, before returning his attention back to his brother.

She'd been dismissed.

Instead of anger, she'd felt an overwhelming sense of sadness.

A heavy sigh rushed from Andrea before she pushed aside her thoughts. Her daughter was waiting. There was a purpose to her stride as Andrea headed toward the stables.

* * *

Victoria Malvey

The Yule log burned brightly in the hearth, spreading cheery warmth through the family salon. Flickering lights could be seen through the tall windows, creating a wondrous sight across the lands at Leighaven. Nicholas sat between his wife and daughter, both of whom were near twitching with excitement. Lady Anne shared a settee with Miriam, who was passing out the gifts.

"This is for Marissa and this last package is for you, Andrea." Miriam sat back, her own gifts resting on her lap.

"Can I go first? Can I?" chimed Marissa, shaking a package.

"We wouldn't think of allowing anyone else that honor," said Nicholas in lazy amusement.

Andrea's hand dropped onto his thigh as she leaned forward to watch Marissa. Nicholas's gaze slid over her glowing face to her belly, which was just beginning to round, and back again. Andrea now clothed herself in soft, full dresses that she had ordered from London before their departure.

With her high color and ripening fullness, Nicholas found her more beautiful than ever. Andrea sent him a bright smile before returning her attention to Marissa. He thought of his gift for her and felt a sense of rightness.

His life would be wonderful, if not for the continued threat to his family. Although there had been no further attempts on his life, he would be a fool to relax his guard. The Bow Street runner's report had told Nicholas that Harry was in deep financial debt and his family had virtually disowned him. However, there was nothing beyond that which incriminated him. The added information that Harry had been Andrea's most ardent suitor in London during his absence all those years hardly came as a shock.

It frustrated him to realize that he was no closer to solving this mystery. No leads, no clues, no real suspects. Only three—one nearly successful—attempts upon his life.

Fear clenched in the pit of his stomach, but he thrust it away, refusing to allow it to sway his path. At his daughter's exclamation of pleasure, Nicholas focused on her joy, setting aside his dark thoughts.

"Thank you, Grandmama," Marissa said quickly, her face covered with a wide grin. "It is the most beautiful glass I have ever seen." Her eyes were wide with wonder as she turned the small glass globe in her hands. Inside the globe was a chestnut mare. The globe was filled with water and golden sparkles, giving it a magical appearance. The entire object was only six inches tall, but it was exquisite in detail. "The horse looks just like Stargazer. He and I are friends from my riding lessons with Mama."

A pleased smile lit Miriam's face. "When I saw it, I thought of you."

Carefully, Marissa placed the globe on the table before tearing into the next gift. She opened the top of the box to reveal a pair of beautiful leather gloves, doeskin soft, off-white in color. Marissa hurried to try the gloves for size.

"Young ladies should always protect their hands from unsightly marks," Lady Anne advised. "You must remember to wear them whenever you handle the reins."

Marissa held up her hand, the glove perfectly shaped to her slender fingers. "They are perfect. Thank you, Grandmother."

Lady Anne dipped her head in acceptance of the thanks. The gloves were placed next to the glass globe before Marissa tore into her last package. Inside the small box was a tiny collar.

Victoria Malvey

"Papa?" Marissa questioned, confused at the odd gift.

"The collar belongs to a certain little puppy which remains nameless."

"A puppy!" shrieked Marissa, launching herself onto her father. "Where is he? What color is he? How old is he?" Her words stopped abruptly as another thought hit. "Wait a minute. Is it a boy dog or a girl dog?"

Everyone laughed at her excitement. "Perhaps you should see for yourself, Marissa. Jamieson is trying to keep him from destroying the kitchens at this very moment."

"Oh, thank you," she exclaimed, moving from him onto her mother. Andrea received an enthusiastic— though swift—hug from Marissa before she ran from the room in search of her new friend. The door slammed shut behind her.

"It appears she is pleased with her gift," Nicholas said, laughing.

"What was your first clue, darling?" Andrea patted him on the thigh.

"Amusing, Andrea," he murmured, glancing at her.

She smiled at him, before asking, "Who shall be next? Miriam?"

"Why, certainly," Nicholas's mother replied. Picking up one of the two packages in her lap, she began to carefully pull the tissue away from the small box. She lifted the lid to reveal a beautiful flower pendant in the shape of a tulip, made from diamonds with emeralds creating the stem. "Oh, my," Miriam gasped, her mouth open in amazement. "This is . . . well . . . it is simply the most beautiful piece of jewelry I have ever seen." She snapped the lid down, holding the box out to Nicholas. "It is too much. I cannot accept it as my gift."

Nicholas shrugged lightly. "I am afraid that you will never be able to convince my wife to return that particular trinket. Once she laid eyes upon it, she was positive it was perfect for you."

"Andrea, it is too much," Miriam protested to her smiling daughter-in-law.

Andrea shook her head. "Nonsense. I know how much you love your gardens and as soon as I saw it, I, well, I just knew it was meant for you."

Blinking back tears, Miriam whispered, "Thank you, my dear. Both of you." Drawing a deep breath, she continued, "Shall we see what is in this next package? Is this from you, Anne?"

"Indeed it is."

"What could it be?"

"There's but one way to find out," Lady Anne said, a smile tilting up her lips.

Miriam gently grasped the paper and pulled it back, revealing a large book. "Herbs and Their Many Uses," she read off the cover. A bright smile curved her lips. "Anne, this is marvelous. How did you know?"

"It requires little guessing when you spend every spare hour in the gardens. I thought perhaps you might find that book of interest."

"Thank you." Miriam covered Anne's hand, squeezing lightly in affection.

"Let us see what Father Christmas brought for me, shall we?" Without waiting for anyone's response, Lady Anne began to unwrap the first of her packages. "What a charming wrap, Miriam. I do so enjoy this particular shade of blue." The embroidered shawl spilled through Anne's fingers, its silken texture caressing her hands. "I am quite confident that it will match one of my new gowns."

"I am so glad you like it, Anne."

"How could I not?" she questioned, gently laying the wrap in its box. She moved on to the next present, a small box from Nicholas and Andrea. Confusion drew her eyebrows together as she lifted a key from its bed of blue velvet. "A key? I presume there is some significance to this, as there was to the collar."

Andrea's laughter rang out. "Of course, Mother. It is a key to the London town house."

"The town house?"

"Since you prefer the civilization of town to the wilderness of Leighaven, we felt you might enjoy un-limited access to the family holdings there," Nicholas clarified.

"There could not possibly be a gift more suited than this one." She looked directly at Nicholas. "Thank you for your generosity. Though I must admit, I find it a bit startling."

"Gracious as always, I see," Nicholas murmured.

"Well," Andrea interrupted brightly, unwilling to allow their wonderful evening to disintegrate into an argument. "Nicholas? Perhaps you would like to be next?"

An indulgent smile softened his expression. "You wish to savor your turn, is that it?"

"You know me so well."

"I like to think so," he said softly before turning his attention to the three packages that lay on the settee next to him. The first package held a book on the art of fisticuffs from his mother.

"I have seen you exercise out in the field with Thomas and I thought you might enjoy reading that book," she said quietly.

"Thank you, Mother," he said, leaning forward to kiss her cheek.

The second box was from Lady Anne, and con-tained a beautiful silk cravat, white with elegant stitching around the edges. The soft material wound itself about Nicholas's hands as he lifted it from the box. "Thank you," he said softly.

Lady Anne nodded briskly. "I thought it might be of use if you ever return to town. Since you two generate so much attention, it is best if you are dressed properly," she finished.

"Mine next," Andrea urged her husband.

His eyes were filled with laughter as he lifted the last box. He raised it up and down, gauging the weight of the package. "It is quite heavy."

"You will never guess what it is, so just open it," Andrea laughed.

"Since I have been advised not to upset a woman who is enceinte, I will do as you request," he teased, removing the paper to reveal an exquisite wooden box, inlaid with a rich pattern of wood, stones, and a few precious gems. He traced the swirling design as he murmured, "It is magnificent, Andrea."

"Open it," she urged.

Surprise widened Nicholas's eyes as he gazed at his wife. He had assumed that the box itself was the gift, never imagining that something might be encased in such a unique fashion. Carefully, he lifted the heavy lid.

His breath caught in his throat as he looked down at the two antique daggers cradled on a bed of red velvet, their gleaming blades giving proof of their intended use. He lifted one of the daggers into the light. The knife was obviously old; the weight alone attested to the fact that the metal was forged from the heavier steel of days past.

"They are spectacular." He pressed a gentle kiss upon her mouth. "Thank you."

Pulling back, he said, "It's your turn now, Andrea." He looked down at the single package accompanied by an envelope resting on her lap. "My gift is meant for only the two of us. I would prefer to share it with you later."

"Please, let us not address such personal matters," Lady Anne asked, waving her hand. "Andrea, if you would, please continue."

Nicholas suppressed a retort.

"Perhaps I shall open your gift first then, Mother," Andrea continued, picking up the cream envelope from her mother. It contained a bill of sale from Thomas House, Master Craftsmen. "What is this?"

"I ordered a special rocking chair for you. It will be soothing to your spine as you progress in your maternal state. Your father purchased one for me and I still remember the comfort it brought," she stated.

"I shall treasure your gift and the thought behind it."

Lady Anne nodded. "You are exceedingly difficult to buy for."

Nicholas could clearly see the disappointment Andrea felt from her mother's comment. He felt like taking the older woman by the shoulders and demanding that once, just once, she give her daughter the gift of acceptance. Now, that would be something of value.

Andrea sat up straighter before glancing at her mother-in-law. "This is a good-size box. I can't imagine what it could contain."

"I do hope you will be pleased, Andrea. Like your mother, I was at a loss as to what you might enjoy, so I got a little help from Marissa," Miriam confessed with a shy smile.

"In that case, I am sure it will be perfect." The package was soon opened. Andrea's cry of delight caused Nicholas to peer curiously into the box. His wife picked up the various brushes, clippers, and metal pieces contained in the package. "I desperately needed another set."

"Another set of what?" Nicholas asked.

"This is a new grooming set for my horses," Andrea said excitedly. "My old brushes were worn down to nothing. I meant to replace them, but now that won't be necessary. Aren't they wonderful? This hard bristle brush will make Wildstar's coat shine."

"Wildstar? Hartnell's horse?"

"Yes," Andrea agreed, distracted by her inspection of the set.

"I thought Hartnell had taken his mare to London with him when he left months ago."

"He did," she said, giving Nicholas her full attention, "but Wildstar is returning to our stables next week. She's expecting a foal in the spring and has been showing signs of trouble."

Nicholas's features hardened. After reading that report by the runner, the last place he wanted Hartnell was around his wife. "Will Hartnell be coming also?"

"I expect so."

Displeasure rippled through Nicholas. He didn't see any point in telling Andrea what the report had said about Hartnell. If he told her of the investigation, it would only lead to further questions whose answers he'd rather not share. It wouldn't do to have his expectant wife worrying. That was his responsibility as her husband and as head of this family.

Knowing his wife as he did, he highly doubted that she would share his sentiments. More than likely, she'd be furious at him for ordering an investigation of everyone, including Harry. It was doubtful that Harry's involvement in seedy deals with less than reputable characters would soften her anger.

As long as Harry was around, Andrea was going to

have a shadow—whether it be him, Jamieson, Hampton, or Thomas.

"Are you ready for my present now?" Nicholas asked, forcing a smile.

Before Andrea could respond, Lady Anne got to her feet. "I am going to retire for the evening. Thank you all for your lovely gifts. I shall enjoy them enormously."

Miriam gracefully rose to her feet, coming forward and leaning down to give light kisses to both Nicholas and Andrea. "Thank you both for my lovely pendant. It will always have special meaning for me," she said, smiling brightly.

"I'm pleased," Andrea returned. "I only regret that Thomas couldn't have joined us this evening."

Miriam nodded. "I'm sure he's sorry also. He told me his business in London was unavoidable and regretted not being able to spend the Yuletide at Leighaven."

"Perhaps next year," Nicholas added, fully aware that the business Thomas was investigating was a matter of life or death—his. His younger brother had a meeting with Wiley the day before. Both Nicholas and Thomas were eager to see if the runners had uncovered anything of use—anything at all—if only to give them a starting point.

His mother's cheerful voice brought him back. "I believe I shall search out my granddaughter and see how she is enjoying her new puppy."

Standing, Nicholas held out an open hand to his wife, which she readily accepted.

He tugged lightly, assisting Andrea to her feet. "You really should begin to watch your diet, my dear. I detect a new weight to your frame."

"That is not amusing in the least," she retorted, batting a hand at his arm.

His reply was a deep chuckle before he led them from the now empty room. Their hands remained clasped as he led her up the stairs and down the hallway to their bedroom.

Drawing a deep breath, Nicholas brought his wife over to the bed, easing her down onto the edge, before retrieving a package he had in his wardrobe. "I thought on many different gifts for you this Christmas, but I wanted it to be truly special." He sat on the bed next to her. "There was this wonderful saddle I came upon, and while it was unique, it wasn't something that would have deep meaning for you."

Andrea leaned toward him. "Anything you choose for me will have sentiment for the simple reason that you alone decided on it."

"That would not have been enough," he insisted. "You've come to mean a great deal to me, Andrea, and I wished to bestow upon you a gesture of my deep admiration and affection."

"Oh, Nicholas."

Her breathy whisper convinced him that he'd touched her heart. Slowly, he sank onto the floor, kneeling before her. "Our fathers arranged this marriage and it was not a matter of choice for either of us." He gazed into her eyes. "Since my return, I have truly come to know you. I've watched you with our daughter, seen your courage even through your defiance of me—"

They smiled at each other over the memories of their disagreements.

"—and admired your intelligence and wit. With this in mind, I give you my gift."

Nicholas handed her the small box, apprehension tightening his nerves, hoping he hadn't made an error. He had to concentrate on breathing as she lifted the top off the box.

Slowly, she removed the shimmering ring from its nest. "Nicholas?"

He took the emerald ring from her, reaching for her hand. "If I had complete freedom to choose a wife to call my own right here and now, I would choose you." He slid the gold band onto her finger. "Allow this gift to remind you that you are, and always will be, my choice, my perfect mate."

Tears glistened in her eyes. "Thank you. I could not imagine a gift I will treasure more than your pledge."

In her glowing expression, he found all he'd ever searched for, making the thought of hiding behind his fear unbearable.

The time had come for his leap of faith.

"I love you, Andrea."

A cry of pure joy burst from Andrea as she launched herself into his arms, pressing kisses all over his face, words of love murmured between them.

Nicholas enfolded her beloved form within his embrace and closed his eyes, knowing he held his world in his arms. He'd stepped out from behind the shadows of his fear to bask in the warmth of love.

"Let me love you," he entreated, burning with the need to express his love.

A breathtaking smile curved on her lips as Andrea stood, clasping his hands to draw him upward. She arched into him, capturing his mouth with hers. Instantly, Nicholas wrapped her tightly against him, drinking deeply of the love she offered him, the unending acceptance she gave him, the unconditional affection she showered upon him. The hunger that had eaten away at his soul while in prison, bit by bit, nibble by nibble, ached to be appeased within the healing embrace of his wife.

Restless, she arched against him, trying to move

closer. Her mouth broke from his so she could urge, "Help me take off my gown."

Immediately responsive, Nicholas loosened his hold, reaching for the fastenings that lined the back of the dress. His natural grace abandoned him, his fingers slipping time and again off the hooks. Impatience began to grow within him, as did his fierce desire to consummate their love. Summoning the ragged remains of his self-control, he patiently tried to release the closures once more.

A low moan purred in Andrea's throat while she arched her hips against his swollen manhood. She dipped her tongue into his mouth at the same time, gently mimicking the act of lovemaking.

It proved to be his undoing.

Nicholas closed his fingers about the neck of the gown and pulled sharply, tearing the fabric, sending buttons flying about the room. Shocked at his loss of control, Nicholas broke off their kiss. "Dear God, Andrea, I didn't mean—"

Her sensual laugh shot fire through his veins, his hardness swelling. She stepped back to slowly remove the remains of her gown. Her eyes were locked with his; promises flashed in their emerald depths, intimate knowledge shimmered from them. Piece by piece her clothes fell while he stood still, entranced by her beauty.

Bared to his searching gaze, Andrea stood proudly. Her nipples were hardened into aching buds, yearning for his touch. She lay down upon the bed, reaching a hand toward him. "I love you, Nicholas."

"Andrea," he whispered hoarsely, his eyes darkened with an undefined emotion as he stripped off his clothes. The muscles in his arms quivered as he lay her down upon the bed, covering her with his body. Lust roared through him, heady and strong. He brushed his lips down her arched throat, tasting, nipping, pausing to lick at her damp flesh.

Andrea arched upward, her hands clenching against his shoulders, silently urging his sweet mouth to her breast, his knowing fingers on her womanhood. She twisted her legs against his, her hips moving in perfect counterpoint. "Please, Nicholas."

He nipped at the curve of her neck. "Please what?" he teased, licking her collarbone. "Please kiss you?" Immediately, he covered her mouth with his, tasting her, arousing her, consuming her. He broke off the kiss after a long moment of exchanged heat. "Please touch you?" He trailed his fingers upward from her waist, their light touch causing tingles to vibrate through her. "Please caress your beautiful breasts?" His hand closed about her lush fullness, pressing against the aching flesh. "Or perhaps you mean please kiss them." He lowered his head, flicking over the taut bud with his tongue, causing Andrea to moan loudly, her back arching up into him.

He lifted his head, his burning gaze catching her dazed one. "Well? Which is it?"

Her eyes shone bright with the devil's glint. "All of those, Nicholas. And more—much, much more. Shall I show you what I had in mind?" she purred, her voice low and sultry.

He felt a trace of wariness at the realization that he had pushed her too far. Before he had a chance to question her, Andrea pushed on his shoulders, catching him unaware, tumbling him back onto the covers. Immediately, she scrambled on top of him, her legs straddling his.

The moist heat from her womanhood rubbed against his abdomen, causing him to buck upward in compulsive need. A smile of pleasure curved her lips. "Shall we begin, my lord?"

Without waiting for his response, she began to move down his body, sliding her lips along his neck and onto his chest.

The intensity of her touch destroyed any sense of control. Never before had Andrea been the aggressor, and the sensations storming through him were too exquisite to deny.

He caressed the fine line of her shoulders, the graceful arch of her back, the slender perfection of her neck. He kept his eyes closed so that he could savor the exaltation that was raging within him. He could feel her smile against his skin and a smile of pure joy and unadulterated passion curled his lips in return. He felt like laughing. He felt like shouting out loud. He felt invincible.

And it was all because of the woman who was flowing over him like a healing balm.

Her hair washed over his chest, gently floating against his skin like a silken web of mist as she kissed, caressed, and rubbed her way down his body. She nipped lightly at his hip before kissing the spot in supplication.

Nicholas's breath caught in his throat, his hands buried in her hair, as her lips whispered across his flesh toward his near-bursting tumescence. Her kisses sweetly extracted all the bitterness, all the pain, all the suffering.

Strands of hair caught on his turgid length, wrapping about its heat, a silky caress that drove Nicholas insane with wanting. Her hot breath feathered over his hardness as she lifted her head to look at the proof of his passion. Hesitantly, her lips lowered onto his shaft, closing about the swollen tip. Tasting him, she swirled her tongue around the tip.

A shout burst from Nicholas, part curse, part prayer. He didn't know which and he didn't care. He was beyond thought. The touch of her mouth had sent him into the realm of pure ecstasy, his senses were alive with feelings, his mind a pulsating mass of need. He clenched his fingers in the soft length of her hair, unconsciously guiding her untutored motions as she licked up and down his length.

When his desire was about to explode, Nicholas guided her onto her back. With his mouth, hungry, searching, he caressed her breasts, kissing the underside, licking the swollen nipple, before following the curve of her waist, taking a foray across her navel, and heading relentlessly toward her core. Spreading her legs wide, Nicholas knelt between their lengths, feasting on her with his gaze.

Open, vulnerable, Andrea arched upward, silently pleading with him to continue. Unable to deny himself, Nicholas lowered his head to lick at the sweetness of her womanhood, sending raw pleasure crashing through her.

Unable to hold back, Nicholas lifted himself up, thrusting into her still quivering body, her heat wrapping his length in welcome, her inner flesh gripping him in strong, pulsating warmth. He covered her mouth with his own, each tasting the other, mingling, becoming one as their bodies were one. Finesse was forgotten as Nicholas drove into her, hard, fast, deep.

Together they climbed, higher, higher, into the heat of passion, until finally Andrea erupted beneath him and he swiftly followed. Nicholas lowered himself onto her, their flesh touching, his arms propping him up. He rested his forehead against hers, their eyes closed, their breathing labored, lost together in the aftermath of perfection.

Nicholas opened his eyes to find Andrea watching him, a soft smile of pleasure curving her lips.

He had never seen such a beautiful sight.

"I love you," he said, the words coming easily.

A single tear slid from the corner of her eye. "You managed to find the perfect Christmas gift after all."

"I'm delighted you love the ring," Nicholas said, shifting onto his back.

Andrea raised herself onto her elbow to look in his face. "I wasn't speaking of the ring, though it is lovely." She cupped his cheek with her free hand. "I meant you."

Her meaning couldn't have been more clear. How foolish he'd been to deny himself the joy that came from opening his heart. Love warmed him to his very soul as he turned his head to press a kiss into the palm of her hand. As Andrea settled down into him, Nicholas enfolded her close.

Right next to his heart.

Ten

Andrea glanced down at her hopelessly tangled threads. "I fear I shall never complete this sampler for the new baby," she admitted with a wry smile.

Miriam touched Andrea's knotted embroidery. "Perhaps if you tried to—"

"I assure you any effort is in vain," Lady Anne interrupted, continuing to smoothly slide her needle through the material strung upon her embroidery stand. "I have tried for years to assist my daughter in this womanly art to no avail."

The easy note in her mother's voice made Andrea laugh. "It's true," she agreed, setting down her needle. "I had wanted to make something for the new baby, but it obviously is not meant to be."

Miriam reached over to pat Andrea's hand. "I shall complete any sampler you desire."

"I have already begun one." Lady Anne turned her stand toward the settee where Andrea and Miriam were seated. "Do you approve of the design?"

Andrea looked upon the beautiful unicorn that was surrounded by letters. She appreciated her mother's efforts, but wished that she'd been able to have input into the design itself. Something less ornate. As always, her mother had forged ahead and chosen something she deemed appropriate. Feeling ungrateful, Andrea forced her less than generous thoughts aside and focused upon her mother's good intentions. "It is lovely, Mother."

Lady Anne smiled, turning the embroidery stand around to face her again. She picked up her needle and resumed her stitching. "I hope to finish it by week's end."

"So quickly?" Andrea didn't see the need to rush. It was only mid-January and the baby wasn't due until March.

"I plan on returning to London next week."

"What?" Andrea gasped.

"Is there a problem?" Lady Anne snipped off a thread.

"The roads are disastrous, Mother. It would be far too easy to have an accident on the ice-covered journey into the city." Concern for her mother's welfare overrode all else.

"I must agree with Andrea on this," Miriam added, her hands stilling on her embroidery.

"While I appreciate your concern, I must insist that I will be perfectly safe."

Andrea shook her head at her mother. "Why now? Why can't your journey wait until the spring?"

"The roads are naught but hole-filled ruts then," Anne said, threading another strand of yellow through her needle. "At least during the winter months the roads are hard and thus less jarring. Besides," she added, piercing the material, "it will afford me the opportunity to see the latest fashions being lined up for the next Season."

"Mother, I do not—"

Lady Anne cut off Andrea's protest. "Enough on this, Andrea. My mind is set." She smiled to soften her words. "Do not worry over this matter. The fact that Thomas made the journey just this morning should ease your mind."

"Thomas has returned?"

"He is in the study with Nicholas," Miriam replied.

It would be the ideal time to discuss her mother's unwise plans with her husband. Perhaps Nicholas would be able to dissuade her. Since Christmas her relationship with Nicholas had deepened, strengthened. Andrea curled her fingers over the golden band resting upon her finger. Nicholas would be sure to assist her.

Andrea stood, smiling down at her mother and mother-in-law. "I believe I shall go welcome Thomas home," she said, excusing herself.

The door to the study was cracked open a few inches, so Andrea didn't bother to knock. Her hand was upon the handle when she felt a sharp kick from her baby. Stopping, Andrea pressed both hands against her protruding stomach, feeling her child shift beneath her touch. Wonder caught in her heart as the miracle of life moved within her.

She stood just outside the study, dazed, when her husband's voice caught her attention.

". . . no need to inform Andrea. As always, this information is to be kept between us."

Her hands fell to her sides.

"But, Nick, don't you think it's time we told the family that there was an attempt to poison you?" Thomas's voice was filled with concern.

"No, it shall be between us, as always," Nicholas insisted. "No one else needs to know."

Andrea felt her blood chill within her veins.

"Not even your wife?"

"No one."

Nicholas's pronouncement pierced her happiness. She'd truly believed that he was learning to trust her, but she could no longer hide behind this foolish hope.

Her husband would never think of her as an equal.

Andrea pushed opened the door to reveal herself.

Nicholas looked startled, but he swiftly recovered, moving around his desk to walk toward her. "Andrea? What a lovely surprise."

She stood, frozen, beneath his kiss upon her forehead. Nicholas drew back and she could see from his expression that he was trying to gauge how much she'd overheard.

She tilted her chin upward. "What is going on, Nicholas?"

Again, she saw the calculating light in his eyes. "Nothing of importance. Thomas and I were simply discussing a business matter."

Another piercing pain lanced through her, this latest lie only making it worse. "Is this your attempt at denying all until you see how much I've overheard?"

His dull flush answered her question. "Please come in, Andrea, so we might discuss this in private."

She allowed herself to be escorted into the room, too numb to care one way or the other if the door remained open. She turned to face Nicholas. "How could you keep this from me?"

He must have decided to discard his charade, for he answered, "I thought it would upset you too greatly."

She felt as if he'd just slapped her. "How kind of you to take my delicate sensibilities into consideration."

Her dry tone made Nicholas narrow his eyes. However, it was Thomas who answered. "There was no need to burden you with this, Andrea. At least not until we received all the reports from the Bow Street runners."

"Runners?" she gasped, suddenly realizing there were depths to their deception beyond those she'd overheard. "You were concerned enough to hire investigators, yet you did not see fit to inform me?"

Nicholas's jaw tightened. "It was a recent development, Andrea."

"How recent?"

Her gaze remained upon Nicholas even as Thomas moved to stand next to him. "Since Nick was shot," Thomas said.

Andrea stumbled into a chair, unable to fathom the length of this charade. Had everything been a lie? Her emotions were reeling. "When I questioned you after the accident, you told me it was more than likely a freak incident."

"Not when combined with the time he'd had an arrow shot at him," Thomas said.

"What?"

Nicholas grabbed Thomas by the arm. "You are not helping matters."

Thomas took one look at Andrea's distress and nodded. "Perhaps it would be best if I withdrew and left this to you for resolution."

"Thank you," Nicholas said. He fell silent until Thomas was gone.

Nicholas's expression was the calmest she'd ever seen. He could explain all he wanted, but nothing was going to soothe her. It seemed that all she had left was her pride.

Resolved, she stood once more, facing her husband on equal terms. "I want to know everything."

Nicholas crossed his arms, leaning back against his desk. "Soon after my return to Leighaven, someone shot an arrow at me."

"Why did you not tell me?"

He shrugged lightly. "At the time I considered it a stray shot from a poacher."

She could concede to his logic there. She nodded once. "Please continue."

"Then, as you are aware, I was shot in the shoulder."

"Go on."

Nicholas thrust himself from the desk, his movements agitated. "What is the point of this, Andrea?"

She stood firm. "The point being that, as your wife, I am entitled to know what occurs within this household."

"Therefore subject to my consideration."

"Indeed, but not your trust." All the pain and hurt inside her joined together in a raging fury. "How long I prayed for your avowal of love, Nicholas, longing to hear the words from you. Little did I know how empty they would be once I received them."

He stormed over to her, anger blazing from his eyes. "How dare you belittle my troth. I gave you my love."

"And naught else."

He grabbed her hand, holding it up in front of her face. "Do you not remember my praise when I gave you this ring?"

"Words are easy, Nicholas."

He stiffened. "I don't deserve that remark. My treatment of you has been attentive, especially during this past month."

"What is love without trust?"

Andrea watched Nicholas as he spun away from her, running his hands through his hair. "Why are you doing this?"

"Why did you lie to me . . . virtually since your return?"

"Can you not see that all I did was with your welfare in mind?" He returned to her, holding on to her shoulders. "You are my wife, Andrea. It is my duty, nay, my moral obligation, to protect you."

"Protect me, true, but not to keep all from me." She took a step backward, breaking his hold upon her. "I am a woman of substance, Nicholas. When you were gone, I alone held this family together through sheer determination and hard work. If you knew me at all, you would realize that I cannot abide being sat in a corner and told to mind to my own."

"I have given you more than I ever imagined possible, Andrea. My love for you only makes it more important that I protect you." He faced her. "I take my responsibilities as head of this household very seriously, and if I deem it necessary to withhold information for your own good, then you must honor my wishes."

Slowly, she shook her head. "Love without respect is of little value. You must trust me, make me your confidant, allow me to share the burden you carry." She took a step forward. "Do you not see, Nicholas, that together we are invincible? But only when we are two equal halves, combined to form a whole."

It pained her to look at his raw expression. Nicholas seemed to draw into himself, his features growing cold as he straightened his shoulders. "I am sorry, Andrea, but you ask for too much. You are my wife. You carry my child. I would be unable to live with myself if I did not do everything within my power to protect you."

Her world, in an instant, was gone. Andrea felt cold, frightened, and so very alone. "I'm sorry for both of us," she whispered, tears making her throat tight.

Woodenly, she moved past Nicholas to leave the room. He reached out, catching her arm. "I love you, Andrea."

The raw words ripped at her heart. Tears began to slide from her eyes as she looked up at him. "I know, Nicholas. As I love you." She stood tall and proud as her cheeks grew moist. "But sometimes love isn't enough."

He dropped his hand as if burned. "What do you want from me?"

She'd already told him all he needed to know, and if he were unable to understand now, there truly was no hope for them. Without a word, she resumed her walk to the door.

"What do you want from me?"

The wounded cry made her flinch. Softly, Andrea shut the door behind her.

Andrea ran her hands over Wildstar's swollen belly. "The foal appears to be positioned correctly. I only pray that she holds off delivering her baby for another month."

"Even for February, this weather is bitter," Harry agreed, his eyes fastened on Andrea. "Are you warm enough with only that shawl for protection?"

"Yes." Andrea closed the door on the stall. Her gaze flicked over to where Nicholas stood leaning against a post, silent, watchful. He had followed her out to the stables for her meeting with Harry, even though she'd told him it wasn't necessary. Even in this, the smallest of matters, he did not trust her.

Unfortunately, it came as no surprise. For the past month they had declared a cold truce. Neither acknowledged the other beyond polite necessities and the connecting door between their bedchambers had remained firmly closed.

Andrea had discovered Hell on earth.

She turned toward Harry, dismissing the difficulties of her marriage. "I am quite warm."

"Are you certain?"

She splayed her hands wide over her protruding stomach. "This baby is an internal heating system."

Harry's throat worked, his face instantly turning red. "Andrea, please," he protested.

"What is it, Harry?" Bewilderment marked her countenance.

"It is most unseemly to speak of . . . of . . ." His hand waved toward her.

"Speak of what? The baby?" she asked incredulously.

His head bobbed, bright red still coloring his cheeks.

Nicholas's dark chuckle sliced through the awkward silence. "Have you forgotten, Andrea, that polite members of the female persuasion retire to the privacy of their immediate family once they begin showing, declining all public appearances?" A sneer twisted his lips. "According to the numerous dictates of our pretentious society, your appearance, my dear, is offensive."

Andrea stiffened beneath Nicholas's gaze. Still, it wouldn't do to show the rift between them to anyone else, never mind a man who had literally thrown himself on her only months ago. "Perhaps," she conceded, returning her attention to Harry, "but Harry doesn't mind. Do you?"

A faltering smile appeared on Harry's face. "To be perfectly frank, your delicate condition does require some . . . er, that is, a person needs to accustom themselves to . . ." Harry's stuttering words trailed off.

Nicholas's laugh was a cold, mocking sound.

Andrea faced her husband, anger vibrating through her frame. Despite her longing to unleash her temper, her need to remain professional overrode her desire. Instead, she said in measured words, "Then it is indeed a blessing that my personal attributes play no part in my professional relationship with Harry. Furthermore, you are embarrassing not only Harry and me, but yourself with this ridiculous conversation."

Nicholas sketched a mockery of a bow.

Her lips tightened as she turned back to Harry. "I believe we need to adjust Wildstar's diet. There are some sores in her mouth that concern me. She might need salt added to her feed. It is imperative she maintain her health, because we can't run the risk of her suffering from a high fever."

"That would be a disaster." Harry was clearly shaken by the notion.

"True. After all, a high fever could cause her to abort the foal."

The color drained from his face. "I thought Wildstar was beyond the critical time for a miscarriage."

"And she is," Andrea concurred. "Except in the case of extremely high fevers, which is why we should keep a close eye on her."

"What type of sores?" Harry rushed, panic widening his eyes.

"Let me show you." Before she could reenter Wildstar's stall, a footman came into the stable, accompanied by a blast of frigid air.

"Pardon, my lady, but Lord Fielding has just brought in his roan, which fell and is bleeding from its foreleg."

Concern immediately etched itself on Andrea's features. "Please excuse me, Harry." She glanced at Nicholas. "My lord," she murmured before following the footman out, closing the door behind her.

Nicholas didn't even feel the cold. How could he when he'd been frozen inside for a month? He shifted his gaze onto Hartnell, glad to be afforded a quiet moment with the man.

"I believe it is time we talked, Hartnell."

Harry looked wary, bringing a sense of satisfaction

to Nicholas. "I don't have anything to say to you," Hartnell boldly pronounced.

"That suits me just fine," Nicholas said grimly. "All you have to do is listen." He gave Hartnell his fiercest glare, trying like hell to intimidate the man. "I want you to keep away from my wife."

It failed miserably.

A mocking smile curled Hartnell's lips. "As she is caring for my horse, how do you propose to accomplish that?"

"I *propose*, my dear Harry, that you contact her through written communication only." Nicholas strolled over to stand in front of the shorter man.

"Preposterous."

A chilling smile played on Nicholas's face. "Is it? Then you leave me no choice but to act upon some interesting bits of information that I gathered while in London."

Wariness stiffened Harry's body, his pale blue eyes suddenly alert. "What the deuce are you talking about?"

Nicholas's gaze sharpened. "You, my proper Lord Hartnell, are destitute. Your family has cut you off, and only the promise of repayment from the monies collected when you sell this foal are keeping your creditors at bay." Nicholas reached out to straighten Harry's elaborate cravat. "It also seems that a year ago, you told these very same gentlemen that you were about to be wed." His fingers tightened on the stiff fabric, wrinkling its crisp perfection. "Now, I wouldn't care about this particular rumor except that your intended was none other than my wife."

Harry wrenched free from Nicholas's grasp. "What ridiculous accusations. You can't be serious!"

The smile slipped from his face as Nicholas replied tersely, "Oh, but I am, Harry. I just don't understand how you planned to accomplish this since Andrea already had a husband."

Harry's pretense of ignorance was dropped. "You were missing for years. I was going to petition the courts to annul your marriage. No court would refuse such a request. Besides, you were never coming back—or so I thought. After all, everyone knows that unless you can afford to buy your freedom, no one survives the Bastille."

"No one?" Nicholas lifted his eyebrow mockingly.

A dull flush of anger heightened Harry's color once more. "It was no secret that your family fortunes were gone, so I knew your release wouldn't be bought. You are probably one of only a handful of men to escape with your life."

"But I didn't escape, Hartnell. My family did arrange for my freedom," Nicholas pointed out. "It makes me curious, though, as to why you were so very positive that I would never return."

Harry's lips tightened. "I wasn't sure, only hopeful. Andrea could be a superb wife with the right tutelage."

Nicholas's laughter rang out, startling Wildstar, who stamped her hooves in agitation. "If you believe that Andrea would ever mindlessly follow your dictates, you are as big a fool as I."

Harry jutted out his chin, but remained soundless.

Nicholas's smile faded. "Remember, Hartnell, I don't waste my time on empty threats. Stay away from my wife. Choose some other unsuspecting female to con with your perfect gentleman routine. As you can see, this one already has a husband."

"That could be taken care of," Harry mumbled, his gaze locked on Nicholas's retreating back.

Already heading for the door, Nicholas halted, spinning around to look at Harry. "Are you threatening me, Hartnell?" he asked, his words dripping ice.

Harry was the first to glance away.

Nicholas murmured scathingly, "I didn't think you had the nerve for open confrontation. No, I had better watch my back with you, though. Isn't that right, Hartnell? What a fine example of the eternally honorable Englishman you are." Deliberately, Nicholas turned his back on the man and left the stables, completely missing the fervid hatred in Hartnell's expression.

"We need to come up with another plan, I tell you. The situation is even worse than before." Hampton sat down at the table in the kitchen and looked at Jamieson.

Jamieson sent a pointed look toward Marissa, who was awaiting a snack. "Even if I were still open to this discussion, this would hardly be the place or time for it."

Hampton frowned. "Why are you refusing to talk about this anymore, Jamie?"

The butler rolled his eyes. "Have you forgotten how Lady Andrea came upon us?"

"She wasn't in the least bit put off."

Jamieson was finding it increasingly difficult to retain a hold on his valued composure. "I was," he ground out.

"All I know is that something needs to be done again and I think I'm the one who should decide upon it. After all, everyone knows that I'm responsible for bringing Master Nick and Lady Andrea back together the last time." Hampton puffed out his chest as he looked at Jamieson across the width of the kitchen.

"You old windbag," muttered Jamieson, sending Hampton a glare as he set a glass of milk down in front of Marissa.

"If I hadn't locked them in the cellar, then—"

"Of all the preposterous ideas! All that debacle did was prove to all and sundry that you're an old fool."

"You're just jealous because you didn't think of it," Hampton retorted, giving Marissa a broad wink.

"It was a great plan," the little girl chimed in, earning a smile from Hampton and a disciplinary frown from Jamieson.

"Don't pay Hampton any heed, Miss Marissa."

Her eyes were innocent pools as she gazed up at Jamieson. "But it was a splendid plan, Jamieson. You saw how Papa was kissing Mama so hard that I thought he was hungry."

"More than likely he was," chuckled Hampton.

Jamieson swatted Hampton on the arm. "Fine thing to say in front of the little one."

"Ouch!" exclaimed Hampton, rubbing where Jamieson's hand hit. "Will you stop knocking on me?"

"Then desist in your crude remarks in front of the family."

Hampton scowled at Jamieson before he headed from the room. "You're being a true pompous ass, Jamie. Indeed you are."

"What's an ass?"

Marissa's question followed by Jamieson's groan made Hampton laugh as he left the room, leaving Jamieson alone to field that inquiry. After all, Hampton thought, heading up the stairs, it was a smart man who knew when to retreat.

Yes, sir, it was.

"Where are you off to?" Nicholas stood in the open doorway of the study, wearing a curious expression.

Pulling on her gloves, Andrea glanced over at her husband. She bit back a sigh. Lately, it seemed that Nicholas wanted to know exactly what she was doing every minute of the day. "Do you remember Lord Fielding's roan?" At his nod, she continued, "The wound has reopened and Lord Fielding feels it may be infected. I ordered the carriage to be brought around."

Nicholas's steps echoed in the foyer as he strode toward her. "Why can't he bring the horse here like he did last time?"

"If the limb is infected, it could cause damage to ride him," she explained. "This is not a matter of your concern."

"I believe it to be," he countered. "You are growing unwieldy, Andrea, and it might be best if you remained at home."

She froze. "Yet another dictate, Nicholas?" She tied on her winter bonnet. "How weary I have grown of them."

He frowned at her. "I do only what I think best for you, Andrea. Can you begrudge me that?"

She gazed up at her husband's beloved features. Even set in annoyance, she found them near to irresistible. How often she had longed to end this feud between them, only to realize that she would be unable to live with her compromise. Lord knew, she was so very tired of fighting not only him, but herself as well. She wished she could go back to that lovely month of ignorance when she'd thought her life perfect.

Weary, she rubbed a hand on her temple. "I will be fine, Nicholas."

"I don't like you going out today. It is frigid outside."

"Sydney is a competent coachman and I will be perfectly safe inside the warm carriage," she said, heading for the door.

Resolve darkened his gaze. "Wait. I will get my cloak and accompany you."

She shook her head. "I refuse to be treated as a child, Nicholas. I will return in an hour." She hurried from the house and ordered the carriage away.

"Andrea," Nicholas bellowed, frustrated at her refusal. Cursing under his breath, he rushed to the closet, pulling out and slinging around him the first cloak he found, and followed her.

Too late. The carriage was already halfway down the drive. Nearly blinded by the brilliant white of sunlight reflecting over the fresh snow, Nicholas squinted at the black carriage, a vicious curse falling from his lips. Determined to follow, Nicholas was headed toward the stable to fetch a horse when a scream pierced the crisp air.

He looked down the drive again in time to see the team of horses race down the lane without the carriage. The coachman, Sydney, was thrown into the snowbank as the carriage careened unguided down the icy lane. His heart stopped beating as Nicholas watched the carriage containing his most beloved treasure crash into a thick oak, rolling onto its side after the jarring impact.

"Andrea!" he yelled before breaking into a run. *"Andrea!"* he shouted again and again as he slipped his way down the icy track, the need to reach his wife, to hold her, to ensure her well-being, overcoming everything else. His stride widened as he raced toward Andrea, praying to God, the Holy Spirit, and anyone else who might be listening for the safety of his wife.

"Andrea!" he shouted again, his voice hoarse. Catching the upturned side of the carriage, Nicholas hoisted himself on top, fighting to control his panic. The door was stuck, but he pulled at it, his veins surging with adrenaline, painfully aware of the lack of response coming from inside the carriage.

Panic pumping through him, Nicholas practically ripped the door open, its weight slamming against the side of the carriage, the sound echoing across the snow-laden fields. He squinted, trying to pierce the darkness of the interior, before looking at Sydney, who was now squatting next to him. "I am going to lower myself down. I will need your help getting her out of here."

Without waiting for a response, Nicholas swung his legs into the open doorway. The muscles in his arms bulged with effort as he carefully lowered himself into the darkness, knowing that his wife lay silently within. Once inside, he felt around like a blind man. Finally, beneath overturned cushions, he found her.

Her shuddering breath made him tremble with relief. She was alive.

Emotion choked him as he gently lifted her into his arms. When Nicholas raised her into the light that was streaming through the open door, his arms tightened convulsively at the sight of blood staining the side of her face. She had a small cut on her forehead and God only knew where else she was hurt.

"Sydney?"

The coachman peered into the open doorway from above. "I'm here, my lord."

"I'll hand her up to you, but be very careful. She's been injured."

"Yes, my lord."

"Grab her under her arms and gently lift her out," he ordered, his hand shifting to press against her derriere in order to lift her higher. "What the—" Nicholas felt his heart lurch when he touched the wetness of her skirts. Instinctively, he knew that she was bleeding.

The baby.

Determination streaked through him. After all he'd sacrificed to protect her, it seemed far too cruel that he might lose her this way. He lifted her unconscious body up toward Sydney's outstretched hands.

"Got her," Sydney shouted.

Nicholas jumped up, grabbing hold of the opening and pulling himself out. His wife's pallor was alarming, but not as much as the brilliant red staining her skirts.

"God save us," the coachman whispered, crossing himself as his eyes focused on the blood.

"We can't depend on Him alone," Nicholas said, leaping down into the snow. "Lower her down to me. Gently."

Sydney crossed himself again before easing his mistress down into Nicholas's outstretched arms. The minute she was clear, he jumped down, too.

"Run ahead and alert Jamieson," Nicholas barked, moving as fast as he could without jarring Andrea. "And send someone to fetch a doctor immediately."

Sydney hesitated. "What about the team, my lord?"

"Damn the bloody horses. *Go!*" Nicholas roared.

The coachman dashed off to follow his orders.

Nicholas dared a quick glance down at his wife, his arms squeezing her gently into his warmth. "Fight, Andrea. I know you have it in you. Fight with everything you are worth, with everything you are." His gaze focused on the house. It seemed a million miles to reach it, although in reality it was only a few yards away.

Pandemonium reigned. Jamieson hustled down the steps, unmindful of the cold, while Hampton held open the door for Nicholas. Miriam, pale, her features set, stood at the top of the stairs. "Up here, Nicholas," she urged.

As soon as he reached the bedchamber, Nicholas

tenderly laid his wife down upon the coverlet. "She's bleeding."

"I know," Miriam murmured, her hands hurrying to remove Andrea's damp clothes. Nicholas stood back, watching in helpless frustration as his mother took over caring for his wife. Miriam spared him a glance. "Go downstairs, Nicholas."

"No," he said, shaking his head. Andrea belonged to him and he'd fight God himself for her. His panic hardened into cold determination. "I stay."

Nicholas moved toward the bed and held his wife's hand as his mother pressed clean cloths between Andrea's legs, trying to stem the trickle of blood.

He grasped her hand tightly, trying to give her his strength, unable to imagine life without her.

"She might lose the baby."

Nicholas flinched at his mother's soft warning. "What of my wife?"

"I don't know."

His mother's response held no reassurance. Nicholas lifted Andrea's fingers to his mouth for a kiss, before pulling a chair close to the bedside.

He sat down, unmindful of his own wet, blood-stained clothes, to keep watch over the center of his life.

Shadows filled the room while Nicholas kept his vigil, never releasing Andrea's hand. His mother had gone to speak with Marissa after the doctor had come. The prognosis was favorable. If the baby survived the next twenty-four hours, then the chances of miscarriage were slim. Andrea's head wound was minor, but when combined with the loss of blood, she had yet to regain consciousness.

Jamieson had brought in a tray of food for Nicholas, but he was unable to force anything down. The clock chimed the passing hours and Nicholas's eyes grew more bloodshot.

The door cracked open and Jamieson peeked around the frame. "Master Nick, I do believe you should come downstairs. Sydney has discovered a startling fact."

"What?" His voice was hoarse.

"It is most urgent, my lord." Jamieson glanced quickly behind him before whispering, "It appears Madame's accident was deliberately set."

The shock settled into deadly intent. He'd thought he'd taken all the necessary precautions to protect his family. He'd kept vigil against poisoning, not allowed any family member outside without escort, and made sure he was aware of his family's whereabouts at all times. And still, it hadn't been enough. Someone had slipped past all of his security measures, daring to harm his wife. Rage—hot, intense—seared through him. This had to end *now*.

He looked at his wife and knew what course must be taken.

"Please ask my mother to watch over Andrea for a few minutes and tell Sydney that I will be down directly. Has Thomas arrived from London yet?"

"Just a bit ago," Jamieson answered before heading off. A few minutes passed before Miriam arrived. "Nicholas? Jamieson said you needed me."

As much as he hated to leave Andrea, he needed to end this nightmare. "Please keep watch over Andrea and tell me immediately if there is any change in her condition."

"Of course," his mother replied, taking over the chair he had just vacated.

Nicholas leaned down and kissed Andrea's forehead. It was time to catch a would-be killer, by means fair or foul.

* * *

"Tell me what you've uncovered," Nicholas demanded, his fierce glare swinging to touch upon Sydney, Jamieson, Hampton, and Thomas.

"The team just returned, my lord," Sydney began, "and when I examined their harnesses, I found this." He held out the long length of leather.

Nicholas examined the harness closely. Only a small section of the leather had been ripped. It was obvious that a knife had sliced through the leather, leaving only enough to hold it together until the carriage was in motion.

Nicholas fingered the jagged edge. "When could this have happened? Don't you care for the tack after each use?"

"Most definitely, my lord," Sydney said briskly. "Before we put the harness away, we oil it and check for stress."

"Then the damage must have occurred since then," Nicholas concluded. "When was this harness last used?"

Sydney tapped his fingers against his leg. "I don't believe the carriage has been used since we took Lady Andrea's mother to London."

"A month ago," Nicholas murmured.

"Shall I notify the magistrate?" Jamieson asked.

Nicholas shook his head. "All that pompous ass would do is inform us that it was another unfortunate mishap. No, it is our mystery to solve." His boots slammed down on the floor as he paced back and forth. "Was Andrea the target or was she merely the victim?"

Thomas sat down. "If you account for past history, the answer is obvious."

Nicholas drew to a halt, his gut churning at the thought that his wife was lying unconscious because of him. "Indeed."

"Did you not say you were planning a trip to London soon?" Thomas asked.

"Yes," he replied. He had made clear his plans to attend a meeting in London. He just hadn't mentioned that it was with the runners.

"But who could be doing this, Master Nick?" Jamieson asked, concern furrowing his brow.

Nicholas looked at Sydney. "Thank you for your assistance today and for bringing this to my attention. I will not forget it. Now, if you would please leave us, I need to discuss this matter in private." The coachman nodded, heading for the door, only to be brought up short by Nicholas's call. "And, Sydney, everything that transpired here today stays in this room. Understood?"

"Without question, my lord," the young man replied before leaving the study.

"Gentlemen, I am going to need your cooperation in order to trap our assailant."

"Who are we trying to catch, my lord?" Jamieson asked.

"Hartnell."

"Lord Harry?" squeaked Jamieson, his composure obviously ruffled.

"That nanny boy?" Hampton exclaimed.

Thomas smiled over Hampton's insult, but he became serious again when he looked at Nicholas. "How can you be so sure?"

"His background check has already revealed that Harry has no morals when it comes to how he earns his money, not to mention his notion of marrying my wife."

"None of those things makes him our attacker," Thomas protested.

"True, but he is the only real suspect we have. He's been close by whenever an incident has occurred.

We've eliminated all other possibilities, which makes him the most culpable."

"But he's off gallivanting about London, Master Nick. He couldn't have done anything to the bridle."

Jamieson agreed to Hampton's observation with a nod.

"This could have been cut any time since Lady Anne's departure and, as Harry left only a week ago, he might have done it then. He had the time, he had the access, and he had the motive."

The three men were silent before Thomas finally said, "All right, then, Nick. What do you want us to do?"

Satisfaction settled in Nicholas's heart. "I want you to return to London, Thomas. I'm going to send a missive to Harry requesting his presence at Leighaven."

"Will he come?"

"Oh, he'll come, all right, if I threaten to expose him."

"And what do we do with him once you get him here?"

Instead of answering Thomas's question, Nicholas turned to the two older men. "Jamieson, Hampton, I'd like for you to stand on the other side of the connecting door to the library, so you'll be able to testify that you heard his admission of guilt."

"Don't you think you're being overly optimistic? Why on earth would Harry admit to anything?"

Nicholas eased a smile at his brother. "Because I've decided upon a plan to make him feel as if he's achieved his victory over me."

"And how do you propose to accomplish that?"

"By utilizing my sharpest weapon—you."

Thomas pressed a hand to his chest. "Me? Surely you jest."

He shook his head. "You, my dear brother, are going to be the bait to trap a rat."

Thomas grinned broadly. "Now why does that appeal to me?"

Nicholas's laugh echoed with triumph. "Now, gentlemen, we need to review my plan."

The four men leaned together, hushed whispers racing between them, as they plotted to catch the assailant in their midst.

Eleven

Nicholas had resumed his vigil at Andrea's bedside. Almost twenty-four hours had passed since her accident, yet aside from some restless stirring, she had not regained consciousness. He rubbed wearily at his eyes, lack of sleep making him groggy. In these morning hours, it was hard to keep his mind from replaying the horrific scene of her carriage crashing into the tree. Over and over, he saw Andrea's carriage hurtling across the drive, shuddering against the tree, and falling onto the fresh snow.

Dear God, he had almost lost her.

An eternity of darkness yawned before him at that thought. Little by little, Andrea had begun to change his existence, spreading light, laughter, and happiness throughout it. If he lost her now, he realized bleakly, his world would once again plunge into a chasm of despair that not even Marissa could pull him from.

This past month had been hell for him. To have her love withdrawn after he had basked within its warmth for such a short time had nearly destroyed him. He still hadn't thought of a way to resolve their problems.

All he'd ever wanted was to protect her, to keep her safe.

Yet here she lay, unconscious, and all of his efforts had been for naught. The distance between them had become less than meaningless. The only thing of true importance in his life was his family—with Andrea at its heart.

Andrea's head moved upon her pillow, her features shifting slightly. It was only a small movement, but it was enough for Nicholas. Eagerly, he leaned forward. "Andrea? Can you hear me? Wake up, darling."

Her eyelids fluttered.

"That's it, Andrea. Come back to me. It is time to wake up now," he crooned softly.

"Nicholas?" she whispered, confusion mingled with weariness in her voice.

"I am here," he murmured, shifting to sit on the edge of the bed, stroking her tangled hair off her forehead.

Her lashes lifted. "What happened? Why am I here?"

"Do you remember the accident?" he questioned softly.

Her brow drew downward. "Yes. What happened? All I remember is the carriage swaying back and forth, out of control. My last memory is pitching forward." She shook her head. "Then nothing."

Nicholas stroked the back of his hand down her cheek.

Suddenly Andrea reached for her stomach. "What about my baby? Is everything all right?"

"Yes, Andrea, everything is perfect," he hastened to comfort her. "There was some initial bleeding and things were a bit precarious earlier, but the most dangerous time has passed."

"Bleeding?" Andrea asked hoarsely.

"Everything is fine," Nicholas repeated, his tone soothingly calm. "The doctor will visit again this morning, so you can speak with him directly. I know he'll reassure you."

Tears welled in her eyes, emerald pools of green. "If anything happened to—" Her choked voice broke off.

Nicholas gathered Andrea into his arms, pressing her head against his strong chest, rocking her, murmuring, "I know, I know."

He lay down next to her, cradling her against him, holding her tight. Even after she'd drifted off to sleep, Nicholas held her close, pledging to keep her safe from harm.

The Trent crest cooled in the wax, sealing his missive to Hartnell. A cold sense of satisfaction settled within him. Finally, he thought with a rush of anticipation, the game was about to move into the final phase.

He longed to achieve victory over Hartnell, end this continued threat, and move forward with the things of true worth: his family, their happiness, Andrea's love.

Grasping the letter firmly in his hand, Nicholas strode to the door. In the foyer, he asked a passing maid, "Do you know where I might locate Jamieson?"

The maid pointed to the stairs as she answered, "I believe he is with the Countess."

Nicholas smiled. Andrea. She had proven to be about as cooperative an invalid as he had. After three weeks of confinement to her bed, her patience was completely gone, destroyed by boredom.

Tapping the letter against his palm, Nicholas took the stairs two at a time. His half smile widened into a full grin as he heard the conversation floating down the hallway.

"Jamieson, you are not being reasonable."

"I can only offer my apologies once more, your ladyship, but the Earl has specifically requested that you remain at rest." Jamieson's voice was stiff with discomfort. "I strongly request permission to leave. This is most . . ." The butler's words faltered, giving further evidence of his unease. ". . . most improper," he finished on a firm note.

Nicholas paused on the threshold of their bedchamber. Still in her robe, Andrea stood directly behind Jamieson, who wore an expression of long suffering. Miriam stood apart from the disputing pair, clearly at a loss as to what she should do to ease the situation. It was clear no one knew how to handle Andrea.

Nicholas made the appropriate response.

His booming laughter shot through the room, causing everyone to jump in surprise. His mirth grew louder as he saw the varied responses; blatant relief on the faces of his mother and Jamieson, and a fierce glare in Andrea's eyes as she turned the full portion of her frustration upon him.

"This is not in the least amusing, Nicholas. I assure you." Andrea frowned at him as the volume of his laughter increased.

Finally Nicholas managed to contain his amusement, but was unable to wipe the broad grin off his face. "Now, would someone please explain to me exactly what is happening?"

All three spoke at once.

"My lord, the Countess would like . . ."

"Andrea feels that she should be . . ."

"The doctor told me that three weeks . . ."

The result was another round of mayhem.

Andrea spun about, fixing Miriam with a stern look. "Please, Miriam, I need to discuss this with Nicholas."

"I know, dear, but first he must be aware of the situation."

"Then I am the one who will inform him."

"With your pardon, Lady Andrea, I feel it is my duty to—"

Andrea pointed a long finger at Jamieson. "If my wishes had been considered from the first, we wouldn't even be having this conversation."

Jamieson grew rigid. "Your pardon, Countess, but I beg to differ. After all, it is not I who—"

"Enough," Nicholas said quietly, his voice slicing through the jumbled discussion.

Like a child's top, Andrea pivoted toward Nicholas once more. "No, it is not enough. I am going insane here in—"

"Please, Andrea. Enough." She flushed prettily as she fell silent. Nicholas looked at his mother. "Do you feel Andrea is well enough to be up and about?"

"From all indications—"

"Why are you inquiring after my health from your mother?" Andrea interrupted, obviously put out by his question. "After all, she's not the one—"

"Andrea, please!" His wife frowned at him in displeasure and pointedly looked away. Nicholas fought the urge to grin as he returned his attention to his mother. "You were saying?"

Miriam glanced at Andrea, before replying, "The bleeding has long since stopped and her strength has begun to return."

Jamieson cleared his throat loudly. "Master Nick, if I might . . ."

There was no way to hold back his broad smile over Jamieson's obvious discomfort. Nicholas took mercy upon their butler. "Thank you for your assistance, Jamieson. I believe I can handle the situation from here."

Jamieson tugged down on his vest. "You have my deepest gratitude, my lord," he pronounced, causing Nicholas's smile to widen further. Jamieson straightened his shoulders before he began to walk from the room.

"Jamieson?" Nicholas's question stopped the butler's exit. "Would you please post this letter today?"

With his normal decorum now in place, Jamieson merely accepted the missive before bowing slightly. "Of course, my lord." His exit from the room was immediate.

Nicholas turned his full attention upon Andrea. "Very well, my dear. There seems to be no reason to delay your—shall I say—freedom?"

She relaxed, sensing victory. "Ah, yes. I do believe freedom is the correct term."

"I thought so," he murmured, still amused. "I shall leave you to your ablutions." Nicholas excused himself.

Andrea stared at the closed door, stunned by Nicholas's warm humor. Since her accident, he'd been nothing but loving and attentive, and yet she was unsure how to respond to him. There was so much she wanted to ask him. Could he have realized that his rigid beliefs served no purpose other than to tear them apart? Still, she hesitated to upset the delicate balance of their new relationship. While he seemed so responsive now, the past month had taught her to be wary.

"Shall I fetch your lovely lavender walking dress?" Miriam asked, breaking into Andrea's thoughts.

Still too exhausted to sort through her jumbled thoughts, Andrea let them slide away. "That would be lovely, Miriam. Just lovely."

Two days later, Lord Harry Hartnell strode into the St. James club in search of Thomas Leigh. Checking his outer cloak, he searched the large room for his target. Finding Thomas, Harry stepped quickly toward him.

Thomas glanced up at Harry, folding his paper onto his lap. "Good day, Hartnell."

"Not likely," he grumbled, taking the chair next to Thomas.

"Oh? What seems to be the trouble, Harry?"

"You know."

"I do?"

Harry's mouth thinned. "It is about the damn note from your brother."

"A note?" Thomas sloshed the remaining brandy around in his glass. "I am at a loss."

"Are you?" he asked, surprised. "Since you recently returned from Leighaven, I assumed you knew of your brother's plans."

"Do you honestly believe he takes me into his confidence?"

The bitter undertone in Thomas's question caught Harry's attention. "He has demanded my presence at Leighaven."

Thomas took a sip. "Are you going?"

"I have chosen to oblige your brother." Harry didn't see the need to mention Nicholas's threat to expose his financial situation if Thomas did not already know.

"Perhaps we can travel together."

"You are returning so soon?" Harry knew Thomas had arrived back in town only days before.

Thomas shifted in his chair. "I received a message this morning that Nicholas would like my return."

"Do you have an inclination as to the reason?"

Thomas remained silent.

Curious, Harry leaned forward. "None of my business, really. I was just wondering if you knew, is all."

"I have an inkling," Thomas admitted slowly.

"Do tell."

Thomas shook his head. "It is far too personal a matter."

"Then who better to lend an ear but one who is close to your family," Harry replied, hoping his confidential tone would loosen Thomas's tongue.

"I believe it has to do with his wife."

"Andrea?" Harry was stunned.

Thomas slammed a fist against the arm of a chair. "The arrogant bastard returns home, flinging outrageous accusations at us, not even pausing to consider the possibility of innocence."

Now this was an interesting tidbit. Harry leaned closer. "Are you implying that your brother accused you of a liaison with his wife?"

"Utter nonsense, I know," Thomas said, "but it is nearly impossible to convince him otherwise."

Harry eyed Thomas thoughtfully. "She is a beautiful woman," he admitted.

"Do you think me blind?" Thomas rubbed a hand down his face. "Now I must go and face his bloody anger once more."

"So that's the way of it. He beckons and you come running," Harry sneered.

A flinch shook Thomas's shoulders. "As long as he holds the purse strings, I do." Arching his throat, Thomas drained the snifter. "As galling as it is, I find I enjoy the luxuries of life far too much to give them up by deliberately angering the man who pays for them all."

"Damnable situation, isn't it?" Harry said, looking deeply into the fire. He'd never before realized how much he had in common with Thomas.

Thomas nodded in agreement.

"Upon consideration, it seems the situation would have been better for both of us if your brother had never returned."

Thomas set down his empty snifter. "Unfortunately, he has, and we must accommodate his demands."

"Yes," Harry agreed, careful not to add the words "for now."

"You requested an audience?" Andrea asked as she entered the study.

Nicholas rounded his desk to assist Andrea into a chair. She accepted his help with a smile. There were shadows beneath her eyes, making her appear fatigued. Nicholas silently asked himself again if he was doing the right thing.

Here sat his wife, bruised and battered, looking frail and delicate. Yet, underneath, he knew there was a core of strength that would never be defeated.

She was his wife, his love . . . his equal.

"Thank you for joining me, Andrea," he began, taking a seat opposite her. "Now that you've had time to recuperate, we need to discuss a few matters of importance."

Andrea folded her hands on her lap. "Fine."

"Your accident was deliberately set."

Andrea stared at him. Of all the things she imagined he'd want to discuss, this had never occurred to her. He'd caught her off guard. "Pardon me?"

"The harness on our carriage was cut to the point where it would snap if any strain were applied. When your horses started forward, the leather broke."

She leaned back in her chair, too stunned to answer.

"I believe I was the intended target and you were merely injured by mistake." Nicholas dropped his head onto his hands. "God, Andrea, I would do anything to keep you from being harmed. Even after all those other attempts, I never imagined they would attack in that fashion."

Comprehension began to set in, and with it, hope. "Why are you telling me this, Nicholas?"

He reached for her hands, clasping them within his, as he moved to his knees before her. "The distance between us tormented me, but I believed—truly believed—it would protect you from harm. Despite all I was denied at my insistence, I still thought it would keep you safe. That is worth any price, Andrea."

"But I was harmed regardless."

His fingers clenched upon hers. "Do you not know that that realization terrifies me?"

"I am fine, Nicholas," Andrea reassured him, praying that she would never awaken from this dream.

"Thank God," he said, the words heartfelt. "I suddenly realized that I can never fully protect you. If my measures can't ensure it, then what purpose does it serve to push you away from me?"

"All it does is rob us of happiness during whatever time we may have together." Andrea waited for his response.

"I cannot deny us anymore." He leaned down to kiss their clasped hands. "I shall not attempt to shield you from anything, Andrea. From this moment forth, we are equal halves to a whole."

Elation spilled into her heart as she pulled her hands free, wrapping her arms around him, holding him close. "Oh, Nicholas. I love you so."

He stroked her back, pressing kisses on each inch of her face, her neck. "I love you," he murmured. "I've missed you so dreadfully."

She arched her throat, unable to get enough of the husband she loved. "And I you. So often I caught myself from going to you and begging you to forgive me."

He cupped her face between his palms. "Forgive

you?" His smile made her catch her breath. "Why should I forgive you for being right?"

"I just wanted us to be as we once were."

He shook his head, the tenderness in his gaze bringing tears to her eyes. "No, my love, it shall be far better."

All she'd ever wanted was here in front of her. Nicholas leaned forward, scooping her up, before settling into her chair, holding her quite comfortably on his lap. "Shall I tell you of the troubles plaguing Leighaven?"

Andrea leaned against Nicholas and gave him her strength. "I wait upon you."

He smiled down at her and started at the beginning.

"You look most presentable," Hampton said as he straightened Nicholas's cravat.

"Thank you, Hampton," he replied, looking at himself in the long mirror. In many ways this was his suit of armor. After all, today was the day he did battle against his enemy.

Nicholas bid his manservant a good day and left his room. Last night had strengthened him, he knew, for he had spent it in the arms of his love.

Andrea had made a few suggestions to his plan to catch their assailant. Resolution flowed strongly through him. He'd never suspected that simply talking about troublesome issues eased one's mind. They were truly united, and as one, he felt invincible.

His confident step faltered when he caught sight of his mother-in-law at the base of the stairs. "Good day, my lady. To what do we owe this pleasure?"

Lady Anne turned toward him, removing her heavy gloves. "Need I a reason to return to Leighaven now? Was it too presumptuous of me to think this my home, too?"

Nicholas took a deep breath. "Certainly not."

She nodded regally. "Thank you . . . and if you must know, I decided to return in order to help my daughter with the birth of her child." Lady Anne handed her cloak to a nearby maid. "Her time is rapidly approaching."

Warm memories of stroking Andrea's stomach as the baby kicked within flooded Nicholas. His minor irritation over Anne's appearance faded away. Despite their lack of a close relationship, his wife might indeed appreciate the presence of her mother. "Your consideration is much welcomed."

"So noted," she replied before glancing at the maid. "Please arrange for a large pot of tea to be brought to my chambers. I vow I am frozen near to the bone."

Nicholas smiled politely at his mother-in-law as he stepped around her and headed into the study.

A few hours later, Jamieson interrupted him as he worked on the ledgers to announce the arrival of Thomas, along with Lord Hartnell. Anticipation surged through him. All was in place. "Please ask Thomas and Hartnell to join me in the study in fifteen minutes. You and Hampton need to be in position by then."

"Very good, my lord." Jamieson closed the door behind him, leaving Nicholas alone in the room once more.

"Let the games begin," he murmured softly.

Andrea and Miriam sat on the floor in Marissa's room, playing with the little girl and her new puppy. Marissa's shout of glee brought smiles to their faces.

"Look at what Spangles can do, Mama," she exclaimed, pointing at her puppy, who was bouncing around from person to person. "Sit, Spangles. Sit."

The dog wagged its tail wildly, his tongue lolling out

of his mouth as he searched for the next hand to pet him. Marissa tried again, this time a little louder. "*Sit, Spangles. Sit.*"

Still the puppy ignored the command, yipping at Marissa, instead. The little girl's expression crumpled. "I don't understand it. He did it for me yesterday."

Almost as if sensing his playmate's disappointment, the small dog sat down with another bark. "Yay," she shouted, scooping the fuzzy animal up into her arms. Marissa's laughter was infectious as Spangles licked her face. "You did it, Spangles. Good doggy!"

Andrea and Miriam exchanged smiles.

"Oh, dear Lord, you allow that animal into her bedchamber?" Anne's shocked voice ended their laughter.

Andrea looked at her mother, smiling. Not even her mother's censure could spoil her mood this day. "Welcome home, Mother. I was not expecting you today."

"I decided to return from London to ensure your health and to assist with your birthing."

"How thoughtful." Andrea ran her hands down her protruding stomach. "I still have a month to wait."

"I am aware of that. However, I thought it best to return while the roads are still passable."

"Quite often, we have horrendous weather in March," Miriam agreed.

"Would you like to see the tricks I taught Spangles, Grandmother?" Marissa asked brightly.

Lady Anne smiled at Marissa. "Thank you for your offer, darling, but I must visit with your father for a spell."

That caught Andrea's attention. "Nicholas?"

Her mother lifted an eyebrow. "Is there a problem with that idea?"

"I believe Nicholas is unavailable at present."

"Even for his mother-in-law?" Anne asked, incredulous.

Andrea shifted beneath her mother's stare. "He has a meeting with Thomas and Harry."

"Lord Hartnell?"

"Yes."

Andrea hoped that would end the discussion, but her mother lifted her chin. "I fail to see how their meeting could be more important than my problem."

Andrea decided to try another route. "Perhaps if you inform me of your troubles, I might be able to help you sort through them."

"There is no sorting through lack of funds, Andrea." Anne's voice grew sharper. "I had a few extra expenditures while in town and need to request additional monies to cover my overdrawn accounts with various shopkeepers."

Andrea sighed, recognizing her mother's strident tone. There would be no dissuading her. The best she could do was to accompany her mother into Nicholas's office, hope that the meeting had yet to begin, then hustle her out of the study as quickly as possible.

Andrea leaned over to kiss Marissa. "Excuse me, angel. I need to visit with your papa for a little while. I promise to return and play with you and Spangles a bit more when I'm finished."

"Are you going to leave, too?" Marissa asked Miriam, sadness entering her wide golden eyes.

"Certainly not. I want to stay and see more tricks from Spangles." Miriam touched a finger to the tip of Marissa's nose.

The little girl smiled widely. "He doesn't know any more, but perhaps we can teach him to lie down. What do you think, Grandmama?"

"I believe it shall prove a challenge. We'd best begin immediately," Miriam stated in serious tones.

Marissa nodded in solemn agreement.

Andrea shifted about, trying to lever herself up from the ground. In her advanced stage of pregnancy, there was no easy way to accomplish that feat.

"Oh, for heaven's sake," Anne muttered under her breath, steadying Andrea by the arm and helping to lift her the rest of the way up to a standing position. "We would be here all day if I didn't help you."

Andrea smiled at her mother's exasperation. " 'Tis true. I'm often baffled as to why they refer to this as being in a delicate condition. Nothing could be farther from it."

"Andrea, please," Anne protested softly, obviously discomforted by the topic.

Andrea smiled at her daughter and mother-in-law. "I will return shortly."

"Good-bye, Mama," Marissa said, holding her puppy on her lap.

Anne frowned. "You truly should forbid that animal from the house."

Andrea waved farewell to Miriam and headed from the room. She glanced at her mother. "I would appreciate it if you would refrain from making such disparaging remarks in front of Marissa."

Her mother appeared stunned.

Andrea stopped walking and reached out to hold her mother's hand. "I realize that you only say those things because you care for us and want us to behave in a proper fashion, but they must come to an end, Mother. I am a woman grown and, as such, can make the decisions that affect me and my family."

Her mother nodded stiffly. "Very well."

Andrea watched her mother walk away and sighed before hurrying to catch up with her.

Twelve

Nicholas turned at the knock. "Enter."

Thomas and Harry came through the doorway one after the other, each wearing a matching expression of wariness. Nicholas smiled in expectancy. It would all end here. He leaned back against his desk.

Thomas sat in one of the armchairs in front of Nicholas. He waited until Harry took the other seat before asking lightly, "We have done your bidding, Nick. Now what did you need to say to us?"

"Hartnell will need to be patient while you and I have our discussion," Nicholas responded, his arms crossing over his chest.

Thomas frowned. "About?"

Nicholas dropped his arms to his sides, standing erect before his brother. "About a little accident my wife suffered a few weeks ago. I don't suppose you would know anything about that, now, would you?"

Thomas shook his head in denial. "What accident? What are you talking about?"

"After I thought about it, there could be no other logical answer to the question."

"What question?"

Nicholas paused. "The question of who is trying to destroy me."

"How utterly preposterous," denied Thomas, raising his voice.

"Is it?" Nicholas murmured, his tones silky. "Who is better positioned to gain from my demise? Who would inherit not only the title, but the fortunes as well?"

"Have you gone mad, Nick?" Thomas leaped to his feet.

"And what of my wife?" Nicholas continued, ignoring Thomas's outburst. "While you would be unable to wed, you could certainly enjoy the privileges of an intimate association if you were discreet."

"I don't have to listen to this rot." Thomas turned to leave the room. "Are you coming, Harry?"

The other man shook his head. "I'm rather enjoying this. Listening to your brother make ludicrous insinuations is fascinating."

"Keep out of it, Hartnell," Nicholas ground out before grabbing Thomas's arm. "Don't go off just yet. I think you need to hear everything I say unless you'd rather hear it from the magistrate."

Thomas shook off his brother's restraining hold. "You have nothing on me. No proof whatsoever."

"Are you so sure?" Nicholas asked.

"You are merely inventing ridiculous theories. You have no evidence." Thomas pointed at Hartnell. "Why, you could just as easily have chosen Harry to lay the blame upon."

"Never," Nicholas said, dismissing Harry with a glance. "That would be impossible."

"How can you be so sure?"

"Look at the man," Nicholas scoffed, gesturing toward Harry, who stood in offense. "He is a soft, *refined* dandy. I doubt if he has enough passion in his veins to do anything that might dirty his hands," Nicholas sneered in disgust.

"Hold up, Trent," demanded Harry, his voice raised in agitation. "I resent your insults toward my manhood and—"

"What manhood, Harry?" Nicholas's gaze swept over Harry's pudgy body, his lips twisting into a mockery of a smile. "I see no man before me and I certainly see nothing which would indicate a definable manhood."

Harry vibrated with anger. "Damn you, Trent. Why did you have to come back?"

"It would have been better for everyone if you'd remained dead," Thomas added, sidling next to Harry.

Anger twisted Harry's features. "The only solution is to send you into an early grave."

"But you've found it rather difficult to dispose of me, haven't you, Hartnell?" Nicholas asked, taunting him. "You're no match for me, you fool. Not now, not ever."

"I almost got you once," he spat, a crazed look overtaking his normally bland face.

Satisfaction soared through Nicholas as he received the proof to his suspicions.

"You almost . . . what?" Thomas asked, his eyes widening. "It was you, Harry. You were the one who shot Nicholas."

Harry dropped his facade. "Yes, both times. I missed the first time, but not the second, did I, Trent? I nearly got you. In fact, I would have, if that little brat of yours hadn't come running up and ruined everything."

Harry turned toward Thomas. "It's not too late, Thomas. We can still have everything. If we get rid of your brother, I can marry Andrea, you receive the title, and we can share the fortune."

"Just the two of us?"

"And one other," he said quickly, before turning to glare at Nicholas. "Now all we need to do is think of a way to rid ourselves of him.

Slowly Thomas moved away from Harry. "What about the reins, Harry? Did you think of that, too?"

Harry shook his head violently, too focused on Nicholas to notice Thomas's withdrawal. "I didn't think up any of them, but I could have. I know I could have."

"Who helped you, Harry?" Thomas asked.

Harry ignored Thomas's question. Spittle flew from his mouth as he cursed Nicholas. "Everything would have been just perfect if you hadn't shown up, back from the dead. Now your brother and I are going to make sure you stay there forever."

Thomas walked over to stand next to Nicholas. "I don't think you quite understand the situation, Harry."

The cool voice of his compatriot jarred Harry from his near-hypnotic state. His eyes darted back and forth, from brother to brother. "What are you doing, Thomas? You stand to benefit from his death, too. You loathe your brother. You despise having to go begging to him for everything you have, everything you want. We can get all we want if we work together."

Thomas shook his head. "I could never betray my brother. I led you to believe it true, but I have no use for the title and never once thought of Andrea in any manner other than sister."

"You concocted this scheme to . . . to . . ." Harry stuttered, confusion darkening his features.

"To coerce you into admitting to your crimes."

Harry's eyes grew wild. "No, no. You said that you hated him. You told me so."

Thomas lifted his shoulders in a nonchalant shrug. "I lied."

"No," Harry mumbled, looking about him like a trapped animal. Desperate, he darted toward Nicholas's desk, where the box of knives Andrea had given him lay open. Triumph blazed in his expression as he pointed a sharp blade at Nicholas. "I shall finish you both."

"It will hardly appear an accident," Nicholas pointed out.

"No, but it will be even better. Imagine what the magistrate will be led to believe. Two brothers fighting to the death over a woman. I shall, of course, be on hand to comfort Andrea after the blood is cleaned."

Nicholas smiled, not intimidated in the least by the weapon in Harry's possession. "We are still two against one. The odds are not in your favor."

"Shut up." Harry began to sweat.

Nicholas crossed his arms. "We've got you, Hartnell. There's nothing you can do."

Andrea caught up with her mother in the corridor outside of Marissa's room and matched her, stride for stride, as they quickly walked down to the study. The sound of raised voices made the two women stop abruptly.

Andrea knew she couldn't allow her mother to enter the room, well aware of the confrontation taking place. "It is impossible for you to see Nicholas now."

Anne frowned slightly before she finally said, "Very well. Nicholas would probably be very uncooperative in his present state. The meeting does not appear to be a soothing one."

"Thank you for understanding, Mother."

"I believe I shall return to my chambers." Anne

turned, heading up the stairs. "Are you returning to Marissa?"

Andrea waved her mother on. "Not at the moment."

"As you please," Anne said, ascending to the upper corridor.

Andrea waited until her mother had disappeared up the stairs before she walked across the foyer. Her family had been threatened, her husband shot. She had every right to witness Harry's accounting.

Andrea stepped into the study.

"Andrea!" Nicholas shouted, lunging for her.

But he was too late.

A strong arm wrapped about Andrea's neck, dragging her backward. Hot breath rushed over her ear as her assailant asked, "Now who holds all the cards?"

Harry. She was unable to utter a word; the blade held to her neck convinced her to remain silent.

She was in serious danger.

Andrea fought back her panic, knowing it would not help her plight. Jamieson and Hampton came bursting into the room, causing Harry to flinch. The knife bit into the soft flesh of Andrea's neck, bringing a roar of anger from Nicholas. Blocking it all out, Andrea focused on ways to escape Harry's clutches.

"Let her go, Hartnell," Nicholas demanded, his voice raw with emotion.

The sound of Harry's laughter grated in her ear. "Do you really believe I would be that stupid? I realize that you will never allow me to simply walk away from this room. My only hope for escape is to take Andrea with me. You'd never harm her."

Nicholas took a step forward. "If you hurt her, I will track you down until you are dead." The words were a vow.

Harry shook slightly at the promise he heard in Nicholas's voice, but still he continued with his bravado. "I will see you in Hell first."

His bitter laugh worried Harry. "I've been there, Hartnell, and I survived. What else can you threaten me with?"

"I can send Andrea there, too."

Nicholas curled his hands into fists as he took another step.

"Don't come any closer," Harry admonished, pulling Andrea backward.

The movement caused the knife to slip downward. It was the chance she'd been hoping for. Andrea smashed her elbow into Harry's middle, bending him over in pain. She spun free even as Nicholas launched himself past her, his fist slamming into Harry's face.

Hartnell crashed to the floor, the knife skittering away in the fall. Thomas rushed forward, placing a foot upon Harry's throat to keep him on the ground while Nicholas reached for Andrea, pulling her close.

Hampton and Jamieson moved next to Thomas, looking down at the prone man. "Well done," Jamieson said.

"Nicholas," Harry groaned from the floor.

Hampton tapped Thomas on the arm. "I don't think you're pressing hard enough, Master Thomas."

With a grin, Thomas stepped harder, eliciting a choking sound from Harry.

Slowly Nicholas released Andrea and moved to stand over Harry. Wordlessly he gazed down on the man who had threatened his family.

"You think you have won," Harry whispered, his voice raspy from the pressure of Thomas's foot. "But you haven't. She is smarter than you. She is smarter than all of us."

"She?" Nicholas asked quietly, his body tensing once more.

A chuckle of pleasure escaped Harry's beaten body. "It wasn't me who came up with these plans. No, it was—"

A shot rang out in the room.

Nicholas watched in shock as a crimson patch of blood blossomed across Harry's chest. Death claimed him instantly. Nicholas twisted to face the assailant.

Lady Anne stood in the doorway, her gun now trained on Nicholas.

"Mother!" Andrea gasped.

Lady Anne's mouth tightened, but she kept the gun pointed at Nicholas.

"You've killed him," Andrea whispered, barely able to speak. "You shot Harry."

"He brought it upon himself for betraying me," Lady Anne snapped. "I always knew Harry was weak. When he called on me in London to tell me of your husband's letter requesting his presence, I was afraid that Nicholas was planning something of this nature."

"Which, of course, is the true reason for your visit," Nicholas concluded.

Lady Anne glared at him. "Damn you, Leigh, for forcing my hand like this. If you'd never returned, I wouldn't have needed to take such drastic measures."

Andrea was too shocked to move. "Why are you doing this?"

"I am saving us," Anne insisted, keeping her attention focused on Nicholas. "He will destroy us."

"How can you say that?" Andrea asked, finding it difficult to think logically through her horror. It was incomprehensible that her mother had been trying to kill her husband.

"Did you learn nothing from your childhood, Andrea?"

"My childhood?" she asked, unable to follow her mother's defense. "How does that affect anything? Good Lord, Mother, you're standing over a man you just shot and you're asking me of my childhood?" she finished in a hysterical rush.

"Think, Andrea. Think upon all the times we begged off relatives, and how your father would grace us with his charming smile while he stole the clothes from our backs."

Andrea watched her mother's face contort in anger.

"When I found out he'd run through the inheritance, I could bear no more. It was quite simple, really. A few pieces of poison root in his meal and he was gone."

The calm admission staggered Andrea. "He was my father," she whispered, retaining a fierce hold upon her tears.

"He was destroying us!" Anne shouted, sparing a glance for Andrea. "Don't you understand that? Even if we'd managed to recoup our losses and replenish our accounts, he would have run through that money as well, leaving us destitute once more. There would have been no end to it."

"Oh, Mother." Andrea leaned back against the wall. "How could you?"

"How could I not?" Anne grew rigid. "I could not live in fear of poverty for the remainder of my life."

Andrea wanted to curl into a ball and pretend none of this had happened. But it was her mother who stood before them, wielding a gun. That made it her responsibility to find out all the facts. She straightened, facing her mother.

"How could you do this to me, to us? I offered you a home here at Leighaven after my father was kil—" She couldn't bring herself to say the word. "—after my father's death."

"It was no hardship to take me in. The Trent fortune was massive and could easily sustain another." Her lips tightened. "Though it did gall me to accept their charity. However, the match was my idea, thus I was deserving of the assistance."

"Why try to destroy me? You already had everything you wanted." Nicholas kept his gaze fixed on the gun.

"You wanted to ruin me!" Anne exclaimed. "You came home, took control of the family fortune, and ruined everything. I didn't rid myself of your father simply to—"

"*My* father?" Nicholas interrupted.

Anne allowed herself a smile of mockery. "I poisoned your father, too."

"Oh, no, Mother." Andrea felt ill. Her mother had destroyed so much.

"He had spent a fortune, literally, on bribes in order to find out Nicholas's whereabouts." Anne waved the gun. "Once again, a man was destroying all that I'd worked for. I couldn't allow him to continue, so I used the easiest method available. Besides, it had worked so well in the past."

"You monster," Nicholas accused.

Anne drew back her shoulders. "It is so easy for you to judge, isn't it, Nicholas? You've never been helpless while someone else decided your fate."

"What do you think my years in prison were?"

"Ah, but your hands were tied. Mine weren't." She looked at him boldly. "If you had been afforded the opportunity to alter your fate, to free yourself from threat, would you not have taken it, regardless of the cost?"

"I could never be so duplicitous in my methods," Nicholas avowed.

"You think yourself so noble?" Anne sneered. "In

my position, you would have acted as I did. I was given an opportunity to free us from your father before he ran through the family fortune, and I took it. Little did I know his youngest son would complete the task, emptying our coffers once more."

Thomas shifted uncomfortably.

"Unfortunately, I did not find out about his losses until Andrea had accepted responsibility for our welfare. There was no need to dispose of you, Thomas, because you withdrew from your responsibilities." Anne glanced at Andrea, smiling slightly. "I was so very proud of your success, my daughter. You opened my consciousness to a whole new way of thought. I'd been raised to believe that a woman was nothing without a husband to guide her. Yet you proved that an intelligent female can accomplish great wealth and power without the assistance of a man."

Andrea pressed a hand to her stomach, exerting control over her raging emotions. "I only wanted to save the family."

"As did I, and the glorious part is, together we succeeded. Between your financial expertise and my clearing your path, we have rebuilt the Trent fortunes beyond their original glory."

Andrea wrapped her arms around herself, unable to bear the pain she'd unintentionally helped create.

Anne took a step closer. "Your mistake lay in securing your husband's freedom, then in handing over control of our finances. However, I accept blame for your actions."

Andrea shook her head, unable to follow her mother's logic.

"It was I who raised you to believe in the rights of the husband, little knowing that it would haunt me one day." Anne looked at Nicholas. "If I had known, my lessons would have been far different. Now, all we need do is rid ourselves of these few men and return to the ways of the past."

"No, Mother." Andrea walked over to her husband, grasping his hand. "No more. This ends now. Put down the gun, Mother. Please."

Sadness filled Anne's gaze. "Oh, my poor dear. You fancy yourself in love with him, don't you? It's not too late, Andrea. Step away, come to me, and we can secure the future for your daughter."

"Not at this cost, Mother." A tear slipped free. "No more."

Anne's hand trembled as she said, "Then you leave me no choice."

Nicholas stepped in front of Andrea. "You cannot mean to harm your own daughter, Anne. It is me you want."

Hatred twisted Anne's features. "How I loathe you, Nicholas. My daughter must die because of you."

"It is still not too late. What if I gave you enough money to satisfy your needs and allowed you to leave without interference?"

"And take your word you would not hunt me down? You think me the fool, Nicholas," Anne returned. "You, above all else, must die for the heartache you have brought upon me."

"You brought it upon yourself, Mother," Andrea said, moving again to Nicholas's side. She entwined her fingers with his and smiled tremulously up at Nicholas, love for him flowing through her.

He returned her hold fiercely.

"Oh, Andrea, you disappoint me so." Anne shook her head. "You are throwing away everything for him."

"No, Mother. I am gaining all by standing with him."

Anne scowled at Nicholas. "If this buffoon, Hartnell, had succeeded with that arrow, this would never have come to pass."

"Did you use my wife as the bait to secure Harry's acquiescence?"

"He was an even bigger idiot than the rest. He actually thought that once he killed you, he would marry Andrea, and inherit the fortune." Anne shot a mocking glance down at the dead man. "Clear thinking was never one of Harry's strong points."

"He never suspected that you would frame him for the murder and he would be sent to rot in prison if he didn't meet the hangman's rope."

"Precisely," Anne agreed. "He actually believed he was safe since he knew my identity."

"As if any sane person would actually believe a macabre tale such as this one," Nicholas concluded. "Even if he did lay blame upon you, who would have believed it?"

"How astute," Anne murmured. "Harry's death is very convenient. Imagine my distress at walking in upon Lord Hartnell, in a jealous rage, as he shoots my beloved family before turning the gun upon himself."

"Our incompetent magistrate will never question a thing," Nicholas agreed.

"Quite right," Anne agreed. "I fear, however, it is time to end this pleasant conversation. Rest assured, Andrea, that I will care for your daughter and will correct the mistakes I made with you. Marissa will be raised to believe in her own fortitude and strength. Never will she look to a husband to secure her happiness."

"Don't do this, Mother," Andrea pleaded.

Tears slid down Anne's cheeks as she pointed the gun at her daughter. "I shall regret this more than you know."

"No!" Nicholas bellowed as he launched himself at

Anne. He knocked the gun away as he fell to the floor, landing heavily. Stunned, he managed to roll over. He pushed slowly to his feet, keeping his gaze fixed upon Lady Anne, who scooped up the knife Harry had dropped. She lunged toward him just as a shot rang out from the gun now held securely within Thomas's grasp.

Lady Anne's manipulations were at an end.

She lay lifeless upon the floor, a bullet wound piercing her heart, the knife lying within her hand. Sobbing, Andrea rushed to Nicholas, wrapping him in her arms, burying her face against his shoulder.

"It's finally over," he said, stroking her back. "I'm so sorry, darling. So very sorry."

Andrea stood before the window, staring out into the dark night. Thoughts of her mother pained her.

"Andrea?" Nicholas came up behind her, pulled her back against him, and wrapped both his arms around her. "Are you all right, my love?"

"She was my mother."

"And she loved you," he said.

Andrea flinched. "How can you say that? She would never have done all those horrible things if she had."

"You must understand, Andrea. She did them *because* she loved you."

Words were beyond her.

"Your mother truly believed that her actions protected you and herself. She never wanted to harm you."

"Do you so quickly forget that she was pointing a gun at me just this afternoon?" Andrea grew colder at the memory.

"She didn't use it, though, Andrea. In the end, she couldn't bring herself to kill you."

"You knocked the gun from her," Andrea protested, unable to separate the image of her mother from that of the murderess.

"There were those few seconds before I reached her where she could have pulled the trigger. She knew I was coming, she knew it would mean the end of her scheming, yet she couldn't do it. She could not end your life, Andrea. In her own way, she loved you and only wanted what was best for you."

Tears slid silently down Andrea's cheeks. "How did I not see?"

Nicholas sighed. "She was your mother. Why would you ever suspect her?"

"She took so much from us," Andrea said, spinning away. "My mother destroyed your family. She killed your father and tried to kill you."

Nicholas held out his hands. "Andrea, my love, don't torment yourself. It is all in our past now."

"But how do I live with that past?"

"You cannot allow it to affect your future," Nicholas said softly. "You need to understand that you are not responsible for your mother's actions. She made her own choices in life, as we must make ours."

He walked toward where she stood, frozen and so very cold. "I choose you, Andrea. Now and forever."

Nicholas wrapped her in a loving embrace, warming her to her soul, allowing her to grieve for her mother despite all the pain she'd caused.

In doing so, Nicholas showed her a place of wonder. Heaven.

Epilogue

Chelmsford, England—August 1811

"*T*his is one sleepy child," Andrea said, gazing down at John, her sweet baby boy.

"He's a big boy and needs his rest." Miriam smiled at them. "I wager he'll be as tall as his father."

Andrea looked at her husband, who was wading in the brook with Marissa, the two of them laughing. Happiness flooded her. They had just returned from London yesterday and had decided to picnic in their usual spot. The sun shone brightly upon them as they lounged before their meal.

"How are you feeling, Andrea?"

Miriam's question caught her off guard. "Quite well," she answered.

"I wasn't inquiring after your health." Miriam gazed out over the sunlit field. "I wondered how you felt about returning to Leighaven."

Andrea understood the question now. Her mother. She kissed her son's fuzzy head, inhaling his innocent scent. "I've come to peace with the memories of my mother. Somewhere along the way, she got lost and never found her way back."

Miriam reached out to touch Andrea's arm in silent empathy.

Andrea smiled at her mother-in-law. "How could hatred live in my heart when I am constantly surrounded by love?"

"Marissa seems to be recovered from the tragedy."

"We simply told her that her grandmother had been shot. She does not need to know anything beyond that."

Miriam nodded in agreement. "I am also thankful that our constable accepted the incident without further inquiries."

"For once the man's incompetency was for the best. He never questioned Nicholas's tale of how Harry had been stealing the banknotes in the study when my mother stumbled upon him."

"Did he not even ask after the fact that there was only one gun at the scene?"

The images were too painful for Andrea to envision. "Might we discuss something else?"

"How thoughtless of me," Miriam said. "My apologies, Andrea."

Andrea eased her sleeping child away from her body, laying him on the blanket. "There you are, my sweet baby."

Little John slept on contentedly.

"I'm disappointed Thomas didn't join us."

Andrea smiled at Miriam, thanking her without words for changing the topic. "I do believe he prefers the sights of town."

Miriam laughed softly. "Undoubtedly he will accept one of the offers he received to visit in Scotland later on this month."

"He is happiest when unencumbered, our Thomas."

"If he doesn't settle down within a few years, I vow I'll send Jamieson and Hampton to accompany him." Miriam's eyes sparkled. "Those two will find him a wonderful match."

"And make him crazed in the process," Andrea agreed with a grin.

"They did fine by you."

Andrea merely lifted her brows.

"With a bit of help from me," Miriam conceded.

Andrea gazed down at her husband and daughter and nodded. "I couldn't agree with you more."

"This water is *freezing!*"

His daughter's giggle made standing barefoot in the middle of a cold brook worthwhile. Nicholas smiled at Marissa, who sat upon the bank removing her slippers and stockings. "Hurry it up, darling, before my toes break off from the cold."

Another giggle was his reward. Marissa stood and held out her hand. "Come and help me, Papa."

Nicholas started back, carefully finding his footing upon the slick rocks of the streambed. A few feet from his daughter, he stepped down on a rock—only to have it move underneath his foot. With a yelp, Nicholas jumped back, his arms waving frantically as he tried to find his balance.

The loud splash of his bottom landing in the water was nearly drowned out by the peals of laughter coming not only from Marissa, but from his wife and mother, who looked down upon them from the hill. The frigid water soaked into his clothes as Nicholas shifted off a pointed rock. He watched the turtle he'd stepped on swim off.

"Oh, Papa. That was so funny." Marissa clutched her stomach. "You looked like this," she said, flailing her arms wildly, her mouth wide open, her eyes rolling, before dropping onto the soft grass.

"Hold up a moment, young lady. You get to land on grass, but I had to sit down on this!" Nicholas reached underwater and pulled up a pointed rock.

Her eyes widened. "That must have hurt."

Nicholas tossed the rock over his shoulder, ignoring the water that splashed up onto him. "I'm your big, strong papa," he stated in a deep voice. "A rock can't hurt me overmuch."

Andrea strolled up, her hands on her hips, as she looked down at him. "For such an intelligent man, you certainly are sitting in that cold water for a very long time."

He shifted back and forth. "It's rather invigorating, Andrea. Would you care to join me?"

Andrea waved him off with her hand. "We can play later, Nicholas. I came down to fetch you and Marissa for some dinner."

Nicholas slowly shifted to his feet. Andrea glanced down at her daughter. "Why don't you head up to our blankets, angel? Your papa and I will join you."

Marissa nodded happily, racing off toward her little brother and grandmother just as Nicholas made it to the bank. He reached out and grabbed Andrea, pulling her against him. Her laughing shriek made him smile.

"Let go of me. You're freezing!"

He held on tight, delighting in her playful protests.

Andrea squirmed against him. "Nicholas. Our children are watching."

"Marissa will merely think you're helping me to dry off."

"And what of your mother? I highly doubt she'll be fooled," Andrea retorted.

"I'm sure she'll be kind enough to look the other way," he said, nuzzling her ear.

"Stop, Nicholas."

Her halfhearted protest did little to deter him.

"Your mother is waiting upon us for dinner," Andrea murmured, tilting her head to the side in spite of her words.

Accepting her offer, Nicholas began to kiss her neck. "And just what would you like me to feast upon?" he murmured suggestively to his wife, nipping gently.

"Right now, we're having chicken." She arched into him, a soft moan breaking from her. "But later we'll partake of a different delight." Her breath feathered over him. "And Nicholas, I'm very hungry."

A sigh broke from Nicholas as Andrea stepped back, out of his arms. "You never want to play," he grumbled.

Andrea tilted back her head, laughing. "Oh, my poor, long-suffering baby. Later, Nicholas. I promise." She turned and walked through the field a little way before turning back and stretching out her hand to him. "Come on, darling."

For a moment, Nicholas gazed at the life before him: a loving wife standing in the sunshine, with his daughter and son lying on a blanket next to his mother. Just like before, it seemed too perfect to be real.

A smile curved upon Nicholas's mouth as he hurried forward and, grasping his wife's hand, stepped into the picture.